LIFE
SUBTRACTED

David Hailwood

Biomekazoik Press

With thanks to Stuart Giddings and Debbie Moon for getting the body count off to a good start, and to the Hastings Writers Group, Illiterati, and the University of Chichester Creative Writing MA group for their years of encouragement.

Special thanks must also be made to Andrea Samuelson and Richard Wheeler – founding members of the 'Save Grott Society', and to my wife Jenny for all the cups of tea.

One

'Now,' said Grison, addressing the small group of naked people who stood before him on the rooftop, 'you are all going to *die*.'

Cheering. Nods of approval.

'Your bodies will be spread like a magnificent crimson pâté across the pavement thousands of feet below.'

More cheering – slightly less enthused.

Grison cursed under his breath. The mood destabilisers were already beginning to wear off. 'Not that your deaths will be in vain, of course,' he hurriedly added. 'Thanks to your noble sacrifice, millions upon millions of the latest thing in designer burial wear will be sold.' He gestured grandly to the pairs of Adios trainers that adorned the otherwise naked individuals feet. 'Thanks to the single selfless act you are about to perform you will no longer be unrecognisable faces in a featureless crowd. You will be known. You will be celebrated. Popular musicians will compose jingles in your honour.'

A small hairy hand went up. Grison studiously ignored it.

'The memory of your deed will live forever on in the minds of consumers and advertising agencies. Immortality is but a few short steps away, and far be it for me to stand in the path of your destinies. So, without further ado, tie laces, fix backpacks, and chaaaa–' Grison froze mid-speech. His eyes strayed back to the small hairy owner of the small hairy hand. They looked slowly down, and narrowed. 'What, pray tell, is that, Mr Grott?'

The small Neanderthal-type looked down towards his crotch; the object of Grison's attention. 'My thermal undies, Mr Grison. Bit nippy up here. A man could catch his death of cold.'

Grison's heavy brow wrinkled in disgust. 'They've got *unicorns* on them.'

'Yes, Mr Grison,' said Grott with a totally unfounded sense of pride.

Grison yanked a leaflet from one of the backpacks and thrust it into Grott's suspiciously moist hand. 'Read!' he commanded.

It was a command Grott followed with considerable difficulty. His tongue lolled from side to side as his eyes attempted to study the page. 'Adios trainers,' it read. 'Go out in style.'

'Now,' said Grison, 'I want you to think long and hard before you answer this one. Does it mention anywhere on that leaflet anything about unicorn motif undergarments?'

Grott scrunched up his face in concentration. He began to re-read the leaflet.

'*No!*' Grison bellowed, tearing it from his hands. 'It does not. You were all expressly forbidden from wearing anything that might detract from the sponsor's product, otherwise it could invalidate the whole contract. Do you want these people's deaths to be in vain?' Grison swept out a muscular arm to take in the long line of dishevelled-looking snuff streakers. 'Do you want your death to be without meaning?'

'To be honest, I'm not entirely sure that I want to die at all, actually.'

Grison almost fell to his knees. 'You *what?*'

'Well, you see, I've had such a lovely time this morning. Met some smashing people, thoroughly enjoyed the complimentary tea and scones and everything. And, well, I don't want to appear ungrateful, but I think that flinging myself off the roof might put a bit of a downer on the whole day.'

Grison massaged his temples. 'I'm willing to bet you didn't actually drink the tea, did you?' He stared deep into Grott's eyes. They weren't dilated, bloodshot or anything. This was a very bad sign.

'Oh no, it wasn't my brew. But the scones were *very* good.' Grott favoured Grison with a grin full of crumbs.

A shudder of repulsion ran through Grison's immaculately dressed body. If ever there was a man who deserved to die, it was Mr Grott. 'Don't you *want* to kill yourself?' he asked incredulously.

'I'm not terribly sold on the idea, no.'

'Oh come on man, you must. All these other people are doing it. Go with the flow…live a little.'

'I've never been one to follow trends, Mr Grison.'

'But think of all the money your family stands to gain. The Adios trainers corporation has agreed to make a more than generous donation to each and every one of the bereaved.'

'I don't have a family.'

'Relatives then.'

'They all disowned me.'

'Bloody hell,' said Grison, allowing a rare smile to creep across his terminally grim features. 'That must be a bit depressing.'

'I suppose it is, now you come to mention it.'

'So depressing in fact, that if I was you I'd probably want to kill myself.'

Grott's podgy face scrunched up like play-doh in the hands of a mental patient. 'You would?'

'Why, most certainly.' Grison was positively beaming.

The rusted cogs of Grott's mind struggled to turn. He gave his head a vigorous scratch, liberating a few lice.

'Well,' he said eventually, 'lucky you're not me then isn't it, Mr Grison? Else we'd be in a right old pickle.'

An involuntary muscular spasm caused Grison's right eye to twitch ever so slightly. Other than that, his composure remained rock-solid. It was clear to him now that a new approach was needed; a simple plan for a simple man. 'Look around you, Grott,' he said. 'What do you see?'

Grott looked around him and coughed. 'Smog. Thick, dark smog.'

'And?'

Grott looked down at the sprawling cityscape that lay below, its ugly grey megastructures reaching up out of the polluted depths like jagged teeth in the mouth of a leper. 'Factories,' he said. 'Buildings and factories as far as the eye can see. Which isn't that far, on account of the smog.'

'That's right, Grott – buildings, factories and smog. A wonderful sight, is it not?'

Grott stroked one of his many chins in thoughtful contemplation. 'Not really, no.'

'Exactly. Would you really want to live in a world as polluted and overcrowded as this?'

Grott scratched his head again, forcing Grison to step back to avoid the contagion. 'I guess when you put it like that it does seem a little foolish. So you, er, really think I should kill myself?'

'Mr Grott, I have never been so sure of anything in all my life.' Grison noticed with relish that Grott's will was beginning to waver. Time to put all those motivational speech seminars to good use, he thought. 'Without death,' Grison began, 'life has no punch line. It is but a badly written joke told by the gods to keep mankind in a perpetual state of misery.' Grison clenched his hands together, voice trembling with emotion. 'Dispel that misery. Put joy back into your life. Put joy back into everyone's lives.' He laid a hand on Grott's shoulder and fixed him with a look of absolute warmth and compassion. 'Kill yourself. I *implore* you.'

Tears streamed from the eyes of all assembled. Grott removed his undergarments and blew his nose on them.

'R-right you are then,' he said. 'And thank you, Mr Grison. That all means rather a lot to me.'

'That's the spirit, lad. Knew I could depend upon you.' Grison gave the small man a hearty pat on the back.

'*Aaaaaaaah!*' said Grott, as he tumbled from the rooftop.

Grison rubbed his hands together and grinned. 'Right then, positions please, ladies and gentlemen. I suggest you all follow Mr Grott's fine example. And remember, please try to land head first – we don't want to damage the merchandise.'

Anthony Cresswell cautiously edged his way in through the apartment door. Something rancid was in the air.

'This,' the estate agent said, beaming in the cramped hallway, 'is your lucky day!'

'It doesn't smell like my lucky day,' Anthony said, wrinkling his nose.

'Oh, that's just the air recycling unit, sir. It's specially designed to sift out all those nasty old pollutants in the atmosphere. Your senses probably aren't attuned to air of this particular calibre.' The estate agent delicately sniffed the air like it was the finest of wines. Her face paled slightly.

'It smells a bit like…cabbage.'

'Well,' the estate agent coughed, 'that's clean air for you.' She took a step forward. Something squeaked underfoot. Before Anthony could see what it was, she kicked it deftly into the shadows.

'That sounded like a rat. Does this place have rats?'

A hopeful smile enveloped the estate agent's face. 'Do you *like* rats?' she asked.

'No,' Anthony said, 'I do not.'

'Oh.' Her smile dropped. 'Definitely wasn't a rat, then. *Behold!*' She flung open a door, and gestured grandly inside. 'The living room.'

Anthony appraised the room with a single glance. He didn't even need to turn his head. 'It's a bit small.'

'A bit small?' the estate agent scoffed. 'A bit small? Compact and accessible it may be, but "small" it certainly isn't.'

Anthony looked the petite woman up and down. She was a bit small too, which seemed to be a trait common in estate agents, he'd noticed. He was in fact beginning to get the impression that they all underwent extremely expensive height reduction surgery in an attempt to make the apartments they sold look slightly larger. In this particular case, it hadn't been worth the effort.

'I'll have you know there's usually a twelve-year waiting list for a fully furnished apartment like this,' the estate agent continued, pressing herself against a wall to let Anthony squeeze past. 'It's only your high credit rating that allowed you to skip to the front of the queue. Just come into some inheritance, have you?' She rubbed her hands eagerly together and grinned in a predatory fashion.

'No, my parents took it with them when they made room some years back,' said Anthony, struggling to keep the bitterness out of his voice. 'Booked a place on one of those luxury Sun Runners.' All they'd left him in the way of an inheritance was a crippling debt, and a scorched postcard of the sun, with the words 'wish you were here' scrawled on the back.

'Well, good for them,' said the estate agent. 'Voluntary cremation's a very popular retirement option these days. Promotion then, was it?'

Anthony nodded.

'Oh congratulations, Mr Cresswell. Let me guess…'

She looked his badly dressed frame up and down, and decided another lie was probably in order. It wasn't that Anthony was particularly unattractive in appearance, he was simply average in almost every way; he had an average height, an average weight, an alarmingly average haircut, and the sort of features that would've driven Picasso insane, as no matter how he rearranged them they'd still look just as bland. 'Admiralty?' she said.

'Accountancy.'

'Accountancy, eh? Very noble profession. It's a wonderful job you people do, keeping those population figures down.'

'Actually, that's more the Sterilisation Statistics department's area. I'm in Junior Accountancy.'

'Ah. So…making tea and fetching biscuits, is it then?'

'Mostly just the tea making,' Anthony admitted. 'I do occasionally encounter the odd hobnob or two along the way.'

'Hobnobs?' The estate agent whistled appreciatively. 'As important as that?'

'Not that it matters any more. I'm moving up in the world.' A serene smile settled on Anthony's face. Finally, after just ten short years, he would have a legitimate reason to use the lift. He'd probably even be given his own laminated lift pass and everything. Bliss! 'Up, up, up!' he said. 'All that way to Senior Accountancy.'

'Yes indeed, sir. If you're lucky, they might even let you make Horlicks.' The estate agent slipped an arm round Anthony's shoulder, and waved a contract in his face. 'Just sign there.'

Anthony pushed it away. 'I think I ought to see a bit more of the apartment before I make any decisions.'

'There's not a lot more to see, apart from the toilet/kitchen combo, and I just know you're going to get a thrill out of that.' The estate agent artfully blocked the route to the toilet/kitchen combo, on the off chance that it proved to be too much of a thrill. 'It's all very clean, very modern, and conforms to the government's stringent recyke policies. As the saying goes, "out one end, in the oth—"'

'Where's the bed?' Anthony asked. Apart from a sofa that had been wedged at an angle between three walls, furnishings were few and far between.

'Ah, yes…the bed.' The estate agent fixed her smile firmly in place, braced herself, and motioned upwards.

Anthony stared unblinking at the mattress glued to the ceiling. 'How am I supposed to get to it?'

'Just flick the switch in the corner and let the zero gravity field take care of the rest.'

'I don't know,' said Anthony, attempting to calculate the angles necessary to attain a good night's kip, 'seems a bit complicated.'

'If it's too hi-tech for your liking, I'm sure it wouldn't be too much of a problem for us to remove the sofa and lower the bed. For a modest fee, of course.'

'But I like the sofa,' said Anthony, tugging one thin thread of optimism free from the descending duvet of despair. 'Blue…' he murmured, running a hand over the sofa's silky sky-blue lining. 'My favourite colour's blue.'

'I'll get you a nice blue pen then, Mr Cresswell.' As the estate agent started to root around in her pockets, a small cylindrical device fell out at Anthony's feet.

'What's this for?' Anthony enquired, bending to pick it up.

'What's what for, sir?'

'This remote control thingie.'

'That's just for the lights, Mr Cresswell.' The estate agent made a frantic grab for it, and missed. 'Nothing to concern yourself about.'

Anthony squinted at the tiny lettering on its side. 'It says "Holographic Generator" on it.'

'Does it? Does it really?' Tugging wildly at Anthony's arm, the estate agent attempted to guide him towards a doorway. 'Let's go see that toilet!'

Click!

The room flickered and faded, replaced by something even less pleasant. Grime and filth dribbled down the once pristine walls – of which now there were only three. In a corner of the room rats and cockroaches fought over the bones of a previous tenant.

And, to top it all off, the sofa was brown, not blue.

'Still want to show me that toilet?' Anthony asked, raising a single eyebrow.

'I think I'd best not under the circumstances.' The estate agent forced a smile. 'I'll put you on our call back list, shall I Mr Cresswell?'

'Oh, who am I kidding?' Anthony sighed. 'I'll take it. Where do I sign?'

'You *will?* I mean, of course you will! You won't regret this, sir. You've got a good deal. No, a *great* deal.'

'No I haven't,' said Anthony. 'It's a dump. Unfortunately, it's about a thousand times better than my current living quarters.'

'Where's that then, Mr Cresswell?' The estate agent hurriedly thrust a contract into Anthony's hands before he could change his mind.

'Pine Towers.'

An involuntary shudder ran through the estate agent's petite body. 'The Coffin Parlour?' She crossed herself, and uttered a quick prayer of protection to the God of Commerce. 'Oh dear me, no you don't want to live there. It has an extremely high tenant mortality rate; all those bodies tightly packed together, with barely enough room to breathe. Might as well just nail the lids shut over those poor devil's caskets whilst they sleep, and be done with it. No, you'd be lucky to survive six months in a place like that. How long have you been there?'

'Ten years,' said Anthony sombrely.

The estate agent took her best stab at a sympathetic smile, and patted him gently on the arm in an attempt to jog a signature out of him. To her relief, it worked. 'And your bank details,' she said, tapping the contract, 'in that corner there.'

Anthony finished carving his details into the paper, screwed it up, and tossed it at the estate agent's feet. 'There, happy?'

'Beyond words, Mr Cresswell,' said the estate agent, grinning like a Cheshire cat who'd just got laid.

'That makes one of us, at least.'

She deposited the contract into a briefcase, span the combination lock, and chained it to her arm. 'Pleasure doing business with you. Shall I show you to the door?'

'Don't bother.' Anthony sighed. 'I'll use the wall.'

The streets outside seethed with pedestrians; several million sardines vacuum wrapped and crammed inexpertly into God Almighty's lunchbox. People stood on top of people, attempting to surf the crowd to freedom. Other people stood on top of them. This was all, in its own way, completely pointless, as no matter how hard they tried, no matter how hard they struggled, the entire crowd was slowly edging backwards.

To Anthony, it seemed as if every living soul in the city had assembled here before him, in a shameless attempt at making him late for work. He glanced at his watch. One hour left…it was going to be tight.

'Lucky I didn't have one of those nasty old walls to slow me down,' he muttered, elbowing the person in front.

The megascraper lay tantalisingly close. He could see it from here – it was impossible not to; the vast grey slab-like exterior of the Ministry for the Administration of Necessary Reductions (or MANRs, as almost no one liked to call them) towered over the city like a tombstone. At its top, a massive holographic epitaph dreamt up by the government's marketing division flickered and spat: 'Your sacrifice makes room for others.'

Anthony painstakingly inched his way across the pavement, wishing with every step that a few people might pay the Ministry's sacred mantra a bit more attention. Perhaps then he'd stand a greater chance of reaching his hover car in time, which he'd foolishly parked in a designated space that the estate agent had confidently assured him was 'but a stone's throw from the apartment'.

Ten minutes remaining…

Anthony attempted with relative success to scale a portly gentleman in front of him, though this small victory was rudely cut short when he was immediately caught by a wave of pedestrian traffic heading in the opposite direction.

He punched, bit and kicked against the struggling tide of crowd surfers, forcing himself onwards, keeping his head low to avoid the deadly hover cars that whirred and buzzed overhead.

Decapitations were commonplace in the city, and mostly regarded as just another of its little quirks.

Five minutes…

With a *'pop'* like a cork from a bottle, Anthony's bruised and battered body was ejected out onto the roadside. A relieved smile spread across his face. He'd landed directly beside his hover car. Finally, something had gone right. As he reached his keys out towards his vehicle, the smile evaporated.

A small naked dead man jutted from the punctured roof of his brand new company car, legs spread upwards in a wide V-shape, like a two-finger message sent by the gods.

Anthony's bottom lip stammered up and down. He looked to the sky for an answer. A leaflet drifted towards him. He snatched it out of the air and examined it.

'Adios trainers,' it read. 'Go out in style.'

'Morning, Jeff!' Anthony trilled, jogging in through the reception doors. 'Sorry I'm late. Car was hit by a low-flying hobbit.'

The receptionist looked up from his newspaper. 'New shoes, Mr Cresswell?'

Anthony shuffled his newly acquired pair of Adios trainers. 'What, these old things? Had them ages.'

'Seem a bit small for you,' Jeff observed. 'And slightly blood-stained.'

'That's second-hand goods for you. Sign me in will you?' Anthony called, heading for the lift. 'There's a good chap.'

'Afraid I can't do that, Mr Cresswell,' Jeff said.

'Oh dear.' Anthony grimaced. 'Misplaced the old biro again have you? Not to worry – I've probably got one lurking somewhere about my personage.'

'It's a touch more serious than that, sir.'

'Come on out you little rascal!' Anthony said, rummaging in his pockets. 'I know you're here somewhere.'

The receptionist calmly set his newspaper aside. 'You've been *fired*, Mr Cresswell.'

'Aha!' cried Anthony, holding up a biro like it was Excalibur itself. 'Success! A pen!' His smile froze. 'I'm sorry, what?'

'They've had to let you go. Lack of punctuality, and all that.'

'You can't be serious!' Anthony leaned on the reception counter and inspected Jeff closely. His face looked serious. His posture looked serious. Even the ginger toupee that sat at a raunchy angle on his head somehow managed to look serious.

'I *am* serious, sir,' said Jeff, confirming Anthony's suspicions.

'But...but I'm only ten minutes late.' Anthony thrust his watch under Jeff's nose, and tapped it purposefully. 'Eight forty A.M. Ten minutes, see?'

'It's Thursday, Mr Cresswell,' said Jeff. 'You were expected Tuesday.'

Anthony's shoulders sagged, and his defiant expression wandered off in search of a stiff drink. 'Ah,' he said, 'noticed that, did you?'

'You could've phoned, sir.'

'Left my phone in the car, along with my breathing mask, nutri-tablets, cattle prod, everything. Two days on foot, being driven in exactly the wrong direction. No food, no water, no toilet facilities.' He looked up at Jeff, hope radiating in his tear-filled eyes. 'But I got here in the end. That's what counts, eh? That's what counts.'

'Not really, Mr Cresswell. You're still fired.'

'B-b-but –' Anthony stammered.

'As a matter of fact, they've already managed to fill your position. With a *punctual* employee.' Jeff brushed a speck of dust off his tie.

'You…?' Anthony gasped.

'That's right. No more pen pushing for me.'

'You…?'

'I'm moving up in the world,' Jeff beamed. 'I'm going places.'

'But you've got a toupee!' Anthony shrieked, pointing an accusing finger at Jeff's head. 'You'll never make it.'

'It's a little thing know as "Retro-chic",' said Jeff, straightening his hair. 'I wouldn't expect you to understand.'

Anthony slumped to the floor in a miserable heap. 'I've been with the company my entire working life. What am I supposed to do now? I can't get another job, not at my age. I'm twenty-five. *Twenty-five!'*

'I'm not without sympathy, Mr Cresswell,' Jeff said, retrieving a gun from a drawer and placing it on his desk. 'Please feel free to retire yourself against the Wall Of Shame.' He gestured to a wall opposite, covered in bloodstains and riddled with bullet holes. A metallic blood-encrusted sign upon it bore the helpful reminder that Anthony's sacrifice would make room for others.

'Jeff…' Anthony pleaded, struggling to his feet. 'It's *me,* Tony. We played squash together.'

'Yes,' the receptionist said bitterly. 'You beat me.'

'Oh now, surely you can't –'

Jeff forced the gun into Anthony's hands. 'Good day,' he said, reaching for his newspaper.

'Be reasonable…'

'Good day.'

Anthony wandered in a daze towards the Wall Of Shame. He wandered back again.

'This really isn't fair, you know.'

'I expect is isn't sir, no.'

'You really are a bastard.'

'I am indeed, Mr Cresswell.'

Anthony walked back towards the wall. He stopped half way and looked down at the gun in his hands. A thought occurred to him. He wandered back, and pointed it at Jeff. 'I have a gun…' he said, uncertainly.

'I know,' said Jeff, flicking idly through the newspaper. 'I gave it to you.'

'Right, right.' Anthony lowered the gun, and wandered back towards the wall. Well, that was him out of ideas. There seemed only one option left. He snapped the gun to the side of his head, and slowly drew back the trigger. 'Er. I'll be off, then,' he said.

A shot.

A ricochet.

A thud.

A scream.

Silence.

Cautiously, Anthony opened one eye.

Jeff lay across his desk in a pool of blood, looking distinctly unamused.

'Oh dear!' said Anthony, rushing to his aid. 'I'm terribly sorry.' He whipped the toupee off Jeff's head, and attempted to stem the flow of blood with it.

Jeff looked up at Anthony in confusion. He looked back towards the wound, then up at Anthony again. 'You *ducked,*' he observed, and then died.

Two

Anthony sat in a particularly small office, staring up at a particularly large moustache. It belonged to Department Head Macemby Pickler, and it was enormous – it almost looked alive. It took every ounce of restraint in Anthony's body to stop him from leaning forward across the desk to pat it and feed it a biscuit.

'It's a monster,' Anthony murmured, shaking his head in wonder. 'A *monster!*'

Mr Pickler coughed politely and gestured to a sign behind him, which stated in polite yet definite terms: 'Please don't stare at the moustache'.

'Ah,' said Anthony, adjusting his gaze to look down at his feet. 'Sorry.'

Mr Pickler set aside Anthony's personnel file and smiled warmly at him. 'Think nothing of it. Can't say I blame you. It is quite something isn't it?' He ran the back of his hand lovingly across his moustache. Anthony could've almost sworn he heard it purr.

'No need to be modest, sir. It's a work of art.'

'You're too kind Anthony, too kind.' Mr Pickler blushed, lavishing the attention. 'Tell you what, let's cut straight to the chase. How's a hundred thousand creds sound?'

'What?' Anthony's brow furrowed. 'To pet the moustache?'

Mr Pickler sighed. 'Not quite what I had in mind, Anthony. Still, damn fine idea though.' He made a note. 'I meant as your starting wage, not including performance bonuses, and other fringe benefits, of course.' His eyes strayed back to the personnel file. 'I see from our records that you've recently come into possession of a company car, so we won't worry about giving you another one of those.'

'You…want to hire me, sir?' Anthony said cautiously.

'That's right.'

'But didn't you just fire me?'

'Ah, but that was before your unique skills came to our attention. Keeping them secret from us all this time. Shame on you, Anthony. Shame on you!' Mr Pickler waggled an admonishing finger. 'Our department's crying out for people with your abilities. Couldn't possibly exist without them.'

'Well, why didn't you say so?' Anthony leapt to his feet as if a state of world emergency had been declared. 'I'll go stick the kettle on this instant. We'll have you sipping Horlicks in no time!'

Mr Pickler chuckled heartily. 'Come now, Anthony, this isn't the Senior Accountancy department.'

Anthony sat down again. 'It isn't?' He glanced around. 'Where am I then?'

Mr Pickler's moustache fanned itself out to make way for a particularly wide grin. 'Subtractions.'

'Never heard of it.'

'Very few people have, except those who are in the department, and those who encounter it,' said Mr Pickler. 'And those who encounter it generally do not live to tell the tale.'

A cluster of worry lines briefly added a bit of character to Anthony's otherwise bland face. 'You kill people?'

'Oh no, no, no, that would be terribly impolite. No, we don't so much kill people as give them a gentle nudge in the right direction.'

At that moment, a huge fist punched a hole through the door. Anthony and Mr Pickler stared at it together.

'Whoops,' came a voice from the other side. 'Sorry, knocked a bit hard there.'

'Ah,' said Mr Pickler, 'here comes our top nudger now – Philip Grison. In you come, Philip.'

A muscular, bullet-headed man strode in through the remains of the door, picking splinters out of his mighty knuckles. 'Morning, sir. Sorry about the door, though you have to admit it was in the way a bit.'

'That's quite all right. How did this morning's assignment go?'

'A hundred percent success rate as always, sir. Rid the world of a bunch of completely brainless no-hopers.' Grison's eyes fell upon Anthony. They looked him up and down. 'Oh dear,' he said. 'Did I miss one?'

'Anthony Cresswell here's a new recruit. Just joined the department today.'

Anthony extended a hand in greeting. Grison stared at it until it went away.

'He looks a bit wet, sir.'

'It's all in the report. Got a lot of hidden talent, this one.'

Grison snatched the report off the desk and read it through. Words like 'Hopeless', 'Brain dead', and 'Makes a rubbish cup of tea' seemed to crop up with alarming regularity. 'It's very well hidden, isn't it sir?'

'Skip to the end, Philip. Today's entry.'

Grison lowered his eyes to the bottom of the page. His eyebrows arched slightly. 'A ricochet?'

'Er, yes,' said Anthony. 'Sorry about that.'

'It shows some potential I suppose.'

'Oh, come now, Philip. There are those among us who would give their right trigger-finger for the ability to pull off a shot like that.' Mr Pickler clasped his hands together, beaming at Anthony like he was a favourite son. 'The angles and vectors you must've had to calculate…such skill! Such mathematical genius! Oh, you'll do the department proud.'

'I wouldn't be so sure about that,' Grison muttered.

'No need for sour grapes, Philip. I can see how you might feel a little threatened by this feisty young hot shot working his way so rapidly up through the ranks. But when it comes down to it, we're all fighting for the same cause, are we not?'

'What is our cause, exactly?' Anthony asked.

'To ensure the survival of the human race, of course.'

'Right,' Anthony said. 'And we're going to achieve this by nudging people, are we?'

Grison made the universal sign of the fruit-loop. 'You see what I mean, sir? Completely barking.'

'Ah, no, I fear Anthony may have slightly misunderstood me.' Mr Pickler leant forward and peered at Anthony over his moustache. 'When I told you we nudge people, I rather meant it in a figurative sense.'

'Well yes,' said Grison, 'in an actual sense, we blow people's heads off.'

'You *what?*' Anthony screeched.

'Not me, obviously. Some of the other recruits do. Young, twitchy folks with no sense of style. Makes me sick, it really does.'

'So you do kill people? You mean I was right?'

Mr Pickler's round face crinkled in distaste. 'Not "kill", Anthony. Never "kill". It's such an *unfriendly* word. We prefer to use the term "subtract".' His face brightened. 'Yes, a good traditional accountancy sort of word. After all, in many respects we're very much like the traditional accountant.'

'Only we happen to subtract people rather than figures,' Grison said. 'I've personally subtracted over ten thousand people this year alone, and I didn't lay a finger on any of them.' His chest swelled with pride. 'Sponsorship deals, that's the secret.'

'And that's what you want me to do is it?' Anthony locked eyes with Mr Pickler. 'Give people a couple of creds and tell them to snuff it?'

'Not at all, Anthony. The manner in which you conduct your assignments is entirely up to you. Some employees prefer to use a gun, some favour knives, and others prefer less conventional means. As long as someone gets subtracted by the end of the day, everybody's happy.'

Grison laid a firm hand on Anthony's shoulder. 'Doubly so if it's *you*.'

'But surely there must be other ways to deal with the population crisis?' Anthony said, struggling to keep the desperation out of his voice. 'What about the departments below us? Doesn't their work count for anything?'

'I'm afraid not, Anthony. Socially acceptable as their methods may be, with their fancy recycling and sterilisation schemes, they barely make an impact. Most of them exist as a front for our activities. After all, people would probably get a little upset if they discovered the government's best solution to the ever rising population levels was to remove the population from the equation.'

Anthony's bottom lip went for a bit of a wobble.

'It's quite all right, Anthony,' Mr Pickler said, smiling sympathetically. 'You're in Subtractions now. Plenty of time to make up for lost ground.'

'Or to be buried beneath it,' Grison mumbled.

'Philip, be a good chap and show Anthony around the workplace. I'm sure he must be raring to get down to the task at hand.'

'Oh bloody hell,' Grison moaned. 'Do I have to?'

'Much as I'd love to take him myself, it is fast approaching grooming hour.' Mr Pickler ran a hand lovingly through his facial hair.

'Very well, sir. Far be it for me to stand between a man and his moustache.' Grison tucked the report underarm and marched towards the doorway. He glanced back over his shoulder at Anthony. 'Well? What are you waiting for? This way, Cressface.'

Anthony followed Grison down a drab corridor towards a vast, bustling office. Grison pushed his way into the middle of the room and clapped his hands loudly together.

'Okay, listen up people,' he yelled over the hubbub. 'This is Anthony Cressface, a promising new addition to the team.'

A hundred pairs of eyes swivelled towards Anthony.

'At least,' Grison continued, 'that's the official word. Bit of a wet blanket if you ask me, but never mind.'

A hundred mouths sniggered in unison.

'Anyway, please don't bother trying to make him feel welcome, since he probably won't be with us for long. If he is, I'll gladly subtract him myself. Thanks for your time.'

The office activity resumed. Grison returned his attention to Anthony. 'That's the introductions over with. Any questions?'

Anthony's mouth opened and shut a few times.

'I'll take that as a "no".' Grison made to leave.

'W-wait a minute!' Anthony managed to stammer. 'I don't know what I'm supposed to do.'

'Oh yes, almost forgot.' Grison thrust Anthony's personnel file into his hands. 'Take that down to the room at the far end, and insert it into Noddy.'

'I beg your pardon?'

Grison span on his heel, and was gone.

'Er,' said Anthony, looking around for assistance. 'Oh dear.'

Much to Anthony's relief, Noddy turned out to be a state of the art computer system, and not the rosy-cheeked hat-wearing technician he'd found stooped over the control panel.

'Once again, sorry about the mix-up,' Anthony said, the personnel file hanging limply at his side. 'I really can't apologise enough.'

'No problem, mate,' the technician said, dutifully levering a few rogue biscuit crumbs out of Noddy's keyboard. 'Happens all the time. At least you had the common decency to ask my name first.'

The technician's name was Nigel, and he had the universal appearance of technicians everywhere; thin, wild eyed, and bearded. Even though there was barely enough meat on the man to make a very small and disappointing buffet sandwich, his buttocks still managed to hang a good two inches out of his jeans. The overall effect was of a badly disguised stick insect that had been interrupted half way through a rather unwelcome strip tease.

'But why Noddy?' Anthony said, critically examining the machine. It was about the size of an office photocopier, and covered in a bank of brightly coloured flashing lights, along with plenty of knobs, dials and twiddly bits. 'What's it stand for?'

'Doesn't stand for anything,' Nigel said, casually picking his ear with a screwdriver. 'The system designer was a huge Glam Rock fan.' Nigel stirred his tea with the screwdriver, and took a sip. 'Naturally they shot him as soon as they found out. On Noddy's command, ironically.'

'Well, hooray for the system, eh?' Anthony fed his report into a slot at the top of the computer. 'So Noddy's an assassin as well, is he?'

'Oh he's much more than that.' Nigel affectionately patted Noddy's sleek metallic surface. 'The personal details of everyone in the city are stored within this beauty. It's Noddy's job to sift through them all, separate wheat from chaff, and then determine which employee is best suited to –'

'Blowing the chaff's head off?' Anthony said miserably.
'That's it exactly.'

'Where's the bloody cancel button?' Anthony jabbed frantically at Noddy's keyboard. 'I'm not ready for that sort of thing, not yet. It's my first day!'

With a thoughtful click, several really meaty whirrs, and a short, woefully inaccurate rendition of 'Cum on feel the noize', Noddy reached a verdict. A photo shot out of his rear exit hatch.

'Too late for second thoughts,' Nigel said, stooping to retrieve it. 'Let's take a gander at your first lucky client.'

They stared at the photo together, and exchanged glances.

'It's never done that before,' Nigel said.

'Just a mistake, right?' Anthony said slowly.

'Oh yeah, I'm sure that's what it is.' Nigel waved a dismissive hand. 'We'll try again.'

He reinserted the photo, which Noddy immediately spat out. He tried several more times, each with exactly the same result; another photo of Anthony.

'Let me have another go.' Anthony forced the photo into the slot. With an irritated 'click' Noddy grudgingly accepted it.

'You see?' Anthony said. 'All it took was a little –'

The photo shot out again. This time the word 'Subtract' had been emblazoned across Anthony's forehead in large red letters.

'Ah, come on...' Anthony whined. 'Now that's hardly fair.'

Nigel scratched his buttocks thoughtfully. 'Maybe we're taking things a little too literally here.'

'Too damn right I'm taking things literally!' Anthony cried. 'This jumped up juke-box wants me to kill myself!'

'Now I hardly think that's likely. You've got to remember Noddy's a very intelligent machine. He's probably talking on some deep metaphorical level that we're not quite aware of.'

'You really think so?' Anthony inspected the photo again. The word 'Subtract' had been underlined several times.

'Yeah,' Nigel said, sounding unconvinced. 'What he probably means is, y'know, destroy your former self. Sever all ties with your past life, and take on a bold new identity. He must have something very special planned for you. Very special indeed.'

'Sounds a bit far fetched to me. Are you sure there aren't any other interpretations?'

'Only one I can think of,' said Nigel. 'That you're the most useless sod in the entire city, and Noddy wants you to blow your own brains out.'

'Destroy my former self, eh?' Anthony rolled the idea around in his mind. 'You know, the more I think about it, the more it makes sense.'

'If I were you, I'd head down to Rakembalo's Genetic Makeover and ask for a complete overhaul. Nothing fancy, mind. No need to go overboard.'

'Genetically alter my entire appearance?' Anthony clutched himself tightly, as if his body might melt away beneath his fingers. 'But I like the way I look.'

'Do you?' Nigel raised an eyebrow. 'Really? Well, bloody hell.'

'Couldn't I just get a haircut or something?'

'That's not quite destroying your former self, is it? You'll need to remove all distinguishing marks – retinas, fingerprints, DNA.'

'This all seems a little excessive, somehow.'

'You could always consider the alternative, of course.' Nigel tapped the photograph pointedly.

Three

The streets outside were still packed with pedestrians. Anthony was pretty sure he recognised most of them from his walk to work earlier. Forcing his eighteenth Mock-Choc bar deep into his jacket pocket, he stepped off the curb, praying it would be enough to sustain him through the journey.

'Need a lift mate?'

Anthony stopped, and craned his head to one side. He could've almost sworn he heard –

'Do. You. Need. A. Lift. Mate?' The voice came clearer this time, penetrating the thick babble of frustrated pedestrians and excited pickpockets.

Anthony slowly turned around, and immediately wished he hadn't. A car was staring expectantly at him. On any other day, he might have considered this unusual.

'Er, what?'

'Ah, crud,' said the car, rolling its eyes. 'Why do I always get the thick ones?'

'Am I to understand you're offering me a lift?'

''Course I am. I'm a cab aren't I?' the car said in a matter-of-fact sort of way. 'It's what cabs do.'

'Are you absolutely sure about that? You don't look much like a cab.' Most cabs Anthony had seen didn't have pulsating flesh panelling, and they most certainly didn't have two huge muscular legs supporting them at the rear.

The car sighed, and held out an arm for Anthony to inspect. 'What does it say on the tattoo?'

Anthony peered at the tattoo, eyes narrowing in confusion. 'It says "Crab".'

'Close enough though, eh?' The car's left wing-mirror winked at Anthony in a cheerful fashion. 'I'm Derek. I'll be your driver for the day.'

'No you bloody won't,' Anthony said, attempting to force his way into the crowd.

The car gripped Anthony tightly by his arm. 'Come on, give me a chance. You're the first customer I've had all day who hasn't run screaming at the sight of me.'

'Then let go of my arm,' Anthony said stiffly. 'We'll soon uphold that tradition.'

'At least tell me where it is you're trying to get to.'

'At the moment? Wherever you're not. Please let go.'

'Why walk when you can ride in style?' With a sickly wet *'shluck!'* the car door swung open to reveal a soft, pink, squidgy interior.

'I think that answers that question,' Anthony said, his face draining of colour.

'Plush skin-lined seats, comfortable bloated liver footrests and a warm gastrically heated environment.' The wing-mirrors waggled their eyebrows enticingly. 'What more could any discerning passenger wish for?'

'A sick bag and some major psychiatric counselling,' Anthony said. 'I'll walk, thanks.'

'Wouldn't hear of it.' The arm thrust Anthony headfirst into the car, and the door squelched shut behind him. 'Just sit back, relax, and let me handle the driving.'

'Please let me out,' Anthony whimpered. 'I get carsick. You wouldn't enjoy it.'

'That's quite all right.' A huge mouth grinned at Anthony from the dashboard. 'I've got some tablets for that sort of thing. They're in the glove compartment.'

Anthony glanced around him at an interior that looked as if Hannibal Lecter and Leatherface had decorated it, possibly using parts of each other. 'Which one's the glove compartment?'

'That purple veiny sort of object in front of you. Just reach your fingers deep into the crevice and have a good old rummage. They're in there somewhere.'

'Actually,' Anthony said, his voice trembling, 'I'm feeling much better now.'

'Really?'

'Oh yes. Much, much better.'

'Are you sure? You look a bit green there.'

'I like green,' Anthony said weakly. 'Green's a good colour.'

'Well, if you say so.'

With a sudden explosion of deeply unpleasant noises, Derek's organic engine farted into life. 'Just hear that engine purr,' he said proudly.

Anthony gripped a hand over his nose, trying to block out the suspicious-smelling fumes. 'Rakembalo's Genetic Makeover. Close by, is it?'

'Yeah, it's down in The Stacks, just around the corner. We're practically there already.'

'I'd like to go there then.' Anthony fought back the bile rising in his throat. 'Quick as you can. Hurry…'

'Sit tight then. Oh, and you might want to hold your breath for a bit. Takeoffs tend to be a little on the ripe side.'

With an almighty bound, and a vast eruption of noxious gases, Derek propelled himself into the air. Two large, sloppy wet wings unfurled from the roof and harnessed his own personal current of wind.

Two and a half hours later, with a noise like a ruptured zeppelin, he touched down outside a vast collection of work units stacked higgledy-piggledy on top of each other, much like the vehicles parked around them.

'Pretty smooth trip all round, I thought,' Derek said, disgorging Anthony's body onto the roadside. 'Took a bit longer than anticipated, but I thought you'd much rather take the scenic route.'

'Scenic route?' Anthony shrieked, hugging his knees to his chest. 'All I saw were innards!'

'That reminds me, really must get some windows installed one day.'

'And a fan!' Anthony cried. 'For the love of god, get a fan.'

'You're right.' Derek hauled himself upright. 'No time like the present. I'll have a word with Rakembalo and see what he can do.' He extended a hand in Anthony's direction, and coughed politely. 'Of course, all that's going to cost money.'

'You've got to be joking.'

'I'm not a public service, mate. A man's got to earn a living.'

Anthony stormed off towards the door of the genetics parlour, at the bottom of the stack.

'All right, call it twenty creds,' Derek said, following after him. 'I'll even throw in a ride home.'

Inside, the genetics parlour was garishly decorated and perfectly circular, much like its proprietor.

The overweight eyesore waddled towards them as they entered, his expression managing to simultaneously convey agony, pity, disgust and contempt.

'Oh my heavens!' he cried. 'You poor creature! Look at you...you're *hideous.*'

'I know,' Anthony said, casting a backwards glance at Derek. 'That's what I've been trying to tell him.'

Ignoring Derek, Rakembalo marched straight up to Anthony and gripped him by the face. 'Why, I've never seen anyone quite so...*bland* in all my life.'

'Excuse me?' Anthony's eyes darted around, desperately searching for someone else the man might be addressing.

'Helena!' Rakembalo called out to his attractive blonde triple-nosed receptionist. 'Cancel all my appointments for the day. I've got my work cut out for me on this one. At last, a challenge. God, what a challenge!' Tugging at Anthony's cheeks like an overzealous aunt, Rakembalo began to twist and mould his skin into new and increasingly painful positions.

'Ow!' Anthony cried, pulling away from his grasp. 'Get off me, you maniac!'

'Oh my dear boy, do you not yet understand? You are in the presence of greatness! For I am Rakembalo...the artiste. The creator.' Rakembalo clapped his hands sharply together. A swarm of miniature cameras whooshed up from a grating beneath Anthony's feet, and buzzed around him, clicking and flashing away. The panels on the walls around him lit up, displaying Anthony's image on each one.

'Do not fret, my dear boy. Mother Nature is a cruel and unimaginative artist who paints from a selective pallet. But I shall expand that pallet and make you bright as a rainbow and radiant as a summer's day!' The impassioned geneticist clapped his hands together again, and the cameras vanished back into the grating. 'Helena? Some classical music to inspire the mood, if you please.' He screwed his eyes shut, and lifted his head towards the ceiling. The less than elegant tones of 'I'm too sexy' wafted down from hidden speakers. Slowly he began to wobble and gyrate in time with the music.

'I'm seeing...I'm seeing...a pinch of rustic blue...velvet hairline. The scent of thyme...thyme...' Rakembalo sniffed the air. 'Apricot? No, no, definitely thyme...excreting from your pores. Large hands...big claws...good for burrowing. Oh yes, this is it. I can feel it! A masterpiece in the works. A *masterpiece!*'

As he continued to rant, the picture on the panels warped and twisted to encompass his growing vision.

The ranting stopped. The music faded. The picture warped one final time.

'Behold!' Rakembalo cried, opening his eyes and throwing his arms out wide. 'The new you!'

Anthony stared at the panels. A blue hunchbacked thing stared back at him. 'I look like a sodding Morlock!'

'Yes!' Rakembalo enthused, nodding away excitedly. 'Yes! Share the vision. Encompass the dream.'

'I rather think not, actually. I want something that doesn't stand out. A face of the crowd.'

'You *are* a face of the crowd. An uninspired crowd.' The geneticist clenched his hands emphatically together. 'Be one with the inner you. The *true* you.'

'I just want something ordinary.'

Rakembalo's face stiffened. With one harsh motion, he blanked the panels around him. 'Then take a seat in the waiting area,' he said coldly. 'I believe that gentleman was first.' He bustled past Anthony, and moved towards Derek.

'I'm in no rush,' said Derek, who'd rocked back onto his roof like an oversized tortoise, and had his feet resting precariously on a tiny coffee table. 'Quite comfortable parked over here.'

Rakembalo sighed, and turned back towards Anthony. 'Very well, Mr Ordinary. Perhaps we could see about fitting you up with one of our customer cast offs.'

'That doesn't sound very promising.'

'If sir wants something inconspicuous, it is the best place to start.' Rakembalo clapped his hands together, this time with considerably less flourish. The panels filled with hundreds of pictures of increasingly average looking people. 'Whenever a customer gets a radical new appearance, they quite often like to trade in their old appearance against the price,' he explained.

'And that saves money, does it?' Anthony's thin brow knitted in contemplation.

'Don't even think about it, sir. The trade-in value for your present appearance would barely afford you a nose job. Now hurry up and choose, before I grow weary of your presence.'

Anthony marched up and down a row of pictures that looked like they'd been lifted from a police mug shot album, carefully inspecting the unsightly characters. 'Ugly, fat, short, ginger, looks like someone my mum would've dated…' He stopped at the image of a strikingly handsome man, with blonde hair and blue eyes…the sort of desirable features absolutely guaranteed to get the girls. This was the one. Oh yes, this was the one.

'That one there,' he said. 'No doubt about it.'

'Very good s–'

'Hey, that's me!' Derek cried. 'I mean, the old me, before I had the improvements made.' He winked a headlight in Anthony's direction. 'Hey, in a sense I guess this'll make us DNA brothers.'

'Actually,' Anthony said hurriedly, 'I meant that one there.' He pointed to the picture next to it, of a squinty-eyed man with a facial tick and a smile like an angry badger. His hair was beating a tactical retreat up his forehead, and had been combed over to form a question mark motif, though the only question it was likely to raise in any onlooker's minds was why this man had gone to such extravagant lengths to look like such a tit.

'A superlative choice, sir,' Rakembalo said, trying to suppress a snigger. 'If you'd care to follow me towards the DNA mixer.'

Anthony was led towards a booth much like those used for passport photos, except a little less complicated to operate. He stopped in front of the curtain. 'This isn't going to be painful, is it?'

'Sadly not,' Rakembalo said. 'Now please get inside and disrobe.'

'Is that really necessary?'

'Unless you want to be wearing your clothes internally,

I'd certainly advise in its favour.'

Anthony stepped inside and pulled the curtain shut behind him. Clothing rustled as it dropped to the floor.

Rakembalo reached towards the keypad on the outside of the booth, just as Anthony poked his head out.

'Before you start, any chance you could keep my old appearance on file? I may want it back at some point.'

The geneticist eyed him doubtfully. 'Now I hardly think that's likely, sir.'

'It might not be much to you, but I rather like it, thank you very much.'

'Oh, if you insist.' Rakembalo plucked a single hair from Anthony's head. 'Your DNA will be kept in storage for a maximum of thirty days. If you have not reclaimed it by then, it automatically becomes property of the management. Though heaven knows what I should want with it.'

'You're too kind.' Anthony disappeared behind the curtain.

'Ready?' Rakembalo cracked his knuckles back, and twiddled his fingers. 'Then let us begin.' His hand flickered briefly over the keypad. The booth flashed once.

'There,' he said. 'All done.'

Anthony emerged from the booth. Or rather, someone else did. 'Is that it?' he said, running his hands along the contours of his new face.

'You might want to put some clothes on before you leave the premises, but otherwise yes that's it.'

'Colin?' a voice said from somewhere down low. 'Is that you?'

Anthony slowly lowered his head. A woman's face stared back up at him. 'Who the bloody hell are you?' Anthony shrieked.

The head looked around at the body it had unexpectedly found itself attached to. 'Colin!' it screamed. 'What have you done to me, you bastard?'

Anthony looked to Rakembalo for assistance. 'A little help?'

'Something wrong, sir?' Rakembalo asked, smiling innocently.

'Colin!' the head screamed. *'Coliiiiiiin!'*

'Is this your idea of inconspicuous?' Anthony gestured to the small screaming head protruding from his armpit. 'I'll stand out a mile away with this.'

'Ah yes, I see what's happened,' Rakembalo said calmly. 'I must have accidentally stored this customer's DNA *after* the operation rather than *before.*'

'Well, get rid of it!' Anthony snapped, his new facial tick twitching away manically.

'Oh, very well. Step back into the booth and we'll see if we can absorb the extraneous head into your system. Which one would you like me to remove?'

'The one under my armpit would be nice,' Anthony snarled from within the booth.

'If you say so. Though you're making a mistake, if you want my opinion.'

Rakembalo ran his hands over the keypad. The booth flashed.

Anthony emerged, looking like a Colin. He carefully inspected his new self and was relieved to discover he now had the correct number of appendages, and none of them were trying to attack him. He slipped back into the booth and forced his clothes on, which were now several sizes too small.

'I take it you'll remember this little incident when it comes to settling the bill?' Anthony said, as he reluctantly handed over his holo card.

'Indeed I will, sir.' Rakembalo eagerly swiped the card through his machine. 'A removal operation always costs extra.'

'After you with that,' Derek said, trundling towards them. 'I haven't been paid yet.'

'Oh for Christ's sake, here.' Anthony threw Derek a handful of coins from his wallet and marched towards the door.

'Do drop by again when your bank balance has recovered,' Rakembalo shouted after him. 'We're doing a wonderful new line in personality grafts. You might want to consider getting yourself one.'

Anthony had barely got five feet from the exit when a huge pair of hands grabbed him from behind. 'Where do you think you're going?' Derek said, grinning. 'I promised you a lift home.'

'Oh god, no,' Anthony cried as he was bundled head-first into the car. 'Please, no!'

'It's no bother. Just got a few stops to make along the way. Fancy going for a curry? My stomach's killing me.' Derek's engine rumbled noisily into action.

'Funny you should mention that,' Anthony growled, covering his nose. 'It's killing *me* as well.'

'Afternoon, Tony,' Nigel said, turning towards the ill-looking man staggering in through the Assignment Room door. 'Nice to see you're back so promptly.'

'Car troubles,' Anthony said, flicking a speck of vomit off his shirt. 'Got here as soon as I – Wait a minute, how did you know it was me?'

'Same clothes.' Nigel retrieved a battered Insta-Print camera from a drawer. 'You're in a fashion league all of your own. May I?' He motioned to the camera. 'For the records.'

'Just don't expect me to smile.'

The camera flashed, and ejected a miserable-looking photo. 'Any problems getting past reception?'

'Curiously, no,' Anthony said. 'The moment I intro-duced myself, the receptionist screamed loudly and ran from the building.'

'Ah, your reputation precedes you.' Nigel glued the photo down onto Anthony's personnel report. 'Let's see if this works, shall we?' He inserted the file into Noddy.

Anthony crossed his fingers and uttered a silent prayer. Unfortunately for him, God was on a coffee break.

Noddy clicked, whirred and produced a result. It was another photo of Anthony; this time, Anthony as he looked now.

Nigel and Anthony stared at it for a while.

'Oh well,' said Nigel, with a shrug. 'It was worth a try.'

'I thought you said Noddy had something special in store for me.'

'Nah, I was wrong. He wants you dead all right.' Nigel yanked a large, menacing drill from his tool belt. 'Do you want to do the honours, or shall I?'

'Whoa, wait a minute…' Anthony backed away, hands raised in protest. 'Let's not be hasty here.'

The drill in Nigel's hand whirred into life. 'Don't worry,' he said, clumsily waving it around as he advanced. 'I'll try and make this as painless as possible. Not really my field of expertise, but I'm sure I'll soon get the hang of it.'

The computer behind him emitted a shrill beep.

'Stop!' Anthony screamed. 'Noddy's printing something out.'

'Is he? Oh blast!' Nigel switched off the drill, picked up Noddy's report sheet in his grimy fingers and read it through.

'Well?' Anthony said, licking his lips nervously. 'What does it say?'

Nigel gloomily thrust his drill back into his tool belt. 'Looks like you get to live after all. Damn, I could've been onto a new career there.'

Anthony snatched the report out of Nigel's hands, and skimmed the page. 'It's not me in the photo,' he concluded. 'It's a man named Colin Frogfertler.'

'That's right. From what I could gather, Noddy wants you to subtract him, use his appearance to infiltrate the resistance, find out who's in charge, and subtract them as well. Not bad for your first day.'

'I didn't even know we had a resistance,' said Anthony. 'What are they resisting against?'

'Us, mostly. They seem to think the department's methods are a little overzealous in nature.'

Anthony glanced at the drill dangling from Nigel's tool belt. 'Fancy that.'

'They also believe the solution to the world's population problem somehow lies in cloning.' Nigel shook his head. 'Which is bloody ridiculous, if you ask me. World's already crowded enough without every Tom, Dick and Harry duplicating himself. It's bad enough we've got sex clones.'

'What's wrong with sex clones?' asked Anthony, who'd been hoping to one day give them a thorough road test.

'Friend of mine had a nasty experience with a sex clone,' said Nigel, his rosy cheeks advancing to beetroot red.

'Friend of yours?'

'Yeah, friend of mine.' Nigel coughed. 'He hired it near the end of its twenty-four hour life cycle, see? One minute he was grinding away, having the time of his life, and the next...' He paused a moment and stared off towards the distant shores of grim reflection. 'I might as well have been dipping my wick in a bowl of soup.'

'They used to sell clone soup, back in the day,' said Anthony, keen to move the conversation in a direction that didn't involve Nigel and sex.

'Yeah, I know, until the great sex clone uprising of 2212,' said Nigel, who wasn't about to let him off that easily. 'It might've only lasted twenty-four hours, but it was more than enough to get their point across; shag it, don't eat it. We'd have won that war too, if it wasn't for all those cold showers.'

Anthony studied his reflection on a metal work surface. 'This Colin…quite high up in the resistance chain of command, is he?' He attempted to rearrange his unappealing features into something that might resemble the heroic pose of a freedom fighter. No matter how hard he tried, he still looked like a badger that was out for blood.

'Oh no, he's nothing – a nobody. His wife Maria, however, was the leader of the resistance. Probably only married him as a cover for her activities. That's her in the photo there.' Nigel tapped the photo of Colin. Anthony followed his finger towards the man in the photo's armpit. Jutting out of it was a disgruntled female head, startlingly familiar in appearance. Anthony recognised it from his incident in the genetics parlour earlier; it was impossible not to. 'Oh yes,' he said. 'I believe I've met her.'

'I doubt it, she's been dead for years. Murdered by Colin, actually.'

'A murderer…' Anthony studied his reflection again. Somehow it all made sense. 'I'm wearing the face of a murderer.'

'Pretty appropriate really,' Nigel said, 'since it's your job to murder him. Subtract, I mean.'

'Why did he do it?' Anthony asked. 'Why did he kill his wife?'

'It's all written down in the report,' Nigel said impatiently. 'Read it yourself.'

'It's a bit difficult to make out the words since you touched it.' Anthony's eyes attempted to weave their way around all the grease and food stains.

'As I recall, it says Colin came home early one night to find his wife in bed with, oh, who was it now?'

Anthony scratched away at a blob of mustard and squinted at the words on the page. 'Terry Thomas?' His eyes widened in surprise.

'That's the chap, yeah.'

37

'But he's dead, isn't he? Has been for a few centuries now.'

'Which only further serves to illustrate the dangers of cloning. Without proper restrictions in place we'd have deceased celebrities popping up and committing adulterous acts all over the bloody place.'

'So Colin killed them both?'

'Not both of them, no. He strangled his wife, and then asked Terry for an autograph. Didn't get it, apparently.'

'What a bastard,' Anthony muttered.

'That's celebrities for you,' Nigel said. 'All up their own arses.'

'I meant Colin.'

'Well the authorities didn't seem to have a problem with his behaviour. Gave him quite a hefty pay out, as it happens. Thanks to his wife's illegal cloning activities, killing her could hardly be considered a crime.'

'If Colin killed his wife, what the hell is he doing with her head grafted to his armpit?'

'He got drunk a few nights back, and went down to the genetics parlour. Woke up with a killer hangover, and a second head. There's a lot of valuable information in that mind of hers, and the resistance will stop at nothing to get their hands on it.'

'So all I've got to do is subtract her and Colin, hide the body, and wait for the resistance to pick me up?'

'That's about the size of it. Shouldn't pose too much of a problem, since you look exactly like Colin.'

'Not exactly like him,' Anthony said. 'Aren't you forgetting one tiny detail?'

Nigel stared at him blankly for a moment. 'Oh my god!' he yelled suddenly. 'You *don't* have a second head jutting out of your armpit!'

'So glad you noticed.'

'This throws a spanner in the works, and no mistake.'

'Yes,' Anthony said, smiling. 'Rotten luck. Guess I won't be killing anyone today after all.'

'I wouldn't be so sure about that. You seem to forget…' Nigel winked confidently, and leant his arm in a bowlful of porridge that also doubled as a mouse mat. 'You're in the company of a technical genius here.'

Thirty minutes passed.

Anthony stood staring at the monstrosity that lurked beneath his armpit.

'Well?' Nigel said, looking at him expectantly. 'What do you think?'

Anthony sighed heavily. Where to begin? 'This is the best design you could come up with, is it?' He gingerly prodded the green object that rested underarm. 'A melon on a stick, with a wig?'

'An animatronic melon,' Nigel said, extending a remote control. 'Look.' He pressed a button.

The melon revolved several times, bobbed up and down, and then exploded.

'Brilliant…' Anthony said, wiping juice from his eye. 'Now I don't even have a melon.'

'Oh well.' Nigel shrugged. 'I guess this calls for Plan B.'

'You mean that *wasn't* Plan B?'

'Oh no, Plan B's a lot less complex.' He handed Anthony a jumper. 'There you go. Sellotape a coupla grapefruits to your pit, and wear that over the top.' He tapped his nose conspiratorially. 'They won't suspect a thing.'

'I'm going to die,' Anthony said quietly. 'You know this, don't you?'

'I should hope so too,' a cheerful voice said from behind.

Grison stood beside Noddy, reading through Anthony's assignment. The smile on his face widened with every paragraph. 'Nice weasely new image, by the way. Really suits you.'

'Oh, hello,' said Anthony as he awkwardly attempted to Sellotape a pair of grapefruits to his armpit. 'Come to gloat, have you?'

'On the contrary,' Grison said. 'I've come to wish you the best of luck.'

'Really?' Anthony's eyes narrowed in suspicion.

'Yes, there's no doubt in my mind that you're absolutely the right man for the job.'

'That's very, er –'

'After all,' Grison said, grinning, 'it *is* a suicide mission. You will almost certainly be horribly and brutally killed.'

'I think Nigel's gone out of his way to accomplish that,' Anthony said, slipping the jumper over his head.

'Is that all the thanks I get?' Nigel tutted. 'That's no ordinary grapefruit, you know. It contains a specially devised homing beacon. Run into trouble, and a couple of our lads'll be right along to mop up any unfriendlies.'

'And whatever's left of your body,' Grison added, thoroughly enjoying himself.

'You really have thought of everything, haven't you? What if the resistance ask me to take the jumper *off*? What then?'

'Ah, well, then, er…then…' Nigel frowned. 'Um…'

'I believe I can answer that,' Grison said. 'You see that melon?' He gestured to the fragments of sticky red pulp that dribbled from walls and ceiling. 'Let us pretend for the moment that its name is "Cressface"…'

Four

By the time Anthony arrived at Colin's surprisingly spacious apartment, the man was already deep in argument with himself.

'You had to bring that up didn't you?' Colin screamed. 'Every bloody time. One small incident and you just won't let me forget it.'

Anthony edged his way in through an open window. A topless man sporting Anthony's unsavoury new appearance came into view, with an angry head peering out from under his armpit.

'You strangled me to death, Colin!' the head countered. 'It's hardly something I'm likely to forget.'

'Let's keep things in perspective, sweetheart.' Colin paced back and forth on his authentic replica Persian rug. 'I found you in bed with a dead movie star, who was wearing my pyjamas and smoking my bloody cigarettes!'

'Maybe it wouldn't have happened if you'd paid as much attention to me as you did my sister.'

'Honey…sweetheart…' Colin spread his arms out wide in an appeasing gesture. 'I was thinking of you when I shagged her.'

'You were on the *phone* to me when you shagged her,' Maria snapped. '"I'm just across the road, shagging your sister. Put on something sexy, baby – I'm feeling horny tonight!"'

'Well I'm sorry, but as you've so kindly pointed out on many, many occasions, I was drunk at the time. I mean, hell, it took a few pints just to get my courage up. That girl's got a face like the back end of a mule.'

'You inconceivable bastard! We're identical twins!' Colin's own hand slapped him in the face. 'That's why I grew up without a father, remember? My mother chose to keep the pair of us and have him aborted instead.'

'It's always about you, isn't it?' Colin said, restraining his wayward hand.

'That's it, I'm going to file for a separation!'

'That's fine by me honey,' Colin said. 'Just as soon as I've raised enough money to reverse the operation, consider yourself separated. I didn't want you back anyway, you were supposed to be a porn star! Donna Kebabs, that's what it said on the sex clone DNA kit I found in your personal effects.'

'That's because you're predictable, Colin. I knew that if anything ever happened to me, it'd only be a matter of time before curiosity got the better of you.'

'If I'd known it was you in there, I'd have flushed it down the toilet.'

'You think I'm happy with the situation?' Maria screamed. 'What sort of idiot gets a head grafted to his armpit?'

Colin's eyes twitched frantically. 'A drunk idiot. But I'm sober now, honey, and that makes me very, very angry!' His hands leapt to Maria's throat.

'C-Colin…' she choked.

'Don't try and talk your way out of this one, you scabrous cow!' Colin's grip tightened.

'T-there's a man in the corner, Colin.'

Colin broke off his attack. His eyes scanned the shadows, and fell upon Anthony.

Anthony looked behind him, keen to see what Colin was looking at. It was then that he remembered he wasn't supposed to be there. 'Er, hello,' said Anthony. 'Don't mind me. Please, carry on.'

'Who are you?' Colin said gruffly. 'What are you doing with my face?'

'Look, I've obviously caught you at an inconvenient moment. I can see you're terribly busy and everything…'

'Colin,' Maria hissed. 'He has a gun.'

'What? Do I?' Anthony looked down at the object in his hand. 'Oh yes.' He raised the gun. 'This thing.'

'He's going to shoot you, Colin. Rush him. Quickly!'

'Sod that,' Colin said. 'He might blow my head off.'

'Then *I'll* rush him.'

Colin's body staggered forward towards Anthony.

'You'll do nothing of the sort, woman!'

The body staggered backwards.

Anthony watched with interest as Colin's body staggered backwards and forwards for some time, as both brains competed for control.

'Damn it, man!' Colin screamed at Anthony. 'Don't just stand there gawping. Shoot her! That's what you're here for isn't it? Shoot her!'

'No – shoot him,' countered the head under Colin's arm. 'I don't need two brains to live. His is barely operational as it is.'

Sweat trickled down Anthony's face as he repeatedly switched from one target to the other. Eventually, he lowered the gun. 'I can't do it. I just can't…'

'What do you mean you can't do it?' Colin spat. 'You've got a gun. You're a killer, aren't you? So kill.'

'It's not as easy as that.'

'Then give *me* the gun.' Colin stretched out the palm of his hand. 'I'll shoot her.'

Anthony's face brightened. 'Hold on, I've got an idea.' He raised the gun to his own head.

Colin and his wife exchanged glances. 'The man's a bloody lunatic.'

'Well he's *you*, Colin. It stands to reason, doesn't it?'

'No, no,' Anthony said, looking around for a convenient surface to ricochet a bullet off of. 'It's perfectly fine, I've done this before.'

'Don't kill yourself,' Maria pleaded. 'You haven't killed Colin yet.'

'Yes, that's it. Go on – blow your own brains out. You can do it, my son.'

'Will you shut up, Colin!'

'Just trying to give the lad some support.'

Anthony located a metallic 'Home is where the heart is' sign on the wall, and began to calculate the angles.

'Don't do it!' Maria screamed. 'Kill Colin first.'

'Maria!'

'Colin!'

Anthony closed his eyes and blocked out the noise. His finger closed around the trigger.

A wave of pain exploded in his skull.

Blackness.

Grison barged through the door to Mr Pickler's office without bothering to open it first. 'I want to speak to you about the new recruit.'

'Ah, Philip.' Mr Pickler beamed up at him from behind his desk. 'Come in, take a seat. Care for a fruity bon-bon?'

Grison's brow caved in under the relentless barrage of English pleasantries. 'What?'

'Fruity bon-bon.' Mr Pickler rattled a sweets tin encouragingly.

'No thank you,' Grison snapped, trying to get his thoughts back on track.

'Oh go on.' Mr Pickler twiddled his moustache playfully. 'They're *strawberry* flavour.'

Grison sighed. 'Oh, all right. Maybe just the one.' He took two.

'Now, what was it you wanted to see me about?' Mr Pickler settled back in his chair. 'Cresswell again?'

'Not this time.' Grison wrestled noisily with a sweet wrapper. 'It's the other recruit I'm currently more concerned about.'

'Oh, you mean Susan,' Mr Pickler said. 'Yes, lovely girl. Cracking personality. I'm sure she'll do the department proud.'

'Sir.' Grison's stare hardened. 'Her chosen weapon is the spoon.'

'Yes,' Mr Pickler said, smiling amiably. 'That's right.'

'But that's not professionalism,' Grison whined. 'That's just taking the piss.'

'Now I won't hear another word said against Susan. She'll be a very useful girl to have around in a crisis.'

'Oh, undoubtedly.' Grison rolled his eyes. 'If said crisis happens to revolve around the urgent necessity to crack into a pudding, I'm sure she'll be absolutely vital to the mission. But that doesn't change the fact that she's going to be a little bit lacking when it comes to the actual subtraction side of the job.'

'She's very accurate.'

'Yes,' Grison said through gritted teeth. 'Accurate with *spoons*. Have you ever seen anyone die of a spoon wound? It's just not possible.'

'I'm sure we'll see results in time. Noddy's been handing out assignments this morning like there's no tomorrow.'

'Then I hope I get lawyers,' Grison snarled, turning towards the fallen door. 'I could do with something to cheer me up.'

He trampled over the door, stormed down the corridor and stomped into the Assignment Room.

'Morning, Smiler,' Nigel said cheerily.

'Oh shut up.' Grison thrust his report file into Noddy's slot. 'I swear, this whole department's going to the dogs.'

Nigel spat on a cloth and smeared it around on a computer monitor. 'I had a dog once,' he said. 'Holographic one, obviously. Matilda, she was called. Gorgeous terrier-shark crossbreed…used to follow me everywhere, even the public baths, though that never seemed to go down well.' Nigel paused with a faraway look in his eyes, and Grison found himself wishing the rest of Nigel would follow it. 'Then, of course, there was that outcry about holographic pets making people sterile. Probably should've hit the delete key there and then, but she was just so damned cute…' He shook his head, lost in memory.

'So you're sterile then?' Grison concluded. 'Jolly good.'

With a quick burst of 'Mama, weer all crazee now,' the computer behind him printed out a result.

As Grison's eyes fell upon the photo, his foul mood instantly evaporated. 'Well, well, well!'

Nigel glanced at the photo over Grison's shoulder. 'That one again? It's been doing that all morning.'

Grison's mouth cracked into a wide grin. 'Better than lawyers.'

Is he dead?

Blackness…

Don't think so. He fainted before he could pull the trigger.

Blackness gave way to a tiny pinprick of light.

Who is he?

The pinprick widened and multiplied.

Dunno. He's not on our files.

Stars swam in and out of focus.

Well, wake him up and find out.

Gasses swirled…vapours formed.

How am I supposed to do that?

Something began to take shape and grow…

Stick a rat in his mouth. That'll get the bugger up.

Anthony awoke screaming.

'Oh that's just effin' marvellous,' said a voice. 'Now what am I supposed to do with this bloody rat?'

Consciousness careened into Anthony like a careless driver. It felt as if an elephant in concrete boots was tap dancing on his skull.

'Oh dear,' said a voice, sounding entirely unconcerned. 'I do believe he's going to pass out again.'

'Well there's a stroke of luck!' said the other voice.

Although Anthony couldn't make much out through the stars and spots that swirled before his eyes, he was pretty sure someone was striding confidently towards him with a rodent in hand.

'I-I'm fine,' Anthony lied. 'Absolutely dandy.' He attempted to put a hand out to steady himself, but discovered they were bound. 'Please don't do anything drastic.'

Through the dark, spinning void, a face slowly emerged; thin, grey and completely devoid of humour. 'Then perhaps you'd care to tell us who you are?'

The pain in Anthony's skull gradually lessened. He slowly looked around in the dim underground light. He was in a dank tunnel, some sort of sewage system by the smell of it. Colin lay trussed up beside him, gagged as well as bound.

'Answer him!' Another face, identical to the last, except for the fact that it was holding a very small, very dead look-ing vole out in front of it, leaned in towards Anthony. 'Or it's the rodent treatment for you, my son.'

'Who do you think I am?' Anthony snapped. 'I'm Colin Frogfertler.'

The real Colin made an angry noise of protest from be-neath his gag.

'Oh really?' the resistance member said. 'Then perhaps you'd care to explain who that is sat next to you?'

'An impostor, of course,' Anthony swiftly replied. 'An assassin sent to kill me. Fortunately you seem to have intervened before he had the chance.'

'Don't listen to him!' a voice cried from beneath Colin's arm. *'He's* the assassin.'

Anthony's confident expression seeped off his face. He'd forgotten about Maria. How the hell could he have forgotten about Maria?

'Well, "Colin",' the resistance member said, 'how do you explain that?'

'That's not your leader!' Anthony cried. 'It's a melon in a wig!'

'A melon?' The resistance member's voice was surprisingly calm and measured. 'You don't say.'

Maria rolled her eyes. 'Are you really going to listen to this –'

'Oh, it may look and sound and act like Maria,' Anthony interjected, 'but if you were to cut her open, all you'd find inside is a mass of wires and pistons, and, and melon pips, and –'

'Whereas under that jumper of yours, you have the head of the real Maria?'

'Er, yes,' Anthony said warily. 'That's right.'

'And not, for example, just a couple of grapefruits?' The grey-skinned resistance member held a pair of grapefruits up to the dim light, and tilted his head at an enquiring angle.

'Ah,' Anthony said. 'This looks bad, doesn't it?'

The resistance member tossed the grapefruits to his vole-swinging companion, and pulled out a gun. 'Let's try this again, shall we?' He pressed the barrel of the gun against Anthony's temple. 'Who. Are. You?'

'Kevin, we've wasted enough time as it is,' Maria said. 'Kill him, and let's get moving.'

'I'm afraid Kevin passed some years back, ma'am,' the resistance member said. 'I'm his clone, Franco. And that's

Zeppo over there.' He nodded in the direction of the second grey-skinned clone, who was attempting to juggle two grapefruits and a dead vole with varying degrees of success.

'Just kill him, Franco. That's an order.'

'Not until we find out who he is,' Franco said. 'He could be of use to us.'

'Let me cut his tongue out!' Zeppo cried, advancing on Anthony with a knife in hand. 'That'll get him talking.'

'No it won't,' Maria sighed. 'You can't trust him anyway. He's an assassin.'

'What kind of assassin holds a gun to his own head?' Franco countered.

'An incompetent one,' Maria said. 'If he's so eager to shoot himself, you might as well do it yourself and save him the trouble.'

'Oh, very well,' Franco said, cocking his gun. 'You're the boss.'

'Wait!' Anthony screamed. 'I'm Anthony. Anthony Cresswell. I only just joined the department today. I'm not an assassin, I've never killed anyone. Well, not intentionally, anyway. I mostly just make tea. I could make you all a nice cup of tea, if you like? Just please, please don't kill me!'

'Terribly sorry,' Franco said, 'but orders are ord–' A spoon whizzed by, and embedded itself in the masonry an inch above Franco's head. He stared at it a while, looking mildly bemused.

'For Christ's sake, Susan!' a voice hissed from the other end of the tunnel. 'There goes our element of surprise.'

'It's the Administration!' Franco cried, firing his gun into the shadows. 'They've found us!'

The two resistance members grasped Colin and his wife between them, and hauled them off down the tunnel, firing wildly as they went.

'Talk about nick of time,' Anthony said, striding towards the figures massing in the darkness. 'Anthony Cresswell, Subtractions department. Boy am I glad to see y–'

A bullet whistled past his ear.

Bit close, that one, thought Anthony. 'Hey, easy there fellas,' he called. 'I'm on your s–'

Another bullet whistled past Anthony's ear, this time taking most of his ear with it.

He flung himself headfirst into the sewage. 'Stop shooting at me! I'm not Colin. I'm on your side.'

The gunfire gradually petered out into a deathly silence.

'Sorry?' an authoritative voice called. 'What was that? Couldn't hear you over all the gunfire.'

'I said I'm not Colin.'

'Aren't you?' the voice said. 'Well, good for you.'

The gunfire resumed, with added gusto.

Anthony scrambled on his belly through the sewage. Fortunately, thanks to the growing popularity of recycled goods, there was precious little for him to crawl through (less fortunate would've been the knowledge that an unhealthy portion of it was currently crawling through his own digestive system in the form of a Mock-Choc bar).

A short way up the tunnel, Franco had taken refuge in an alcove.

'Hello,' Anthony said, ducking in beside him. 'Mind if I join you?'

'Yes,' Franco replied, kicking him back out. 'Bugger off.'

Anthony dodged a hail of bullets, and flung himself back into the alcove. 'I could be of use to you.'

'Good point.' Franco shuffled over, positioning himself behind Anthony. 'Move two inches to your right.'

Anthony obligingly did as he was asked. 'Okay, now what?'

'Well, if any bullets should round that corner, make sure you get hit by them instead of me.' Franco smiled tightly. 'You may be a rubbish assassin, but at least you might make a halfway decent human shield.'

As a gun fired close by, Anthony instinctively ducked. Turquoise blood pumped from Franco's shoulder. 'No,' he said, clutching his wound, 'it appears I was wrong. Oh well.' He knelt down and rummaged in his backpack.

Meanwhile, Zeppo stood in the centre of the tunnel, cackling like a maniac as bullets, and the odd spoon or two, zinged around him. Occasionally he remembered to return fire.

'What the hell are you doing?' Maria cried from an alcove at the opposite side. 'Get down, you fool!'

Zeppo craned his ear over the gunfire. 'What?'

'She said "duck!"' Anthony yelled.

'I can't,' Zeppo called back. 'I haven't got any kneecaps.'

'What did he say?' Maria shouted.

'He said he hasn't got any kn– *what?'*

Franco wrapped a bandage around his shoulder, and then did likewise with Anthony's wounded ear. 'Imperfections in the cloning process. Zeppo got mental instability and a lack of kneecaps, and I got –'

'Turquoise innards?'

'I know,' Zeppo said, 'I'll limbo.' He arched backwards as far as he could go, and continued firing off random shots down the tunnel.

At the other end of the tunnel the Subtractions department death squad stopped firing long enough to exchange confused glances.

'What the hell's that man doing?' one of them hissed.

'Well, I may be no expert,' another replied, adjusting his binoculars, 'but it looks like the Lambada.'

Anthony cautiously poked his head out from the alcove. He exhaled deeply. 'They've stopped firing. Thank god, they've stopped f–' A barrage of bullets thudded into the brickwork around him. He ducked back in.

'They've started again,' Franco observed.

'It's all right,' Zeppo yelled, limboing back and forth amidst the hail of bullets, 'they're bound to run out of spoons sooner or later.'

'Yes,' Anthony said, 'it's the bullets I'm slightly more concerned about.'

'This is hopeless,' Maria cried. 'We've got to fall back. Cut me loose and give me a weapon.'

Zeppo staggered awkwardly towards her, drawing his knife.

'Do you think that's wise, ma'am?' Franco called. 'What if Colin tries to kill you? He's already done so once. The world can't afford to lose you again.'

Zeppo tore the gag off Colin's mouth. 'Are you going to behave?' he snarled. 'Or am I going to have to cut your lips off?'

'Get stuffed, no-knees,' said Colin.

'Knock him out,' Maria commanded. 'It only takes one mind to control this body.'

Colin opened his mouth to protest; Zeppo's fist rammed sharply into it, and Colin's head slumped backwards.

Zeppo sliced through the bonds and handed Maria a gun. She immediately sprang into action.

'Okay, Franco, you provide covering fire. Zeppo and I will fall back to the next junction. Once we get there, we'll return fire at the enemy, giving you a chance to –' The gun in her hand jerked suddenly and fired.

Zeppo stared in confusion at the hole in his chest. He gurgled something incomprehensible, and slumped to the ground.

'Zeppo!' Franco cried.

'It wasn't me,' Maria said. 'It's Colin! He's still got con–'

The butt of Maria's gun slammed against her skull, silencing her. Colin's head reared up, fully alert. 'Right, that's bloody it!' he yelled. 'I don't know who any of you bastards are, but this has got nothing to do with me.' He levelled the gun at Maria's head. 'Now, we're all going to edge out together nice and slowly. Try anything funny, and I'll decorate your outfit with my wife's brains. Okay,' he called, stepping from the alcove, 'I'm bringing them out. Don't shoo—'

Colin's brains exploded out through the back of his head. His body slid down into the sewage, riddled with bullet holes.

'Maria!' Franco screamed. He turned to Anthony, eyes burning with rage. 'Cover me!'

'What with?' Anthony struggled with the hands tied behind his back. 'And how?'

Franco dashed across the tunnel towards the body of his fallen leader. Bullets danced around him, occasionally making contact. He crawled painfully through the sewage, dragging his blood-soaked body.

A loudspeaker switched on and a voice hollered out through the darkness. 'Hold your fire a moment, lads.'

The gunfire ceased.

'Hello?' said the voice on the loudspeaker. 'I say…hello?'

'Yes?' Anthony yelled back.

'This might sound a bit unusual, but me and the lads were sort of wanting to know if you're dead yet.'

Anthony carefully examined himself, and reached a joyful conclusion. 'Not yet, no.'

'Really? Oh dear.' The voice radiated disappointment. 'It's just I could've sworn I shot you a moment ago.'

'No, no,' Anthony said. 'That was Colin.'

'Oh, I see. *That's* Colin, is it?'

'It was, yes,' Anthony replied.

'Oh well,' the voice on the loudspeaker said. 'Fingers crossed this time, eh?' The loudspeaker clicked off. The guns opened fire again, aiming everything they had at Anthony. Bricks and mortar exploded around him.

Franco dragged Colin's corpse into the alcove opposite Anthony, and turned it over. Maria's face stared up at him, blood trickling from her lips.

'That's Colin all over...' she coughed. 'Never did have any brains.'

'Maria!' Franco cried. 'You're alive!'

'Barely.' She coughed again. 'Lost a lot of blood.'

Franco struggled to help Maria up, wincing at the pain in his shoulder. 'We've got to get you back to the professor. If anyone can save you –'

'I'll...never make it...that far,' Maria wheezed.

'You have to!' Franco cried, tears streaming down his pale face. 'Without you the world is lost.'

Maria reached out and tightly gripped Franco's hand. 'Then you know...what to do,' she said. 'The process ...must begin...again.' Maria's face contorted. Her hand fell limp.

Franco leant over Maria's body, gently running a hand through her hair.

'Excuse me?' Anthony called from beneath a pile of rapidly expanding rubble. 'I know this is a very emotional time for you and everything, but could you please get a move on? People are trying to *shoot* me!'

Franco's fingers came away with several hairs wound around them. He carefully deposited them into a small metal box, and slipped it back into his pocket.

Bullets zinged around him as he leapt back into the alcove beside Anthony.

'Can we please get out of here now?' Anthony asked.

Franco drew a knife, sliced through Anthony's bonds, and pressed a gun into his hands.

'What are you giving me this for?' Anthony said.

'So you can lay down covering fire whilst I make my escape.' Franco saluted him. 'Viva la resistance!'

'Tell you what,' Anthony said, handing the gun back,

'I've got a better idea. Why don't *you* lay down covering fire, whilst *I* escape? Doesn't that sound so much better?'

'Listen, you imbecile,' Franco snapped. 'The future of the entire planet is at stake. Our lives mean nothing in comparison. Understand? Nothing.'

'That's easy for you to say, you're a clone. Knock one of you buggers off, and another two'll spring up to take your place. I'm one of a kind.'

'Then let me take a sample of your DNA. I'll resurrect you at the other end. How's that sound?'

'Pitiful. I'd still have to die, and quite frankly it looks like you've got a head start on me there.'

Franco looked down at his blood-drenched uniform. He'd caught a few bullets on the way back, and was looking, by all accounts, dangerously turquoise.

The Subtractions squad began to edge their way slowly up the tunnel.

Franco was out of options, and he knew it. He thrust the metal box into Anthony's hands. 'Guard this with your life,' he commanded. 'It's mankind's only salvation.'

Anthony slipped the box into his pocket, and snapped off a quick salute. 'You can count on me.'

'You have to get it back to Professor Langerman. He'll know what to do.'

'Langerman. Gotcha.' Anthony wrote the name on the palm of his hand. 'Where do I find him?'

Franco handed Anthony a small circular disk. 'Everything you need's contained upon this locator disk. Just slide it into a navigation console and the disk will do the rest. Now go!' Franco leapt out into the tunnel, guns blazing away in his hands.

Anthony fled in the opposite direction.

The crackle of gunfire echoed out behind him, steadily shrinking into the distance.

Several hours later, when Anthony was absolutely, positively sure he was out of range, he retrieved the box from his pocket, and inspected it for a moment.

'Mankind's only salvation?' he scoffed. 'Fat chance.'

He tossed the box into the sewage, and continued on his way.

Half a day later, Anthony was still continuing on his way. He was lost, up to his ankles in sewage, and his ear not only stung something rotten, but had started to smell something rotten too.

He rounded a bend in the tunnel and stopped, blinking in disbelief.

Now, it seemed, he'd begun to hallucinate. Whether it was from hunger, thirst, or the constant throbbing pain in his skull, he couldn't be sure. All he knew was most sewers didn't usually have a pub in them.

'The Last Resort,' the crooked sign at the top of the pub read. 'Eat, drink and be violently sick.' As hallucinations went, this one seemed particularly satisfying in nature. Anthony resolved to immediately head inside and order an imaginary pint.

As he approached the door, he discovered a less enticing sign upon it. This one said 'Closed'.

'Hello?' Anthony rapped gently on the door. *'Hello?'*

He was greeted with silence. He tried again, with more vigour. 'Is anyone –'

The letterbox flicked open. 'Yes?' a gruff voice said from inside. 'What do you want?'

'A pint of lager and a packet of scampi fries, please,' said Anthony.

'Well, that's tough then, isn't it? We're closed.' The letterbox snapped shut.

Anthony stared at it in frustration. He knocked again.

'You again?' said the voice.

'That's right. Could I come inside, please?'

'No, you can't. It's after hours.'

Anthony glanced at his watch. 'But it's only seven thirty.'

'And we're redecorating,' the voice swiftly added. 'It's very dangerous inside. You might get painted.'

'I'll take that risk, thanks.'

A heavy sigh from behind the door.

'Very well,' the voice said. 'Could I see your I.D. please?'

'My what?'

'Proof of age, junior.'

'I'm twenty five,' Anthony said. 'I have stubble. Look!' He pushed his chin up against the letterbox.

'So had I when I was twelve,' the voice said. 'It means nothing.'

'Okay, here.' Anthony thrust his driving licence in through the gap.

There came a long pause from the other side.

'Looks nothing like you,' the voice concluded, handing the I.D. back.

Anthony examined the photo on the licence, and realised his mistake. 'Ah, well, it wouldn't would it? I've had my appearance genetically altered.'

'A likely story,' the voice growled. 'Bloody kids! You don't even try, do you?' The letterbox slammed shut. Footsteps retreated.

'Wait!' Anthony yelled in desperation. 'I have money!'

Silence.

The footsteps advanced. The letterbox flipped open. 'What sort of money?'

Two unfriendly eyes regarded Anthony through the gap. He held up a twenty-cred note. 'The right sort.'

A hand darted out through the letterbox and snatched the note away.

There was the sound of a bolt being slowly drawn back, followed by several more bolts. A couple of padlocks clinked noisily to the ground. Finally, the door edged open.

'Okay,' the landlord said, sliding the twenty-cred note into his pocket, 'your I.D. checks out.' He beamed Anthony a grin full of holes.

Anthony followed the squat, chequer-toothed man towards the bar, and took a seat.

The landlord disappeared behind the drinks counter, and started pulling a pint without waiting for Anthony to make a selection.

Inside, the bar was even more dank and ill lit than the sewer. A jukebox sat festering in the corner, occasionally choking out the strangulated lyrics of some ancient blues hit. A sickly yellow light streamed down from the ceiling, dimly illuminating the sickly yellow paintwork.

Anthony was, unsurprisingly, the only customer.

'There you go,' the landlord said, sloshing a glass down before him. 'Nice pint of Hurler's Best.'

Anthony looked down at the drink. It squeaked at him. 'Could I possibly have one that doesn't have a rat in it?'

The landlord sucked in air through the numerous gaps in his teeth. 'Bit of a tall order, that,' he said. 'If I were you, I'd sip around it.'

'Could I see a cocktail menu, please?' Anthony asked, pushing the drink aside.

'Hold your horses. You haven't paid for your last drink yet.'

'Well, no,' Anthony said. 'There's a rodent doing back-stroke in it.'

'That's what gives Hurlers its unique flavour,' the land-lord said. 'Twelve creds fifty. Cough up.'

'Fine.' Anthony slammed a five cred note down on the bar top. 'Keep the change.'

Grumbling away, the landlord reluctantly pocketed the note and handed Anthony a cocktail menu.

He eyed it warily. It read more like a Spanish Inquisition starter list.

'A Poke In The Eye...A Punch In The Face...An Unexpected Slap.' Anthony ran his finger down the page. 'What's "A Kick In The Bollo–"' He stopped himself just in time.

'Damn,' the landlord cursed, lowering his foot. 'Almost had you there.'

Anthony handed the menu back. 'I suppose you would've charged me for it as well?'

'Too right. Care to see the wine list?'

Anthony paused to consider this a moment. The chances of the landlord being able to squeeze an entire rat into a wine glass, he decided, were slim at best. What he could squeeze out of one, however, was still cause for concern.

'I'll pass, thanks.'

'Oh well, your loss.' The landlord heaved his shoulders. 'Since you appear to have exhausted all the drinks the bar has to offer, I guess you'll probably be wanting to head on your way.' He turned his back on Anthony and started to polish an already well-polished glass. 'Do feel free to stop by again if ever the urge takes you.'

'Actually,' Anthony said, rising from the stool, 'I think I'd like to stay the night.'

The glass slipped from the landlord's fingers and shattered on the tiles. He turned, looking mortified. 'What?'

'Maybe several nights.' Anthony stretched theatrically. 'We'll see how it goes.'

'Now, now, now, look here –' the landlord stuttered.

'Guestrooms down there, are they?' Anthony made for a door marked 'Private'.

'Wait!' the landlord screamed. 'It's not that sort of establishment! Customers don't stay. They *never* stay!'

'This one does,' Anthony said, pushing his way through the door. 'He's very, very tired. Good night.'

'It'll cost money, you know!' the landlord yelled after him. 'Lots and lots of money.'

'Glad to hear it,' Anthony said, smiling nastily. 'We'll negotiate a fee for getting rid of me in the morning.'

Anthony awoke feeling particularly refreshed. Not only had the pain in his head gone, but his ear had also stopped throbbing. More than that, it seemed to be functioning quite well again.

He unravelled the bandage and inspected his ear in the grubby wall mirror. It had grown back. It was slightly greener than the average ear, but an ear nonetheless.

'Gangrene...' Anthony murmured, stroking a finger tentatively across it. It felt mossy to the touch. Something strange was going on...something very odd indeed.

The sooner he got his old appearance back, the better.

Five

Anthony forced open the sewer cover, and pushed upwards into a thick blanket of smog. According to a map the landlord had sold him at a vastly inflated price, Rakembalo's Genetic Makeover should be directly in front of him. Instead, where the genetics parlour once stood, only ash and embers remained.

'No…' Anthony whispered. 'Please, no…'

Above the parlour's burnt out shell, the rest of the work units were smoking away like a chimney, singed but intact thanks to the anti gravity sensors that kept them afloat in an emergency. Once repair work had been carried out, the entire stack would lower itself into the ashes and a new work unit would be added to the top, as if nothing had ever happened.

Anthony approached a grubby urchin who was sat by the side of the road, prodding Rakembalo's blackened corpse with the glowing end of a stick. 'What happened?' he cried. 'Tell me!'

'A fire,' the child said gleefully. 'A big one. You should've seen it, mister. It were awesome.'

Fighting back a descending wave of nausea, Anthony stumbled into the genetics parlour and scrabbled madly through its embers.

'You're wasting your time, mister. No survivors from that one.' The child gave Rakembalo's body an emphatic poke. 'Everything inside burnt to a crisp.'

Singed and bewildered, Anthony dropped to his knees.

Tears streamed down his cheeks, drawing little white lines in the soot.

The child looked at him with sadistic interest. 'Someone you knew in there?'

'Yes,' Anthony sobbed, 'me.' He let the ashes slip through his fingers. 'Now what the hell am I supposed to do?'

'Well, if I were you,' a voice said, 'I'd probably want to kill myself.'

Anthony brushed away the tears, and looked up into Grison's beaming face. 'You! This is your doing, isn't it?'

Grison casually appraised the smouldering ruins. 'Petty arson? Hardly my style.' He tapped his nose knowingly. 'Sponsorship deals – that's where the real money is.'

'Go away, you vulture!' Anthony pushed past him, and then came to a standstill when he realised he had nowhere else to go.

'I'm just trying to do you a favour,' said Grison, draping an arm over his shoulder. 'No point dying on an empty wallet. Stick with me, lad. Together we'll make a killing.'

'You're only interested in lining your own pockets.'

'You've got me all wrong, Terry.' Grison pulled him in close. 'I want to *help* you.'

'It's Tony!' Anthony attempted to wriggle free from Grison's vice-like grip, but it was futile. 'If you want to help me, then call off the Subtractions department's death squad. Tell them who I really am.'

'Wouldn't make a difference, Tez.'

'It might stop them trying to kill me. Those overzealous idiots damn near blew my head off.'

'I'm not surprised,' Grison said, his arm constricting, 'since it was your head they were aiming for.'

'No, you're wrong there,' Anthony said. 'It was Colin they were after – same as me. They just got a bit carried away, that's all.'

The grip on Anthony's shoulder momentarily relaxed. 'Is that what you think?' Grison chuckled. 'Oh dear, oh dear, oh dear…'

'It…wasn't Colin they were after?' That nauseous feeling was back again, and it had brought with it reinforcements in the form of a strong sense of impending doom.

Humming cheerily to himself, Grison drew a crumpled photograph from his pocket and handed it to Anthony. 'Take a look at this and tell me what's missing.'

Anthony's new facial tick went into overdrive. 'Maria,' he whispered. 'It doesn't have a second head.'

'Because it's a photo of *you*, Terry. Noddy's issued the same photo to every member of the department, with the same three words written on the back.'

Anthony turned the photo over and read what was written there: Subtract on sight. His features danced a strange little jig as they shifted from incomprehension all the way through to understanding.

'Oh my god!' he cried. 'Noddy's trying to kill me!'

'Aren't we all, dear boy? Aren't we all.' Grison's arm slid back into place around Anthony's rigid shoulder, and he gently guided him towards a waiting car.

'Why me?' Anthony said, staggering along in a daze. 'What have I done to deserve this?'

'Nothing, Terry. Absolutely nothing.' Grison opened the car door and rummaged around inside. 'But that's the problem, isn't it? You've never done anything worthwhile in your life. You're a failure, Terry, a nobody.' He handed Anthony a thermos and eased him into the passenger seat. 'I can make you somebody.'

'This is wrong,' Anthony murmured, fumbling with the cap of the thermos. 'This is all wrong.'

'It's a cold and unforgiving world, Terry.' Grison gently patted him on the knee. 'You're better off out of it.'

The thermos cap slipped out of Anthony's hands and landed on the driver's seat. As he leant to retrieve it, something caught his eye.

'Terry, my boy, I'll give you a death that's remembered for all eternity, by historians, scholars, and marketing divisions everywhere.'

A tiny smile tugged at the corners of Anthony's mouth. The keys were still in the ignition...

'You will be known,' Grison said, 'you will be celebrated. Your name will echo out through the ages, etched into the consciousness of civilised society. Terry...Terry...*Terry!*'

'For the last time,' Anthony screamed. 'The name's *Tony!*'

The liquid from the thermos hit Grison full in the face. He fell to the ground, clawing at his skin.

The car's engine flared into life, and Anthony rocketed into the sky.

Grison instantly stopped thrashing around, wiped the cold liquid off his face, and watched the vehicle depart.

'Farewell, Cressface,' he said, smiling. 'Farewell.'

Anthony flicked a switch marked 'Autopilot' and looked around at the vehicle he'd just stolen.

The inside was a pure virginal white. An incense burner dangled from the rear-view mirror, smothering the interior with its holy pine aroma.

Stained glass windows at the vehicle's rear depicted the adventures of a variety of religious celebrities as they performed miracles, saved souls, and inevitably, got nailed to things.

As Anthony glanced behind him, he realised even the driver's seat was shaped like a cross.

He yanked open the glove compartment and peered inside, half expecting to find a Bible, some Rosary beads and a compilation of religious choir songs. He wasn't disappointed.

Surrounded by such an overwhelming abundance of religious paraphernalia, a man could easily find himself overcome with spiritual desire. Anthony was no exception.

'Computer?' he said. 'Lay in a course for the nearest drinking establishment that isn't in a sewer, please.'

'We are already on a set path, my son,' a loud evangelical voice boldly declared from above.

Anthony glanced upwards at the onboard computer's speaker system. 'What path? I didn't set a path.'

'The path of the righteous and holy.'

'Terrific,' Anthony said. 'Any drinking establishments on this path?'

'There are no drinking establishments in Heaven, my son.'

'Doesn't sound very much like Heaven to me,' Anthony grumbled. He pressed a button on the navigation console and called up a map. His finger traced the route outlined there. 'This "Heaven"...' he said, tapping the screen thoughtfully. 'It wouldn't happen to be the large structure directly in our flight path, would it?'

'Ah, the promised land,' the computer said wistfully. 'God bless!'

Anthony transferred his gaze from the navigation console to the rapidly growing structure visible through the windscreen. Its massive white pillars towered high into the smog-filled atmosphere, radiating an aura of divinity, holiness, and absolute solidity.

'And we're going to crash into it, are we?' Anthony enquired, in a voice slightly higher than he would've liked.

'Not crash,' the computer said. 'Be delivered into the hands of Our Lord.'

'Marvellous,' Anthony squeaked. 'Absolutely splendid.' Without taking his eyes off the approaching structure, Anthony's finger repeatedly punched the manual override button. Nothing happened, so he punched it some more.

'Manual override has been over ridden,' the computer explained.

'Then override the override!' Anthony growled. He tugged fiercely at the steering wheel. It snapped off in his hands. His foot angled down towards the air brakes. The vehicle failed to slow.

'Perhaps now would be a good time to say a few words of thanks to the Lord our Father?' the computer suggested.

'Sod words!' Anthony cried, flinging the steering wheel aside. 'What I need's a miracle.'

Tink! Tink! Tink!

An oversized finger rapped on the outside of the driver's window.

'Jesus Christ!' Anthony exclaimed.

'Er, no, not quite,' a muffled voice said from outside.

Anthony wound the window down, and was immediately assailed by the unmistakable stench of curry.

An ugly, shapeless face leered at him. 'All right, mate?' Derek said. 'Need a lift?'

Anthony rolled his eyes accusingly towards the heavens. 'Cheers, God,' he muttered. 'Kick a guy when he's down, why don't you?'

'It's just I can't help but notice,' Derek said, 'you appear to be heading towards certain death there.'

'Well, these things happen.' Anthony attempted to wind the window back up. 'Bye now.'

Derek reached out and blocked the window with an arm. 'Don't be like that. I've got my own windows now, and everything.'

'I know.' Anthony shuddered. 'I can see your innards from here.'

'Yeah, nice aren't they?' Derek said proudly. 'Come on over and have a butchers.'

'If it's all the same to you, Derek, I'd rather die.'

'Would you? Oh, fair enough then.' Derek removed his arm from the window. 'Just thought you might want to know what happened to your body, that's all.'

Anthony sat bolt upright. 'What?'

'Have a nice death, mate.' Derek waved at him. 'Let me know how it turns out.'

Anthony struggled with the car door. 'Derek, wait!'

The structure edged perilously closer. It was now possible to make out thousands of scorch marks on its side, where other hapless crusaders had ended their religious pilgrimage burning in the fiery car wreck of righteousness.

'Ten seconds until impact,' the computer said cheerily. 'Just enough time for a quick Hymn or two.'

'Hymns?' Anthony said. 'Ah, Christ!' He wrenched the car door open, closed his eyes, and leapt.

'Well, that's just charming, that is,' the computer said dejectedly. 'Bloody atheists! No commitment, that's *their* problem.'

The car hit the structure and exploded.

The force of the blast sent Anthony spinning through the air. Gravity took a hold on him, and dragged him down…down…down…until finally he stopped falling and hit something hard. Since he was still alive, he assumed it wasn't the ground. He opened his eyes and immediately regretted it.

'Decided to join me then, did you?' Derek said, grinning.

'It was a spur of the moment decision,' Anthony said, struggling to maintain a hold on a huge yellow pustule that protruded from Derek's bonnet. 'I think it might have been the wrong one.'

Derek's smile evaporated. 'Is that all the thanks I get? I waited eighteen hours for you, and what's the first thing you do? You climb into someone else's car!' Derek shook his bonnet sadly. 'Where's the customer loyalty, that's what I want to know?'

'Well, I'm here now,' Anthony said, clearly wishing he wasn't.

'I only nipped off for a quick curry,' Derek sulked. 'I mean, jeez, you could've waited.'

'Tell me about the genetics parlour, Derek.'

'Got you one as well.' Derek waved an oozing container that looked and smelt like a badly packaged cowpat. 'Probably a bit cold by now, but I could always reheat it in my engine fumes.'

'No thank you. The parlour, Derek.'

'You sure you wouldn't prefer to come inside and discuss this?' Derek's door squelched uninvitingly open.

'Absolutely positive.'

'Please yourself,' Derek said. 'Though you're missing out on some quality workmanship, if you want my opinion. I'll probably be worth a mint, now Rakembalo's dead and everything.'

'Yes.' Anthony sighed. 'And perhaps you'd care to explain how that happened, Derek?'

'Oh, very well.' Derek cleared his throat. 'It was a cold November morning. The gods were playing poker with the lives of men. Fate dealt out a bad hand...'

'Get to the point, Derek!' Anthony snapped.

'Just tryin' to colour the scene a little,' Derek grumbled. 'If you must know, I was parked outside Rakembalo's parlour, waiting for a fare, when a figure tore out of the building and ran straight past me. Next thing I know, the whole place goes up in flames.'

Anthony's eyes narrowed. 'This figure...you didn't by any chance happen to get a good look at him, did you?'

'Oh yeah, clear as daylight. Certainly wouldn't have any trouble identifying that shifty-looking bastard.'

The pustule vibrated ominously as Anthony's grip tightened. 'Let me guess. Stocky build, close-cropped hair, face like well-chiselled granite?'

An expression of thoughtfulness flickered across Derek's dashboard. 'No,' he said, 'more like scrawny body, floppy hair, face like a complete git.'

'But that doesn't sound like Grison at all,' Anthony said.

'Well, no. It was *you*.'

Anthony's fingers involuntarily constricted. The pustule burst, sending a rather damp and unhappy accountant plummeting towards the city below. A huge hand caught him by the collar, and hauled him back up.

'Nice one,' Derek said, depositing Anthony on his bonnet. 'I've been trying to pop that bugger for months. Couldn't do a few more whilst you're there, could you?'

'What do you mean it was me?' Anthony said defensively. 'It couldn't have been me. I was down in the sewers having a pint at the time. I have an alibi!'

'The old you,' Derek explained. 'The body you traded in for that one.'

A green vein in Anthony's forehead began to pulse. 'Let me get this straight,' he said. 'Are you trying to tell me that someone stole my body, and then burnt down Rakembalo's parlour to cover their tracks?'

'That's about the size of it,' Derek said. 'Now, how about that curry, eh?'

Anthony's features twisted into a vacant smile. 'I'm terribly sorry, Derek,' he said, 'but I think this has all been a bit much for me.' His eyes rolled back into their sockets, and he slid from the bonnet.

Six

'Aha! Got the little rascal!'

Mr Pickler emerged from behind his desk with a rogue fruity bon-bon clutched victoriously between thumb and forefinger. 'Sorry about the interruption, gentlemen. Terribly pressing sweetie crisis I had to attend to. Where were we?'

The immaculately dressed Kompact Kars representative with the company logo tattooed neatly on his forehead glared at Mr Pickler from the viewscreen. 'This,' he said, 'is a goddamned outrage!'

'Ah, still at that point of the conversation are we? Jolly good. Didn't miss a thing.' Mr Pickler dusted the sweet off on his sleeve. 'Philip? Any views?'

Grison leant against the doorframe, arms folded in defiance. 'As far as I'm concerned, I performed admirably.'

'You were supposed to deliver us a messiah!' the representative bellowed.

Grison casually pointed a remote control at the viewscreen, and turned the representative's volume down a few notches. 'Look,' he said calmly, 'it's hardly my fault Cressface leapt out before the vehicle exploded. Surely you can't hold me responsible for your bad planning?'

'He was supposed to die for our sins!' the man yelled. 'That was the whole damned point of the campaign!'

'I told you he should've been nailed to the seat for authenticity,' Grison countered. 'But no. Not customer friendly enough, you said. Wouldn't send out a positive image to the kids.' Grison leant in close to the viewscreen, his face reddening. 'But it might've stopped the little bleeder escaping though, mightn't it?'

'One hundred press photographers, all lined up at strategic positions along the route, ready to take photos of the messiah as he ascends to heaven,' the Kompact Kars representative said, ignoring him. 'And what happens? He bails at the last minute. You've made us a goddamned laughing stock!'

Mr Pickler's face fell. 'Oh dear,' he said. 'This won't do. This won't do at all.'

The man on the viewscreen adjusted his collar slightly. 'Well,' he said, 'I'm glad we're getting somewhere at last.'

'See?' Mr Pickler held his sweet up for the representative to inspect. There was a gigantic moustache hair curled around it. 'Completely ruined.'

'That's it!' the representative snarled. 'We're pulling out. Expect to hear from our lawyers.'

The viewscreen went blank. A split second later, a chair smashed through it. The screen popped, crackled and fizzed emphatically.

'Sorry, sir,' Grison said. 'Got a bit riled there.'

'That's perfectly fine, Philip.' Mr Pickler chuckled warmly as he picked himself up and brushed himself down. 'Chairs were made to be thrown. Though if you could perhaps give me a bit of advanced warning next time, I might have the chance to remove myself from the chair first.'

'Sorry sir.'

Mr Pickler dragged the chair back towards his desk. 'No need to look so despondent Philip, the contract was only worth a piffling thirty thousand creds. Hardly cause for concern.'

'Even so, I can't help but feel slightly responsible.' Grison dusted down Mr Pickler's chair and helped him into it. 'In fact, if it's all the same to you, I'd like to try to make up for lost capital by selling a few organs.'

'Oh, if you insist.' Mr Pickler cranked the seat's height as far as it would go, and tilted his head at an enquiring angle. 'Any idea whose?'

Grison scratched his chin thoughtfully. 'How about Trevor in Waste Reduction?'

'Ooh yes.' Mr Pickler made a face. 'Detestable little man. Has a totally irrational phobia of moustaches. I'll have his next of kin notified immediately.' Mr Pickler reached for the holo-phone on his desk, but Grison's hand restrained him.

'Let me do it, sir,' he said. 'I *need* this.'

Mr Pickler chuckled again. 'Well, I suppose this sort of thing is more your area. I'll leave the matter in your hands.'

'Very good, sir.' Grison strode towards the door, paused, and glanced back over his shoulder. 'And Cressface?'

'Oh I shouldn't worry about young Anthony.' Mr Pickler popped a hairy fruit bon-bon in his mouth and sucked it keenly. 'No one could've survived a fall like that.'

Anthony awoke to discover that he still wasn't dead. His first reaction was one of disappointment.

'Oh, bloody hell...' he muttered. His head throbbed, and there was an unpleasant sensation in his left ear.

'Aha!' a triumphant voice enthused. 'The patient has awoken.'

'Patient?' Anthony groaned. 'I'm in a hospital then?'

'That's right, yes.'

Anthony experimentally sniffed the air. 'And not another sewer or anything?'

The doctor brayed. 'It may at times smell that way, but I assure you this certainly isn't a sewer.'

'And if I open my eyes,' Anthony said cautiously, 'you're not going to try ramming a dead rodent down my throat?'

'Oh dear me, no,' the doctor chuckled. 'I shouldn't think we'd do that sort of thing at all.'

'Well,' Anthony said, 'that's a relief.' He opened his eyes. A man in a surgical gown and a gimp suit was bent over him, beaming through the zip in his mask.

'Now then,' said the gimp, 'how about a nice scream?'

'Aaaaaaaaaaaaaaaaaaagggggghhhhh!' said Anthony.

The Gimp Master Surgeon shuddered in delight. 'Ooh!' he said. 'That was a *good* one.'

'Who are you?' Anthony shrieked. 'What is this place?' His eyes darted around the room, taking in metallic trays overflowing with bondage paraphernalia, leather-clad medical students prodding and poking one another with a variety of unwholesome implements, and a large sign on the wall that currently read 'Nil By Anus.' Finally, his eyes looked down, and widened.

He was stripped to the waist and manacled to an operating table.

'All part of the service,' the gimp said with a wink.

'What service?' Anthony gave the chains a frantic rattle. 'What's going on?'

'You're in an S&M clinic. That car-shaped friend of yours dropped you off.'

'Derek?' Anthony snarled. 'That bastard!'

'Said you were looking a bit under the weather and could probably do with something to get you back on your feet again.' The surgeon produced a couple of nipple clamps from behind his back, and beamed pleasantly. 'Reckon these ought to do the trick,' he said, attaching them to Anthony.

'Aaaaaaaaaaaaaaaaaaaaaargh!' went Anthony.

'Masterful,' said the gimp, wiping a tear from his eye. 'Nurse!' He clicked his rubbery fingers. 'The testicle-cuffs, if you please.'

A huge, hairy leather-clad nurse, possibly named 'Mungo', bounded excitedly towards a supply cabinet.

'I want to go to a normal hospital,' Anthony sobbed. 'I don't believe you people are trying to cure me at all.'

'Heavens, no,' chuckled the gimp. 'Can't have people getting better in this day and age. That's why there's so many of these alternative medical practices around. And very popular we're proving too.' The gimp gave Anthony a knowing wink.

'Testicle-cuffs aren't there, Mr Skrunk,' the nurse's gruff voice cut in.

The gimp tutted. 'I bet that bloody intern's gone off with them again. Oh well, looks like we're going to have to skip the preliminaries, and get straight down to the malpractice.' The gimp clicked his fingers again. 'Nurse! Scalpel!'

Mungo handed him a scalpel. The Gimp Master Surgeon inspected it for a moment, and then rammed it sharply into his own leg. 'Ahhh,' he said, tears of joy filling his merry little eyes. 'That's the stuff.' He turned to Anthony. 'Right, your turn.'

'No, no, no,' Anthony said hurriedly. 'I'm fine, thanks all the same. You treat yourself, go on.'

'Now, now, sir.' The gimp waggled a disapproving finger. 'I really think you ought to let the experts decide what level of treatment's best for you.'

'I'm fine,' Anthony lied. 'Seriously, fit as a fiddle. Never felt better.'

'Sir,' the gimp said sternly. 'Your face is green, and there's a small branch growing out your left ear.'

Anthony breathed a sigh of relief. 'Is that what it is? I'd begun to wonder...'

'We've still got to wait for your brain scan to come back from the processing lab, along with a couple of rather raunchy photos we took for blackmail purposes. But until then, what say we have a bit of a poke around and see what we can find?' The gimp removed the "Nil By Anus" sign from the wall, and picked up a poker. 'This ought to do the trick.'

Anthony buttocks constricted as self-preservation kicked in. 'That's it!' he screamed. 'I want a second opinion!'

'Oh, very well,' the gimp sighed. 'Nurse! What do you think I should do with this poker?'

Mungo mimed a sharp upwards thrusting motion and said *'Pppppt!'*

'Well then,' said the gimp, advancing towards Anthony, 'that's that settled.'

'But, but, but, this hardly seems fair now,' Anthony stammered, his mouth running on automatic. 'That I should get all this lovely pain, whilst you're forced to stand there and watch.'

The gimp stopped tugging at Anthony's trouser belt. 'Now you mention it,' he said, 'that does seem a trifle un-sporting.'

'Doesn't it?' Anthony said, nodding his head frantically. 'Doesn't it just?'

'Still,' the gimp said, with a dismissive wave of his hand. 'A job's a job.'

'But it doesn't have to be that way. You could lie on the table for a bit, whilst I give you a prodding.' Anthony smiled hopefully. 'How's that sound, hey? Hm? Hey?'

The gimp sucked in air through his face-zip. 'I don't know. You seem a little unqualified.'

'You could talk me through it. Tell me what I'm doing wrong.'

'And what you're doing right,' the gimp breathed, a dreamy look in his deranged eyes. 'Oh, darn it all, you've convinced me. Let's get you out of those nasty old shackles, eh?' He took a key from his gown and unlocked Anthony.

'You know, this is very kind of you, sir,' the gimp enthused, helping Anthony down from the table. 'Very kind indeed.'

'Don't mention it,' Anthony said, bringing his knee sharply up between the Gimp Master Surgeon's legs.

The gimp slumped blissfully to the ground. 'Ah, that hits the spot,' he falsettoed.

'Oi!' snarled Mungo, dragging his knuckles towards Anthony. 'Where's my pain?'

Anthony elbowed Mungo in the face, knocking several teeth out. 'There you go,' he said. As he sprinted for the door, a hand gripped him from behind.

'Where do you think you're going?' the Gimp Master Surgeon squeaked. 'You haven't finished with me yet.'

'Get your hairy palms off me, you damn dirty gimp!' Anthony cried, shoving the surgeon backwards. He fell against the operating table with a sickening crunch.

'My arm! You broke my arm,' the gimp said merrily. *'Exquisite!* Do it again!'

'Ooh, ooh, and mine!' said Mungo, raising a hand.

'Me too!', 'And me!' chorused the med-students.

Anthony backed away towards the door. 'Seriously now,' he said, 'this is getting just a little bit weird.'

He pushed through the door, and ran off down the corridor.

After many wrong turns, and many unwanted sights that no amount of psychiatric counselling would ever be likely to shift, Anthony finally made it out of the dungeon and into the waiting room.

Derek was sat unfurled over several pieces of furniture, idly thumbing through a magazine on crocheting. He looked up to see Anthony charging towards him.

'All right, mate?' Derek said cheerily. 'Feeling a bit better now?'

'Raaaaaaaaaaarrgh!' cried Anthony, leaping to the attack.

Derek calmly outstretched an arm and gripped him by the throat. 'Still woozy from the medication, are we?'

'Medication?' Anthony choked. 'They tried to stick a poker up my arse!'

'Well, I'm sure those doctors know what they're doing,' Derek said, nodding sagely. 'They're professionals, you know.' He released his grip on Anthony.

'Derek!' Anthony snarled. 'This is an S&M clinic!'

Derek stared blankly at him. 'A what?'

'A bondage parlour,' Anthony hissed. He gestured to the receptionist, who was covered from head to foot in so many body piercings that it looked like she was wearing a suit of armour. 'A house of ill repute, a den of vice, a hedonist's playground dedicated to sadomasochistic pleasure through the medium of pain!'

Derek continued to stare blankly.

'He's right, you know,' said a voice from somewhere beneath Derek.

He slowly rolled his eyes downwards. A semi-naked slave-boy masquerading as a piece of furniture waved up at him.

'Sweet Buddha on a bicycle!' cried Derek as he sprang to his stubby feet. 'Sorry about that, mate. Didn't see you there.'

'Think nothing of it, master,' the slave boy shuddered. 'It was *my* pleasure.' He wandered off to find someone else to sit on him.

Derek leant in close to Anthony and cupped a hand to his ear. 'I don't mean to alarm you, Tony,' he whispered, 'but I don't think this is an ordinary hospital.'

Anthony's baleful glare could've melted glaciers.

'Look, you were turning green. What else was I supposed to do? This was the nearest clinic on route.'

'In case it's escaped your notice, Derek, I'm *still* turning green, and there's a branch sticking out my ear.'

Derek looked the branch up and down, and smiled sheepishly. 'All in all, bit of a wasted trip then, eh?'

'I wouldn't say that,' an emotionless voice intoned. 'Hands up, Twiggy!'

Anthony turned towards the doorway, to find the business end of a gun pointing at him. Its grey-skinned owner didn't look at all amused.

'Franco!' Anthony said. 'I thought you were dead.'

'He is dead,' the grey-skinned man replied. 'I'm Chico.'

'Another clone?'

'That's right.' Chico stepped in through the door. 'Now, I believe you have something that belongs to us?'

Registering the newcomer's arrival, the receptionist flashed him an artificial smile. 'Good afternoon, and welcome to Purgatory, sir,' she said. 'Would you care to make an appointment?'

Without taking his eyes off Anthony, Chico aimed the gun over his shoulder and shot her in the face. 'Sorry about that, love,' he said. 'No witnesses.' He twirled the gun around on his finger like a psychotic majorette, and pointed it back at Anthony. 'The box with our leader's DNA...where is it?'

The image of a small insignificant box floating amidst the sewage briefly flitted through Anthony's mind. 'I, er, don't know what you mean.'

'Look, I know you've got it.' Chico rattled his gun. 'So there's no use playing dumb.'

'How do you know I've got it?' Anthony asked suspiciously. 'We've only just met.'

'Because Franco gave you a locator disk that allows us to track your every move, listen in to your every word.'

Anthony fumbled around in his pocket and pulled out the locator disk. A small green light on its casing was blinking rapidly.

'Excuse me,' said a tired female voice, 'but do you want an appointment or not?'

Chico slowly turned round. The receptionist was staring at him with a bored look in her eyes.

'Hang about,' Chico said. 'Didn't I just shoot you?'

'Yes, sir,' said the receptionist. 'I believe you did.'

'Oh, good. Thought I was losing my touch for a moment there.' Chico shot her in the face again, and turned back to Anthony. 'Now, no more stalling. The DNA box…hand it o–'

'I'm waiting, sir,' said the receptionist, drumming her fingers impatiently.

'Oh, for cryin' out loud!' Chico snapped. He span around and shot the receptionist several dozen times.

Each bullet bounced off a piercing.

'Right!' Chico snarled, holstering his gun. 'So that's your game is it?' He pulled a grenade from his belt and turned back to Anthony. 'Just you stay there,' he commanded. 'I'll deal with you in a minute.'

Anthony had already scarpered.

'Once again, Derek to the rescue,' said Derek, spiralling upwards through the dense morning traffic. 'I'd better get a bloody good tip for this.'

Anthony stared out of Derek's window at the diminishing black exterior of Purgatory hospital. 'Wait!' he cried. 'We've got to go back.'

'Oh yeah, that's definitely the thing to do,' Derek scoffed. 'Let's go say a big hello to the nice gun-toting maniac.'

'That gun-toting maniac might be my only chance to get out of this whole damned mess.'

'What mess? What are you blathering about? *Same to you with knobs on!*' Derek made a rude gesture at a lorry driver he'd just cut up, and immediately cut out in front of another one.

'It's perfectly simple, Derek,' Anthony said. 'I work for a group of renegade accountants led by a shadowy super-computer known only as "Noddy". Noddy gave me a mission to infiltrate their deadly opponents "The Resistance" and bring their organisation down from the inside. I failed, and now Noddy wants me dead. Maybe if I –' Anthony's voice trailed off. He glared at Derek, and patiently waited for him to stop humming the theme to the A-Team.

'Sorry, Tone,' Derek said. 'You carry on there, mate.'

'Right,' Anthony sighed. 'Well, maybe if I complete my mission, Noddy might change his mind about how expendable I am, and the Administration might stop trying to subtract me. And maybe, just maybe, somebody somewhere might have an inkling as to why there's a branch growing out of my ear.'

'With an apple on it,' Derek observed.

'What?'

'The branch has an apple on it.'

Anthony gripped the branch and twisted it round to get a better look. There was indeed an apple sprouting from it. 'Well I'll be jiggered,' Anthony said. 'A miracle!' He plucked the apple and took a tentative bite. His face soured.

'Bit waxy is it?' Derek asked.

Anthony nodded grimly, and tossed the apple out the window. It exploded.

'Fancy that,' said Derek. 'Exploding apples.'

Anthony ducked down in his seat. 'Someone's shooting at us!'

'Bastaaaaard!' yelled a distant angry voice from outside.

Anthony gingerly poked his head out the window.

Chico stood poised in a classic surfer pose on the bonnet of a rapidly advancing hover car, the guns in his hands spitting lead in every direction. 'Double dealing, two-faced, treacherous bastard!'

'Wonder what that's all that about?' said Anthony, winding the window back up.

'Still carrying that locator disk, are ya Tone?' Derek enquired. 'You know, the one that allows the resistance to listen in to your every word?'

Anthony glanced at the flashing disk clenched in his hand. 'Ah,' he said. 'Bugger.'

A second attack vehicle burst towards them out of the smog.

'There he is again,' said Derek. 'And there, and over there.'

Six cars, each piloted by the same man, converged upon them from every direction – left, right, front, back, above and below, until Anthony and Derek were completely boxed in.

'Terrific,' Anthony said. 'Now what do we do?'

'I could toot the horn a bit,' Derek suggested. 'Mind you, might need to stoke up the ol' digestive system with some cabbage first.'

Chico leapt from the bonnet, swung himself in through Derek's passenger door, and rammed the barrel of his gun up against the side of Anthony's head. 'Where is it?' he demanded.

'Where's what?' said Anthony.

'You know what I mean. The DNA of our fallen leader. What have you done with it?'

'It's…in a safe place,' Anthony lied.

The clone squinted at him. 'Are you lying to me?'

'Nooooo,' lied Anthony again.

Chico raised a well-primed bunch of fives. 'You are, aren't you?'

'Absolutely not,' said Anthony, going for the hat-trick.

'You know,' the clone said quietly, 'I have ways of determining when people are lying to me.'

'You do?'

'Yes.' Chico gripped Anthony by the nose and gave it a violent tweak. 'Now tell me the truth you little bastard!'

'Ow! Ow! Ow! All right!' Anthony screamed. 'I dropped it in the sewers. There, are you happy?'

The clone's grey skin turned a ghostly shade of white. 'You did *what?*'

'Sorry.' Anthony shrugged. 'I didn't think it was that important.'

'Not that important?' Chico's left eye began to twitch manically. Anthony's facial tick decided to spar with it for a few rounds. 'Through your actions you might well have doomed the entire human race to an untimely demise.'

'I said I was sorry.' Anthony massaged his aching nose. 'Jeez…'

'I'm going to blow your brains out,' Chico stated, in the sort of tone that left no room for argument.

'Oh bloody hell,' muttered Derek. 'I've only just had my interior remodelled.'

The deranged clone twisted round, jerking his gun wildly from floor to roof. 'Who said that?'

'Me,' said Derek. 'The car.' His huge mouth leered at Chico from the dashboard.

'Ah, yes, right, of course.' The clone breathed a sigh of relief. 'For a moment there, I thought it was another receptionist.' He rammed the tip of his gun into Anthony's mouth, and slowly drew back the trigger.

'Mmmph!' said Anthony, with all due sense of urgency. 'Mmm! Mmmph!'

'What was that?' Chico withdrew the gun, and eyed Anthony with suspicion. 'Were you trying to call me a bastard?'

'No, no, no, no, no,' Anthony said hurriedly.

'Well you should've been,' Chico said. 'Because I *am* a bastard.'

'I was trying to say that you don't have to kill me.'

'Don't have to, no,' the clone said, raising his gun. 'But I rather think I'd like to.'

'There still might be a way to get the DNA.'

The gun lowered again. 'Is that so?'

'Just look at me.' Anthony gestured frantically to his trousers. 'I'm covered in the stuff!'

'What are you ranting about?'

'Colin's blood,' Anthony said. 'It's all over me. There's bound to be some of his wife's DNA in the mix.'

The clone scratched thoughtfully at his stubble. 'Let me get this straight,' he said slowly. 'Are you trying to suggest we resurrect our dearly beloved leader using your *trouser scrapings?*'

'Yes!' Anthony said, nodding wildly.

Chico rolled the idea around in his mind. 'It's a long shot,' he concluded, 'but it just might work.'

'Oh, thank god!' Anthony cried. 'Thank god!'

The clone thrust the barrel of his gun back into Anthony's mouth. 'Right,' he said, 'where were we?'

'Mmmph!' said Anthony, his eyes widening. *'Mmmph!'*

With a sigh, Chico withdrew the gun again. 'What is it now?' he said impatiently.

'What are you doing?' Anthony cried. 'You don't need to kill me any more.'

'Well, no,' Chico said, 'but, strictly speaking, I don't need you alive either. All I need is your clothes.'

'Wait!' Anthony said. 'If you shoot me, I'll...I'll *bleed* on them.'

'Good point.' Chico holstered his weapon, and gripped Anthony firmly by the throat. 'I guess I'll have to strangle you instead.'

'Hnnngh!' protested Anthony. 'Gluuuk!'

'I wouldn't do that if I were you,' said Derek.

'Oh, and why's that?' The clone's grip tightened.

'Hnnngh! Gluuuk!' Anthony reiterated.

'Because if you kill him,' Derek said, 'then you're going to have to undress his corpse.'

The grip on Anthony's throat relaxed. Chico looked him up and down, and shuddered. 'Right then, looks like you're coming back to base with me.'

'Swell,' Anthony wheezed.

'Glad that settled,' said Derek. 'Right, where am I taking you?'

'Can't tell you that.' Chico tapped his nose. 'It's a secret.'

'How am I supposed to get you there, if you won't tell me where it is?'

'I will remain on board to guide you. Now, put this on.' The clone handed Derek a blindfold.

'You've got to be kidding.'

'Either put the blindfold on, or I'll put your eyes out.'

Grumbling away, Derek ripped the blindfold in half, and wrapped both pieces around the large eyeballs that protruded from his wing-mirrors. 'This should make for a perfectly smooth trip,' he muttered.

'And one for you,' Chico said, handing Anthony a grubby piece of rag. 'And one for me.'

'Oh, for the love of god…' Derek moaned.

'So that if ever I'm captured,' Chico said, slipping his silk satin blindfold on, 'I will not be able to tell the enemy the way.'

Anthony's fingers strayed towards the car door's handle. He was immediately met with the uncomfortable yet familiar sensation of a gun barrel being pressed up against the side of his head.

'Do not even contemplate trying to escape,' Chico said. 'I have the ears of a llama and the reactions of a stoat.'

'Not to mention the mental capacity of a goldfish,' Derek mumbled.

A grey bunch of fives jabbed him violently in the dashboard. 'I heard that,' Chico said. 'Ears of a llama, remember?' He thrust his head out the window and yelled, 'Okay, Alpha! Beta! Gamma! Delta! Jeremy!'

'Sir, yes sir!' responded four of the clones piloting the other vehicles.

'Yo!' responded the clone named Jeremy.

'Follow me!'

Seven

The remainder of Anthony's journey went a little something like this:

BEEEEP! BEEEEEEEEEEEEP!

'Open your eyes, you maniac!'

'Okay, now turn left once you hear an electrical humming sound.'

WHUUUM! WHUUUM!

SCREEEEECH!

HONK! HONK!

'Learn to drive, cretin!'

'Good, very good. Now dip down slightly…'

NNNEEEEEEEEEEEEEEEEOOOOOOOWWWWWW!

'Aaaaaaaaaaiiiiiieee!'

'Holy Jesus!'

'Trying, of course, to upset as few pedestrians as possible.'

'Aaaaaaargh!'

'My hat! You squashed my hat!'

'Now, in a few seconds, you should hear the shattering of glass.'

'You *what?*'

'Do not be alarmed. This is a shortcut.'

SMAAASSSSSH!

'Ooow! My *face!*'

'Now, make a sharp right turn at the scent of blueberry muffins…'

'Get out of my bakery, you bastards!'

SMAAAASSSSSH!

'Take the second left, after you hear the –'

MUNCH! CHOMPF!

'Hey, these muffins aren't bad…'

'Course correction: turn 180 degrees…'

WHOOOSH!

BEEP! HONK!

'And prepare again for impact…'

SMAAAASSSSSH!

'Remembering this time to get us *all* a blueberry muffin.'

SNATCH!

'Oi! Gerrofoutofit yer bastards!'

SMAAAASSSSH!

MUNCH! CHOMF! CRUNCH! BURP!

'Mmph! Good.'– CHOMP! –'Now, take a left past mphf mphffff mphh.' MUNCH!

'Past what? What did you say? What??'

NEEEEEEEEEEEEOOOOW!

COUGH! CHOKE!

'Oh my god! Turn now! *Turn!*'

SMAAAAAAAAASSSSSSHHHHHH!

'Aiiiiieee!'

'Eeeeeek!'

'Excuse me, sir! This is a private sex clone brothel, for paying customers only!'

RASP! RASP!

CLICK!

'Remove those blindfolds, gentlemen, and I'll fill you full of lead.'

'Aaaaawwww…'

'Spoil sport…'

SMAAASSH!

'Okay, this is it, we're almost there.'

RUMBLE! RRRRUMBLE!

'Reduce speed, and prepare to cut thrusters on my mark.'

'Cut what? I don't have any thrusters.'

RRRRMMMM RRRRRMMMM!

'All right then…reduce speed, and prepare to stop farting on my mark.'

'Roger, wilco, tango and so forth.'

CLAAAANG!

'Mark!'

PPPPTTT!

SCREEEEEEECH!

RUMBLE! RRRRUMBLE!

CLAAAANG!

A brief, welcome moment of silence, and then –

'Gentlemen, you may now remove your blindfolds.'

Anthony removed his blindfold, which didn't make a jot of difference, as it was still dark.

'It's still dark,' he commented.

'Lights!' commanded Chico.

The lights blinked on. Anthony and Derek blinked along with them.

'Oooh,' said Derek, looking around as his eyes adjusted. 'Where are we?'

'The garage,' said Chico, exiting the car. 'So stop pretending to be impressed.'

'Oooh,' said Anthony, as he followed after Chico. 'Whose underpants are those?' He pointed to some frilly crotchless numbers dangling from Derek's fender.

'Mine now,' said Derek. 'Phwoar!'

'Derek,' Anthony said, transferring his gaze to the sticky black substance oozing out of the many punctures in the car's chassis, 'aren't you just a little bit concerned by the amount of glass shards you've got sticking out of your body?'

'Not any more.' Derek held the underpants aloft, and grinned. 'I've got these. *Weheeeeey!*' His eyes crossed, and he slumped to the ground.

'Derek?' Anthony nudged him gently with the toe of his shoe.

'Don't be concerned,' said Chico. 'I'll have one of the other clones tend to his wounds later, and then I'll have him shot.' He turned to regard the procession of clones that had followed him back to the base. It had gotten considerably smaller. 'Alpha!' he barked.

'Er,' came a timid voice from the one remaining car. 'I'm afraid Alpha's no longer with us, sir.'

'What do you mean he's no longer with us?'

'He crashed, sir,' said the voice.

'Crashed?'

'Hit a pylon. Burnt to a crisp.'

'What about Beta?' Chico asked, looking around. 'Where's Beta?'

'Also crashed. Hit another vehicle, sir.'

'Gamma?' Chico said, his voice trembling slightly. 'Surely not Gamma as well…'

'I'm afraid it was Gamma's vehicle. Made quite an impressive fireball, actually.'

'Delta?' Chico squeaked.

'Got caught in traffic, sir.'

Chico exhaled in relief.

'Well, caught *by* traffic. Splattered across the skyway.'

'How about Jeremy? What happened to Jeremy?'

The voice paused.

The tension mounted.

'Alive and well, sir!' said the clone, springing from his vehicle, blindfold still firmly in place.

'Glad to see one of you made it back alive, at least.'

'Glad it was me, sir,' said Jeremy, snapping off a quick salute.

'Though a thought does occur to me, Jeremy,' said Chico. 'And I don't think it's one you're going to like very much.'

'Oh really, sir?'

'Yes.' Chico took a deep breath. 'How do you know what happened to the other clones?'

'Er, what?' Jeremy saluted again out of panic.

'How do you know what happened to the other clones...'

'Uh –'

'...When you were supposed to be blindfolded?'

Beads of sweat formed on Jeremy's grey forehead. 'Well, er, I, uh, might've taken just a bit of a peek –' A bullet exploded out through the back of his skull.

'Right,' said Chico, turning his back on the corpse of his likeness, 'let's go meet the professor.'

'You...you killed yourself,' Anthony said, staring in morbid fascination at the twitching body.

'Secrecy must be maintained, at all costs.' Chico twirled his gun a few times, and returned it to its holster. 'Now, follow me.'

'What about Derek?'

'Oh, I'm sure he'll be fine lying there unconscious for a bit. The rest will probably do him good.'

'But –'

Chico's hand strayed towards his holster.

'You're right, you're right,' Anthony said hurriedly. 'I'm sure he'll be absolutely fine.'

'Good lad,' said Chico. 'Now, close your eyes a moment.'

'Why?' Anthony said. 'What are you going to do?'

'Key in the code on this console here.' Chico motioned to a keypad by the door. 'Very secretive stuff.'

Anthony turned his back, and reluctantly closed his eyes.

'And no peeking. You know what happens if you peek.'

'Yes,' Anthony mumbled, 'you shoot yourself.' The butt of a gun cracked against the back of his head.

'Don't get sarky,' said Chico.

Anthony listened for what felt like an eternity to the 'Blippety! Bleep!' of the keypad, as Chico methodically entered each number in the seven thousand six hundred and fifty six digit code.

A good twenty minutes later, he keyed in the last number.

A pause of contemplation from the console, followed by a noise like a foghorn. *'Key code incorrect! Please try again.'*

A curse, a sigh, a few more half-hearted taps of fingers on keypad, and then:

'Ah, bollocks to it.'

Gunfire. Sparks fizzling. The metallic 'Whuum!' of a door opening.

'You may now open your eyes.'

The first thing Anthony noticed upon doing so was a console, fizzing away from a neat little bullet hole dead in its centre.

Chico stood in the doorway, attempting to conceal his irritation by whistling under his breath. 'Not one word.'

Anthony contented himself with a smirk. The butt of Chico's gun cracked him across the back of his head.

'That includes smirking. Now, follow me.' He strode off down a long, winding maze of corridors, with Anthony trailing after him. 'Making sure, of course, not to step on any booby traps.'

'What?' Anthony froze.

'Don't worry,' Chico said. 'I'll tell you when to *duck!'*

Anthony ducked. A large axe sprang out of the ground between his legs, missing his groin by inches. He stared down at it, paralysed with fear. 'You…said…duck!'

Chico shrugged. 'I meant roll. Easy mistake.'

'That's it, I'm going home.'

'There's only two ways out of this corridor,' Chico hissed in his best Dirty Harry voice. 'By my side, or in a body bag. Which is it to be?'

Anthony weighed up his options. 'Could I have some time to think about it?'

'Move!'

Cautiously, they advanced down the corridor, stepping past a multitude of tripwires and pressure pads.

'Now,' Chico said, 'as we round this next corner, make sure you dodge left.' He disappeared around the corner.

A moment later, there came a twang and a scream.

'Correction,' Chico's voice called back. 'Make sure you dodge *right.*'

Anthony rounded the corner, and dodged right.

Chico was stood waiting for him, an impatient look on his face and a crossbow bolt jutting out of his shoulder. 'Come on, come on. Get a move on!'

'Doesn't that hurt?' Anthony said, gesturing to the bolt.

'Immensely,' said Chico. 'Thanks for asking.'

'Well then, maybe we should turn ba–'

'Hop, hop, skip, jump!' Chico screamed suddenly.

Anthony hopped twice, skipped and jumped.

Chico stood there laughing at him.

'You're just trying to humiliate me now, aren't you?'

'Doesn't take much effort,' Chico sniggered. 'Now, let's see if we can successfully negotiate our way through the mine f–' Something went *'Click!'* beneath his feet. He slowly looked down. 'Oh dear,' he said.

It was Anthony's turn to laugh; a big snorting, wheezy laugh with plenty of guffaws thrown in for good measure.

'I don't know what you're so happy about,' Chico murmured out the side of his mouth. 'You're the one who's going to disarm it.'

'No I'm not,' Anthony said, chuckling away. 'I'm off, mate.' He turned to leave.

'Make one false move,' Chico hissed, 'and I'll step off this mine, and blow us both to kingdom come.'

'Don't believe a word of it,' Anthony said. 'Bye now.'

'What have I got to lose? I'm just a clone, remember?'

Anthony's shoulders sagged. Muttering and cursing, he returned to Chico's side.

'That's more like it,' Chico said. 'Now, ever disarmed a land mine before?'

'I can't say it's ever come up in my day to day work as an accountant, no.'

'First time for everything. Possibly the last time, too. Have you got a screwdriver?'

Anthony patted his pockets. 'No.'

'Some pliers?'

'No.'

'A portable mine disposal kit?'

'Fresh out, sorry.'

'Well, what have you got?'

Anthony rummaged in his pockets. 'Twelve Mock-Choc bars, and a biro.'

Chico returned a cold, unblinking stare.

'Oh, and this paperclip I found stuck to the sole of my shoe.' Anthony held the paperclip aloft.

The clone's drab grey features cracked a rare smile. 'That'll do nicely,' he said.

Five minutes later, the mine was disarmed, Anthony was a nervous wreck, and Chico was happily munching on a Mock-Choc bar.

'Nice work, Tony.' He patted Anthony's trembling back. 'Now all we need to do is scale the pit of death, and we're home and dry.'

'Scale the *what?*' Anthony shrieked.

'Just kidding. The professor's lab is through that door there.' Chico pointed to a solid wall.

'What door where?' Anthony glanced around the dark, deadly corridor.

'That one.' Chico pointed again.

'Doesn't look much like a door,' Anthony said, squinting at the wall.

'Of course not. If the door actually looked like a door, people might walk through it. Where would be the security in that?'

'Makes a kind of sense, I suppose,' Anthony said, not really caring whether it did or not.

'After you, then.' Chico swept his arm out grandly in the wall's direction.

Anthony strode forwards, and marched straight into the brickwork.

'Gets them every time,' Chico chuckled. He inserted a key into a hole in the wall and gave it a twist. The wall creaked open.

A man in a white lab coat was stood on the other side, arms folded, pale blue eyes narrowed in irritation. He was the oldest man Anthony had ever seen; well over fifty, and had the word 'expired' tattooed on his wrinkled grey forehead. This was a common feature in those unsavoury members of society who refused to opt for one of the government's early retirement packages, which encouraged the old and infirm to make way for a younger generation in some terminal yet trendy fashion or other. They were generally referred to as 'The Living Dead'; societies locusts, draining resources with their selfish desire to carry on breathing.

Chico saluted. 'Professor Langerman, I have returned, and I bring –'

'You used the secret entrance again, didn't you?' the professor snapped.

'Sir, yes sir!'

'How many times do I have to tell you? Use the *lift*. It's what it's there for.'

'Didn't want to attract any unnecessary attention, sir.'

The professor tugged despondently at his impressively long white beard. 'You don't think that leading a platoon of airborne clones around the city *blindfolded* might have attracted slightly more attention?'

'Can't say I'd really considered that option, sir,' Chico said, 'but I'll bear it in mind the next time I use the secret entrance.'

Something that was half way between a sigh and a death rattle wheezed out through the professor's throat. 'How many of them made it back?'

'How many of who, sir?'

'The clones,' the professor said testily. 'The small army of clones I sent you out with.'

'Ah, them.'

'Yes, them.'

'Including me, sir?'

'Including you.'

Chico tapped his chin thoughtfully. He clicked his cheeks a few times. 'One?' he ventured.

'Just the one.' The professor buried his face in his chemical-stained hands.

'Oh, and Jeremy.'

Gaps formed between the professor's fingers. His eyes peered cautiously out.

'But I shot him.'

'You did, did you?'

'Yes, sir. For removing his blindfold.'

'Marvellous. Truly marvellous.'

'We've got to take precautions,' Chico said, waving his finger sternly. 'Don't want another massacre on our hands.'

'Chico,' the professor sighed, 'you *are* a massacre. You've managed yet again to single-handedly wipe out an entire batch of clones.'

'Sorry, sir.' Chico grimaced. 'I'll nip over to the cloning machine and run off a couple more copies, shall I?'

'You do that, Chico. Though you might want to remove that crossbow bolt first.'

Chico looked down at the metal bolt protruding from his shoulder. 'Oh yes. Forgot about that.' He motioned to

Anthony, who was sat on the ground, rubbing at his aching head. 'Watch that one closely,' Chico hissed. 'He's a right bastard.'

The clone stepped past the professor, and disappeared through the secret door that was a wall.

The professor helped Anthony to his feet. 'I really am most awfully sorry about that,' he said. 'Chico does tend to get a little carried away at times.'

'Think nothing of it,' Anthony said, brushing himself down. 'No harm done.'

'I believe formal introductions are in order.' The professor shook Anthony warmly by the hand. 'I am Professor Langerman,' he said. 'And you, I believe, are here to kill me.'

Eight

Anthony sat in a vast dining room, watching the mound of mouth-watering yet distinctly purple food products placed before him on a lavishly decorated platter slowly turn cold.

'Feel free to dig in at any time,' the professor hollered from the other end of the long oak table. 'You must be famished.'

'Oh, no, no, I'm fine,' Anthony said, trying not to drool. 'Had a couple of blueberry muffins on the way over. Couldn't eat another bite.'

Professor Langerman cocked his head. 'I can hear your stomach rumbling from here,' he said. 'It's all one hundred percent home cloned produce – almost as good as the real thing.'

Anthony eyed the food on his plate with suspicion. He reached out a tentative hand, and picked up a sausage. Much like everything else, it was purple.

'It's not poisoned,' the professor said, casually sipping from his Champaign glass, 'if that's what you're thinking.'

Anthony let the sausage slip from his fingers. 'Hadn't crossed my mind until now.'

'If I wanted you dead Anthony, I'd have let Chico do it. God knows, he's eager enough.'

'Then why haven't you?' Anthony pushed his plate aside. 'You've already got my clothes.' He glanced down at the tweed jacket and polyester trousers the professor had cruelly insisted he wore to dinner. 'It's not as if you need me any more.'

'I don't want to kill you Anthony, any more than you want to kill me.'

Anthony scratched his head. 'Well, what's that supposed to mean?'

'I know it was Noddy who put you up to it, and that you're still entertaining the foolish notion that by destroying my operation you might get back in his good books. But let me tell you something, Anthony.' The professor raised his bushy eyebrows knowingly. 'When Noddy wants you dead, *nothing* can make him change his mind.'

Anthony's eyes widened in realisation. 'He's killed you before, hasn't he?'

'Yes, a long time ago. Shortly after I created him.'

'You mean to say…'

'Yes?' the professor prompted.

'You're…'

'Yes?'

'You're…'

'Out with it, man.'

Anthony pointed an accusing finger. 'A *Glam Rock* fan.'

The professor sighed. 'Not to mention the fact that I'm responsible for the deaths of god knows how many innocent people.'

'Ah, yes,' Anthony said. 'That too.'

The professor shook his head, making his long white hair flail around like snakes at an orgy. 'And you know what the really tragic thing is? Noddy was supposed to be a karaoke machine.'

'Come again?'

'Oh, you know how it is when you're sat in a lab designing things late at night, and you get a bit bored.'

'Not really, no.'

'An extra circuit here, a few more wires there…' The professor stacked one bread roll on top of another. 'Next thing I knew, the little so and so was completely self aware,

and hell-bent on the destruction of the entire human race.'
He swept his arms out wide, scattering bread rolls in every
direction.

'Why didn't you pull the plug on him?'

'I had intended to, but the government took a liking to
him. Said he presented a viable solution to the growing
population problem. I tried to persuade them that cloning
was the way forward, but they weren't convinced. Except
when it came to creating human clones for "recreational"
use, of course,' the professor said bitterly. 'They were only
too happy to throw money at that particular project.'

Anthony clicked his fingers sharply. 'That's where I
know your name from...Langerman's Lovers. You're the
sex clone guy!'

One of the professor's eyes twitched slightly. 'Hardly
my greatest accomplishment,' he sighed. 'Though sadly it's
the only one I seem to be remembered for, and the only
one that gained any funding, until Noddy came along. The
government wanted something simple, something that
would yield immediate results...something their sponsors
could really get behind.'

'Like killing useless sods like me, you mean?' Anthony
muttered.

'I wouldn't take it personally, Anthony. Once Noddy's
finished with society's less desirable element, he'll turn on
everyone who's left. He won't be satisfied until the human
species is completely eradicated.'

'And karaoke machines rule the earth?'

'Something like that, yes,' the professor said, scowling.
'That's why I moved my base of operations and, with the
help of a few trusted colleagues, continued the cloning research – even after I was well past my sell-by date.' His
calloused fingertips rubbed irritably at the marking on his
forehead.

'Until Noddy had you subtracted?'

The professor winced. 'Please don't use that word. It was murder, Anthony, through and through. The Administration wiped out everyone I loved, everyone I cared for.'

'Including yourself?'

'Especially myself.' The old man blew his nose noisily on a pocket-handkerchief. 'Many great people died in that massacre.'

Chico kicked the dining room door open, and commando rolled in.

'And one slightly mediocre one survived.' Professor Langerman turned towards the doorway. 'What is it, Chico?'

'Sorry to interrupt, sir.' Chico leapt to his feet and saluted. 'I've finished cloning myself. Thought you might like to meet our new recruits.'

Two more clones commando rolled in. They were identical to Chico in every way, except one of them had no eyelids, and the other had no lips.

'I'm Peter,' said the clone with no eyelids. He saluted and stared.

'O,' said the clone with no lips, also saluting.

The professor glanced sideways at Chico. 'O?'

'His name's Bob, sir,' Chico hissed. 'But he can't pronounce it. Doesn't have any lips, see?'

'That reminds me of a joke,' Anthony said loudly. 'What goes "oo"?'

The three clones glared at him, especially Peter who was particularly good at that sort of thing.

'Anthony,' the professor cautioned, 'I don't think this is the right time.' He made shooing motions at the clones as they fumbled for their guns. 'If you could excuse us please, gentlemen? We were in the middle of a rather important discussion.'

'Right you are, sir.' Chico made for the door. 'I'll come back and shoot that one later shall I?' He hoisted a thumb at Anthony.

'No,' the professor said firmly. 'There's to be no more killing. Those days are over.'

Chico's face fell. Then it rose again, accompanied by a wide grin. 'Ha! Yes, very good sir.' He winked at the professor. 'No more killing. Ha, ha, ha. Nice one.'

He commando rolled back out, followed by his chuckling duplicates.

'The only survivor, you say?' A questioning eyebrow rose to the top of Anthony's receding hairline.

'Yes, hard to believe isn't it? What's perhaps even less believable is Chico's explanation as to how his original incarnation survived.'

Anthony grabbed a bowl of purple knobbly things which might've passed for popcorn in a certain light, and settled back in his chair. 'Oh, this ought to be good.'

'Well, according to Chico, or "Kev" as he was known back then, the moment he heard the Administration approaching he crouched stealthily down behind a water cooler. Then, when the moment was right, he sprang out, brutally stabbed one of them in the eye with a water cone, stole his gun, shot his way out, snagged one of my hairs, fashioned a makeshift parachute out of a collection of man-sized handkerchiefs, and leapt nimbly to safety through the two hundred and fifty-sixth floor window.'

'I was wrong,' Anthony said stiffly. 'That was *terrible.*'

'Yes, and the story gets successively taller with each new clone that tells it. I'm sure you'll be thrilled to learn the latest version has a lot more gunplay in it, and some ninjas.'

'What do you think really happened?'

'Who knows? The important thing is Kevin was able to save my DNA, and resurrect me so I could continue my good work.' A frown worked its way through the professor's wrinkles. 'If only I could remember what my good work *was.*'

'That's easy,' Anthony said. 'It's cloning, isn't it?'

'Yes, but which area of cloning? There's so many of them. I mean, hell, I've spent the last three years alone just trying to recreate the banana.'

'Any luck?' Anthony popped a small purple biscuit into his mouth.

'Not really,' the professor said, 'you're eating the end result there.'

Anthony paused mid-chew. 'I thought everything tasted a bit samey.'

'Anyway, as valuable work as banana recreation is, I'm sure my grand master scheme must have extended slightly further afield than that.'

Being as delicate as he could, Anthony spat several million creds worth of cloning research into a napkin. 'Why don't you remember?'

'Part of the downside of the cloning process, I'm afraid. Each time a copy is made it deviates a little bit more from the original. Sometimes the deviation is a physical defect, other times it's mental.'

'Like in Chico's case?'

'Exactly. I'm sure it'll come as little surprise to you that Chico is Kevin's one hundred and thirty eighth incarnation.'

'That explains a lot,' said Anthony.

'My deviation was of the mental variety. I've got gaps in my memory, Anthony. Gaps where there should be knowledge. All I remember is that before Noddy had me executed I was on the verge of a major breakthrough. Something that was going to solve the population problem once and for all.'

'And that knowledge is contained within Maria's mind?'

Professor Langerman nodded. 'Thankfully, my most trusted employee was absent at the time of the massacre. She was out celebrating our latest breakthrough with a black market celebrity sex clone. Alas, her husband walked in on her mid-celebration and –'

'Yes, yes, I know this bit,' Anthony said impatiently.

'Anyway, after the Administration purged the crime scene we thought her DNA was lost for good, and the experiment along with it, until Maria turned up under her husband's armpit a few days ago. Now, thanks to you, we finally have that DNA back in our grasp. Finally we shall learn what the experiment actually is.'

'Shouldn't you be doing that right now, rather than sitting here talking to me?'

'I am doing that right now, Anthony.' The professor pressed the tips of his fingers together. 'I am also at present redecorating the lower guest room, playing a table tennis tournament against myself, and writing out a complex algorithm for sentient baked Alaska.'

'Ah,' Anthony said. 'Cloned yourself, did you?'

The professor smiled grimly. 'The Administration isn't going to catch me out that way again. Anyway, throwing a banquet in your honour seemed like the least I could do. As I'm sure you're beginning to realise, we have a lot to thank you for. If there's anything I can ever do for you in return, be sure to let me know.'

'Well,' Anthony said, 'there is one thing.'

'Yes?'

'You could start by explaining to me why there's a branch sticking out of my ear.'

The professor stared at Anthony thoughtfully, then shrugged his shoulders. 'Bad hygiene, I guess. Anything else?'

'I just want my body back.'

'Is that all? Consider it done.'

Anthony's chair toppled backwards as he leapt eagerly to his feet. 'You know where it is? You've seen it?'

'I don't know who stole you body, Anthony, but then again, I don't need it. All I need do is extract the DNA from your brain.'

'That would work, would it?'

'Of course it would. After all, it is *your* brain, not Colin's.'

'Ah yes,' Anthony said, his cheeks reddening in embarrassment. 'I hadn't thought of that.'

'Once I've extracted the DNA, I'll be able to use it to remodel your body accordingly. I have all the necessary tools in the laboratory. It should be a relatively simple procedure.'

A rare gleam of hope radiated in Anthony's bloodshot eyes. He felt sick with excitement, or possibly food poisoning. Finally, he was going to be himself again.

'Absolutely *nothing* can go wrong,' the professor said confidently.

'What do you mean something's gone wrong?'

Mr Pickler paused with a huge comb – the sort usually reserved for grooming horses – wedged half way into his moustache.

Grison leant against Mr Pickler's desk, attempting to catch his breath. 'Cressface, sir,' he wheezed. 'He's…still… *huuuh*…still… *huuhhh*…'

'Dead?' Mr Pickler hazarded.

'No… *huuuh*… *huuhhh*.' Grison motioned desperately with one arm. 'Other one.'

Mr Pickler sat up straight. 'Alive?'

'That's… *huuuh*…the one, yes.'

'Oh, excellent.' Mr Pickler clasped his hands together and beamed pleasantly. 'That *is* good news. Always knew that one showed potential.' His fingers strayed back towards his comb.

'No, sir.' Grison wheezed. 'Bad news. Very bad news.'

'Is it?'

'Yes, sir.' Grison sucked in a deep breath. 'It's on every channel. Haven't you seen it?'

Mr Pickler motioned to the chair-shaped hole in the viewscreen.

'Ah. Sorry about that, sir. Thought Nigel would've fixed it by now.'

'Take a seat and tell me what this is all about. Please try not to throw it this time though, eh?'

Grison sat and locked eyes with Mr Pickler. 'We might very well be looking at an end to the way of life as we know it.'

'Oh dear.' Mr Pickler bit his bottom lip. 'This sounds terribly serious. Mind if I, uh…?' He motioned to the comb wedged in his moustache.

'By all means, sir.'

'Damn decent of you, Philip. I do so hate to face a crisis only half groomed.'

'It all revolves around Cresswell. Somehow –'

Grison's voice was drowned out by a hideous rasping sound, as Mr Pickler dragged the comb roughly through the dense foliage of his moustache.

'Second thoughts, sir,' Grison yelled, 'perhaps it's best if you do that later?'

'Oh, if I must.' Mr Pickler laid the comb aside.

'As I was saying, the majority of the world's population seem to be labouring under the belief that Cresswell might in actual fact be, well, er…'

'Spit it out, man.'

'The second coming!'

Mr Pickler beamed. 'Terrific! So the advertising worked after all. Get that Kompact Kars representative on the holo-phone immediately. This calls for a celebration.' His hand reached out for the sweets tin.

'It's got nothing at all to do with the advertising. Or Kompact Kars, for that matter.'

'It hasn't?' The hand reluctantly withdrew.

'No, sir. A surgeon down on Purgatory Row found something growing in Cresswell's mind. Something… remarkable.' Grison slapped a couple of photos down on

Mr Pickler's desk. 'These should explain everything.'

'What am I looking at here?' Mr Pickler asked as he rifled through them.

'Stills taken from the news broadcast.'

Grison's boss squinted at the topmost photograph. He turned it sideways. 'Yes, but what of?'

'Well, that one is an x-ray of Cresswell's mind.'

The moustache bristled in shock, making the comb shoot out, and embed itself in the ceiling. 'Extraordinary,' Mr Pickler said. 'Most extraordinary.'

Grison glanced upwards at the comb. 'You're telling me, sir.'

'And this one?'

'That photo is the image magnified. I believe it shows our problem in full.'

Mr Pickler's eyebrows did a baffled little jig. 'Good grief! Are you sure this is authentic?'

'The Prime Minister seems to think so, as do most of the world leaders.'

'And the surgeon that took them…reliable source, is he?'

'None other than Dr Maximillian Skrunk, sir.'

'The world renown bondage doctor?'

'The very same.'

Mr Pickler shook his head in amazement. 'Good god, then they must be genuine.' He stared at the photos again. 'But how? How is this possible?'

'Haven't a clue, sir,' Grison said. 'All I know is this agency is in serious trouble.'

'You're not wrong there, Philip. You must find Anthony before he falls into the wrong hands.'

'And then what?'

'You subtract him,' Mr Pickler said sternly. 'Second coming or not, this is no time for pleasantries.'

'Are you sure that's wise? Those photos seem to suggest –'

'If those photos are to be believed then this agency's work is obsolete, and we'll all be out of jobs. Do you like your job, Philip?'

'Love it, sir,' said Grison, with passion.

'Then find Anthony and subtract him immediately!'

'I'll get right on it.' Grison nodded, and sped out.

Mr Pickler glanced down at the photos on his desk, and shook his head again. 'We'd be doing the lad a favour,' he murmured. 'Good god…'

Nine

Anthony came to in a cold, dank laboratory, with a blood-ied bandage wrapped around his head. Four Professor Langermans were standing over him, with concerned looks on each of their faces.

'How are you feeling?' one of the professors asked.

'A double case of double vision,' Anthony said groggily, 'but other than that, just dandy.'

A fifth professor approached the bed. 'I assure you, Anthony, it's not double vision. My clones insisted on being present for this monumentous occasion.'

'Monumental, I think you'll find,' professor number four corrected.

'Either way,' the fifth professor said, looking around at his clones. 'I'm sure you'll all agree, something truly wonderful has happened.'

'I don't think Anthony would agree,' the fourth professor mumbled.

'The operation…did it work? Am I me again?' Anthony tried to sit up. His head reeled, and he slumped back down.

'I'm afraid not,' the fifth professor said. 'There's been a…complication.'

Anthony groaned. 'What sort of complication?'

'A rather complicated one,' the third professor chimed in.

Anthony clutched his head. It felt like its sides were going to cave in. 'My brain…' he cried. 'You damaged my brain, didn't you?'

'Oh heavens, no.'

All five professors chuckled nervously.

'Well, that wouldn't have been possible,' professor three stated. 'It's not there any more.'

'My brain's…not there?' said Anthony, frowning.

'Let's just say it is, and it isn't.' Professor five gave Anthony a tight lipped smile.

'Let's not,' professor four added. 'It all sounds rather confusing.'

'You're right.' The fifth professor stroked the third professor's beard absently. 'Perhaps it would help if we showed Anthony a few scans we made whilst he was unconscious.'

'I agree,' professors one and two added in unison.

The second professor approached Anthony's bed with a rolled up x-ray under his arm. 'What does this look like to you?' he asked, as he unrolled it.

Anthony peered at the x-ray. It was black, and covered with thousands of tiny white dots. 'It looks like a star chart.'

'No, Anthony,' professor two said slowly, 'that's your mind.'

Anthony squinted at the x-ray. 'Now I'm really confused.'

'And you see that big dot there?' Professor five leaned in and pointed to a huge circular object dead in the centre of the x-ray. 'That's a planet.'

'You don't say?'

'A small one, granted, but it's growing at a phenomenal rate.'

'Oh, that *is* good news.' Anthony settled back onto the bed.

'Still,' professor three said, 'at least it clears up the mystery as to why there's a branch sticking out your ear.'

'Does it now?'

'Yes. Side effects, dear boy. Side effects of the experiment contained within your mind.'

'There's an experiment in there as well, is there?' Anthony whistled in mock amazement. 'Gosh.'

'The planet *is* the experiment, Anthony. One gigantic experiment to clone planet earth. You're the incubator, you see?'

'Ah, so that's what you were working on is it?'

'Yes.' All five professors nodded excitedly. 'Isn't it amazing?'

'Nothing at all to do with bananas then?' Anthony said. 'Or should I expect to encounter one of those growing out the other ear?' He poked a finger in his right ear and rummaged around. It was reassuringly free of bananas.

'No, no,' the fifth professor said. 'No bananas involved.'

'That's something I suppose.' Anthony plumped up his pillow. 'I have a question, if it's not too much bother?'

'Oh no, no. Please, fire away.'

'How did an entire planet get into my head?'

'Ah.' Professor five looked to his clones for assistance. 'Perhaps someone else would like to field this one?'

'Yes,' professor four said, 'it is a bit of a mind bender.'

'The only way it could logically be possible,' professor one speculated, 'is if Maria's DNA was somehow absorbed into Anthony's system.'

The five professors 'hmmed' thoughtfully.

'That would do it, yes.'

'I concur.'

'As do we.'

'Well, that explains everything.' Anthony rolled his eyes, then closed them and settled down under the covers.

'Ooh, ooh, let me tell him the next bit.' Chico elbowed his way through the mass of professors and leant in close to Anthony's face. 'When that planet gets big enough, do you know what's going to happen next?'

Anthony's eyelids flickered open. 'I'm going to have to buy a really big hat?'

'No.' Chico smiled cruelly. 'It's going to explode out of your head with a force to rival the Big Bang.'

'Is it?' Anthony said. 'Oh, jolly good. There's something to look forward to.' He closed his eyes again, and rolled over.

'By then you'll already be dead.'

'Won't that be nice?' Anthony stifled a yawn. 'Now, if you multiple nut-jobs don't mind, I'm afraid I have far more pressing dreams to attend to.' He buried his head under the pillow. Within seconds he was snoring loudly.

'Well,' professors five and three said, 'he took that a lot better than I expected.'

'That's because he thought it was all a dream,' professor four said, shaking his head.

'Oh dear,' the professors chorused.

'Do you want me to slap him a few times, sirs?' Chico cracked his knuckles eagerly. 'Bring him back to reality?'

'No,' professor five said, looking thoughtful. 'Perhaps it's best this way. He might be more co-operative if he believes none of this actually happened.'

Anthony came to in a cold, dank laboratory, with a bloodied bandage wrapped around his head. Professor Langerman and Chico were standing over him, grinning a little too widely.

'Did it work?' he asked.

'Oh yes, absolutely.' The professor gave him the thumbs up. 'One hundred percent success.'

Chico sniggered.

'Shh,' the professor hissed.

'You mean…I'm me again?' Anthony slowly sat up.

'That's right. Welcome back, Anthony.' The professor proffered his other thumb, and added a wink into the bargain.

'Get me a mirror, quickly!' Anthony said. 'I need to see myself.'

The professor's grin faltered. 'Ah. I don't think you're quite ready for a mirror yet.'

'Why not?'

'Because, uh, because…' The professor looked to Chico for assistance.

'You're ugly,' Chico said helpfully. 'Amazingly ugly.' A wrinkled grey hand cuffed him round the ear.

'What my assistant meant to say was the shock of seeing yourself after all this time might bring about a cardiac arrest.'

'I'll take that risk,' Anthony said. 'A mirror. Now!'

'Er…uh…'

'We don't have any,' Chico blurted.

'Don't have any mirrors?'

The professor narrowed his eyes at Chico. 'Ha. No, never needed them. As I'm sure you can imagine, being surrounded by clones all day I'm already well aware of what I look like.'

Anthony glanced around the room, and spotted something on a tabletop. 'There's one over there.'

'No there isn't,' Chico said, stepping in front of it.

'Yes there is. I can almost see myself in it…' Anthony strained to one side.

'No you can't,' Chico said, moving with him to block his view.

'Ooh, look over there!' the professor cried suddenly. 'Someone's brought you *flowers*.'

Anthony looked to one side.

There came a loud bang, and a smash.

When he looked back, the mirror lay in pieces.

'Wow, I wonder how that happened?' Chico said innocently.

'You shot it!'

'No I didn't,' Chico said, tucking a gun into the back of his trousers.

'Yes you did,' Anthony said accusingly. 'I can see a gun tucked into the back of your trousers in your reflection there.' He pointed to a second mirror.

'Oh bloody hell!' Chico raced to grab it, but it was too late. Anthony had already seen himself.

'Hey! I'm still Colin.'

'Yes,' the professor sighed, 'you're still Colin.'

'Then what happened earlier wasn't a dream?'

'I'm afraid not.'

'And there really is a planet in my mind?'

'I'm afraid so.'

Grim reality struck Anthony like a juggernaut. 'Oh my god,' he moaned. 'There's a planet in my mind and it's going to explode out of me with a force to rival the Big Bang!'

The professor laid a kindly hand on his shoulder. 'Don't look so glum, Anthony. It's not necessarily a *bad* thing.'

Anthony squinted up at him. 'It's not a bad thing that my head's going to explode?'

'Too right,' Chico mumbled.

'Okay, it is rather bad for you,' the professor admitted, 'but good for the rest of humanity. You've got to focus on the bigger picture here. Finally we'll have an end to the population problem; a second planet right on our door-step, just ripe for colonisation.'

'No one's colonising my brain!' Anthony screamed, pulling the banana-motif duvet up to his neck. 'Back off!'

'Don't you see, Anthony? This is your chance to do something worthwhile with your life.'

'Yeah,' Chico sniggered, 'end it.'

'It's not every day you get the opportunity to save the human race and become a martyr, you know.'

'I don't want to become a martyr,' Anthony whined. 'Bring that Maria back and let her be a martyr. She looked like she'd love that sort of thing. I'm sure she'd be well up for it.'

'Ah. I'm afraid resurrecting Maria is no longer an option.'

'What? Why not?'

The professor's face became grave again. 'There's been a complication.'

This time the complication came in the form of a short, squat man dangling from the ceiling. He was suspended in a huge test tube, amidst a sea of empty test tubes wired to a large oblong machine that looked like a cross between a sunbed and a photocopier. Even though the little man was covered from head to foot in body hair, it still couldn't disguise the fact that he was completely naked; a factor which became immediately evident to Anthony as he entered the cloning room and looked up.

'Dear god!' he cried, hurriedly averting his eyes. 'What the hell is that?'

The professor and Chico edged in through the door, being careful not to make the same mistake as Anthony.

'We were rather hoping you could tell us,' the professor said. 'One thing's for sure – it's certainly not Maria.'

Anthony risked a quick glance upwards. The small, hairy form was hunched against the inside of the test tube, absently scratching itself. Anthony's nose wrinkled in disgust. When mankind had scaled the evolutionary ladder, this poor fellow's rungs had quite evidently been greased. 'It's hideous!' he cried. 'Where did it come from?'

'We cloned him,' the professor said, 'from a blood sample taken from the inside of your trainers. Sadly, it was the only uncontaminated DNA sample we could find.'

'That thing was inside my shoes?' Anthony scrunched up his face. 'Ugh!'

'You mean to say you don't know this –' The professor struggled to find the right word, and settled for the wrong one. '…gentleman?'

'Of course I don't know him,' Anthony said. 'If you want to track his mates down, I'd suggest you try giving Tarzan a call.'

Chico moved towards the large machine in the centre of the room. 'Do you want me to flood the tubes?'

'What?'

'Drown the little bastard.' He reached towards a button marked 'Purge'.

'Chico, I've already told you – there's to be no more killing.' Professor Langerman looked up at the little man, and shuddered. 'Even if it *is* a mercy killing.'

Chico's hand moved towards a button marked 'Release'. 'Shall I let him out then, sir?'

'Let's not be hasty, Chico. He might be contagious. Seems happy enough in the tube, best leave him be.'

Realising he had an audience, the little man rapped on the side of the tube and waved a hairy hand.

'Uh, sir?' Chico said. 'I believe the little monkey man's trying to communicate.'

The three of them looked up.

The little man mouthed something at them.

'What was that?' asked the professor, straining his ear towards the glass tube.

The little man mouthed the words again.

'No,' the professor said loudly, 'still can't hear you.'

The little man mimed the universal hand gesture for a cup of tea being delicately sipped.

'That's a bit rude,' Chico said, skilfully misinterpreting it.

'Right!' the professor snarled. 'Flood those tubes, Chico. Drown the little sod!'

'He's trying to tell you he wants a cup of tea,' Anthony said.

'It drinks tea?'

'Most monkeys do, sir,' Chico said, matter-of-factly. 'Saw it on the telly.'

The professor slowly mouthed a response at the man in the tube. 'PG tips all right?'

The little man shook his head, and mouthed something back.

Professor Langerman turned to Anthony for his interpretation.

'He said he's more of an Earl Grey man,' Anthony said. 'But thanks all the same.'

'I'll go put the kettle on shall I, sir?'

'Hold up, Chico,' the professor said. 'I think he's trying to say something else.'

The little man jiggled his nether regions at them, and pointed enthusiastically.

'What's he miming now?' the professor hissed.

'I don't know, sir,' Chico said, covering his eyes with both hands, 'but I wish he'd stop it.'

'I think he's trying to tell you he'd rather like some underpants,' Anthony deduced.

'Ah, yes,' the professor said. 'Get that man some pants, Chico. Make it top priority.'

'Yes, sir.' Chico gratefully made for the door.

'And Chico?' The professor raised a commanding finger. 'Your pants, not mine.'

'Oh, but sir –'

'No buts. A man of my intellectual stature does not exchange clothing with monkeys.'

Chico grumbled his way out the exit.

'And don't forget that tea,' Professor Langerman hollered after him. 'How about it, Anthony? Fancy a cup?'

'Perhaps later,' Anthony said. 'First, I'd like this planet removed from my head.'

'Ah,' the professor said. 'Still a bit concerned about that, are you?'

'A little, yes.'

'I was kind of hoping you might've warmed to the idea by now.'

Anthony looked around at the mass of bizarre contraptions clanking and whirring away in the room. 'Surely there's got to be something here for removing stray planets from people's heads?'

'Unless my clones have been insightfully productive behind my back, nothing I'm aware of.'

Anthony approached a machine with a circular hole in its centre, framed by the words 'Insert head here'. 'How about this one?' He poked his head inside, and looked around. A blue light inside the hole automatically flicked on, and the machine started to hum.

'I don't think that invention will quite serve your purpose, but by all means give it a try.'

The humming grew louder and more frequent. 'Well, it seems to be doing something,' Anthony said. 'What's it for?'

'It's a trap. Specifically designed to entice imbeciles to stick their head in its hole.'

The machine clicked, and the hole constricted.

'I'm stuck!' Anthony exclaimed, struggling to withdraw.

'Yes,' the professor said. 'Clever, isn't it?'

'A little help?'

'Just flip the release switch on the underside.'

Anthony's hand fumbled around. There was a 'Click!' and a 'Pop!' as his head came free.

'One of my earlier experiments,' the professor explained. 'Can't quite remember why I came up with it, but I do recall it seemed terribly important at the time.'

'All right, how about this thing?' Anthony approached a large bubbling apparatus, with multicoloured wires and tubes jutting out at all angles. 'What's this do?'

'Ah, now that's one of my third likenesses creations. Haven't quite worked out its main purpose yet,' the professor admitted. 'At the moment, we mostly just use it for distilling Cider.'

Anthony inspected a small headband covered in flashing lights. 'And this?'

'Mosquito repellent. The complex light sequence gives them seizures.'

A grumble of disappointment escaped from Anthony's lips. Just about every invention mankind had never needed and most certainly never wanted seemed to be present and accounted for. 'Is everything in this room equally useless?'

'My creations are not useless!' the professor snapped. 'They just happen to have very selective functions.'

'How about this?' Anthony picked up a hacksaw and waved it around. 'Could this be used to get a planet out of my head?'

'Anthony, you don't seem to understand. Extracting the planet isn't the problem. The problem is if we removed it we'd have to remove your brain as well.'

'Can't you just cut around it?' Anthony made hacking motions with the saw.

'It's encased within an entire planet's crust.'

'So drill it out then.'

'And risk damaging the planet?' The professor shook his head. 'Whether you like it or not, you and that planet are inseparable.'

Anthony slumped to the ground in a miserable heap. 'Until it explodes out of me, you mean?'

'Best just accept it and move on with your life. There really is no alternative.'

Krrrrk! '–ofessor Langerman?'

The professor jumped, startled.

Krrrrk! '–essor Langerman?' The voice repeated.

The professor fished around in his pocket, pulled out a banana-shaped communication device and flipped it open. 'Yes, Chico? What is it?'

Kkkkrk! '– got trouble, sir.'

The professor craned his ear to the communicator. In the distance, he could hear gunfire. 'What sort of trouble?'

Kkrrrrk! '– out of Earl Grey.' Another gunshot. An explosion.

'Well dammit man, that's no reason to go shooting up the place.'

Krrrk! '– not me, sir.' *Fadoom! Blam!* '– Administration.'

The professor's eyes widened. 'They've found us? Already?'

Krrrk! '–othing I can't hand–' *Fudda! Fudda!* '–esus! God! No!'

– *Krrrssssssssssssssssssssssshh!* –

'Chico?' The professor shook the communicator.

– *Kkrrrrrrrsssshhhhhhhhh!* –

'What's wrong?'

– *Kkrrrrrrrrrrrrrrrrrrrrrrrrrrrrrssh!* –

'Answer me, man!'

Krrrrk! '–orry about that, sir.' Chico's voice broke through the static. 'Milk's off. Smells a bit.'

'Chico!' the professor yelled. 'Get back here now!'

Krrk! '–ith you in a moment. Just straining the bags.'

'This instant, Chico!'

Krrrk! '– you insist, sir.' Krrrsh! '–ing to have a very stewed cup of tea if you want my opi–' *Krrrrk!*

The communicator cut out. The professor thrust it back into his pocket, and clutched Anthony under his arms. 'Come on, Anthony. Up you get.'

Anthony twisted out of his grasp, and slumped back down.

'Didn't you hear? The Administration are attacking. We've got to get out of here!'

'So that I can explode at a later date? Thanks, I'll pass.'

'Anthony, they're going to kill you.'

'I'm dead anyway.' Anthony shrugged. 'What's it matter?'

'If you die now, that planet in your head dies with you, along with humanities last hope.'

Anthony folded his arms defiantly. 'Good,' he said. 'Bollocks to the lot of them.'

Chico stumbled in through the door with a fully laden tea tray. 'Okay, everyone. Tea's up.'

'Chico!' the professor snapped. 'I told you to forget about the –' His eyes widened. The clone was drenched from head to foot in blood. 'Good god, man. You're hit!'

Chico looked down at himself. 'Oh no, don't worry about that – the blood's not *mine*.' He started pouring out the tea. 'Well, technically, I suppose it is. It's Peter's. Got shot whilst he was covering my retreat from the kitchen.'

'So who's holding the enemy back now?' The professor's eyes darted around the room in panic.

'Bob is, sir.' Chico thrust a steaming cup of tea under Anthony's nose. 'There you go, Tony. Wasn't sure how you took yours, so I made it extra milky.'

Anthony batted the cup away.

'Well there's gratitude,' Chico muttered. 'Peter gave his life for that.'

The professor gripped Chico by the shoulders and shook him. 'How many of them are there?'

'Careful, sir,' Chico whined, 'you'll spill the Darjeeling!'

'How many, Chico?'

'Er, well there are three, sir.'

'Just three?' The professor released Chico, and breathed a sigh of relief.

'That's right.' Chico gestured to the tea tray. 'One cup for you, one for Tony, and another for the little monkey fella.'

'Not how many cups of tea!' the professor shrieked. 'How many ruthless killers are marching their way towards us?'

'Oh, right.' Chico grinned inanely. 'Just about all of them, I should think. Hundreds of the buggers, sir.

Swarmed in through the lift shaft. Bob was having a helluva time trying to fend them off with his plank of wood, I can tell you.'

'Plank of wood?'

'That's right, sir. You've gave us specific orders not to kill anyone, remember?'

'You've picked a fine time to obey orders, Chico,' the professor said. 'Shoot to kill, man! Shoot to kill!'

Chico pulled a Mark IV Spleen Splitter from his gun belt and grinned. 'Thought you'd never ask.' He grabbed Anthony by the arm. 'Come on, Tony. No time to slouch around.'

Anthony shook him off. 'Just let me die in peace, will you?'

'Miserable sod. What's up with him?'

'Oh he's just being a bit of a stick in the mud, that's all. Decided it'd be so much better for all humanity if he simply waits here for someone to shoot him.'

'I'll do it if you like,' Chico said, lining up his gun. 'It's no bother.'

'Thanks,' Anthony said, 'but I'd rather not give you the satisfaction.'

'Try to do a guy a favour…'

'Just keep that entrance covered,' the professor commanded.

Chico rattled his Spleen Splitter. 'I'm on it, sir!' He commando rolled towards the door, firing at floor and ceiling as he went.

The professor bent down at Anthony's side. 'Anthony,' he said softly, 'it doesn't have to be like this.'

'Like you said, what choice have I got?'

The professor glanced around cautiously, and whispered: 'There might be a way.'

Anthony slowly peered out from behind his hands. 'You said there wasn't a moment ago.'

'Yes, but only because I didn't want to put the planet at risk. Hardly seems relevant now, since we'll be dead if we stay here much longer.'

'This plan of yours is risky then?'

The professor nodded. 'Very.'

'More risky than having a planet in your skull that's liable to go off at any minute?'

The professor thought about that a moment. 'I shouldn't think so, no.'

'Great, let's hear it.'

'Heads up!' Chico cried. 'We've got company!'

A lone figure charged in through the doorway, and was instantly met with a hail of bullets.

A plank of wood clattered to the ground, shortly followed by Bob.

'Ah,' Chico said, relaxing his grip on the trigger. 'Whoopsadaisy.'

'There goes our last inadequate line of defence,' the professor sighed.

'Not quite, sir.' Chico slammed a fresh magazine into his weapon. 'I'll hold the fort, don't you worry about a thing.'

The professor stretched out his hand to Anthony. 'How about it, Anthony? Ready to save the planet?'

'That depends,' Anthony said. 'You haven't told me what the plan is yet.'

'Now is hardly the time. You'll just have to trust me.'

'Well, I –'

'Put it this way, Anthony. What choice have you got?'

Anthony grudgingly took hold of the professor's hand, and was pulled to his feet.

'Good luck, Chico,' the professor said, saluting the one remaining clone. 'Try not to die or anything.'

'But that takes half the fun out of it, sir.' Chico motioned to the wall. 'Best take the back way out. The lift's already been compromised.'

'Back out the way we came in?' Anthony said. 'You've got to be kidding.'

The professor rapped on the wall, and the secret door concealed within swung open. 'Anthony, I designed that corridor. The traps there are mostly my own creation. I know their workings like the back of my hand. If there's anyone who can safely navigate you through without incident,' he said confidently, 'it's me.'

'Now,' the professor said, stroking his beard thoughtfully. 'Is it red wire before blue wire, or blue before red?'

'This is the *fifth* mine I've trodden on,' Anthony hissed. 'Don't you know the sequence yet?'

'Tell you what…let's try red this time, shall we?'

'Call me unadventurous, but I say we stick with blue,' Anthony said through gritted teeth. 'It seems to have served us pretty well so far.'

'Blue it is then.' The professor cut the wire.

Anthony took a deep breath, stepped off, and completely failed to explode.

'Aha!' the professor cried. 'Success!'

Anthony exhaled, and wiped sweat from his green-tinged forehead. 'Perhaps we should wait here for one of the other professors? Maybe they'd have more –'

Four loud explosions sounded from behind them. A wisp of singed lab-coat drifted by.

'All right, forget it,' Anthony said. 'Let's just keep moving.'

The duo managed to negotiate their way through the rest of the traps with only a minimum of life threatening incidents, and emerged at the door to the garage.

'You see?' The professor said. 'Told you I'd get us through safe and –'

Derek's ugly form lurched out in front of him.

'– soiled,' the professor finished.

'All right geezers?' Derek said. 'Hope you weren't planning on escaping in any of those other cars.' He gestured to the piles of twisted scrap strewn around the garage floor. ''Fraid I had to cannibalise a few odds 'n sods to keep the old ticker ticking over.' Light glinted off his shiny new exterior, which was, in many ways, almost as repulsive as the old one. 'I feel like a new man!'

'Well you look like several,' the professor said, 'and a whole lot more besides.' He gave Anthony a sidelong glance, and hissed: 'What the hell is it?'

'That,' Anthony said glumly, 'is a Derek.'

'You'd better believe it, baby!' Derek's back door squelched open. 'So, where are we all heading? I know this great little curry house, just off Rogue Dog Avenue –'

The professor smiled rather too widely. 'Am I correct in assuming we're to be travelling inside this remarkably smelly gentleman?'

'It's okay, you soon get used to it.' Anthony climbed inside and looked around. His green face suddenly got greener. 'Actually,' he said weakly, 'that was a lie.'

The professor reluctantly followed after him, and the door squelched shut.

'Okay professor,' Anthony said, strapping himself in. 'Care to enlighten us? What's the plan?'

'Very well.' The professor thrust his arms out dramatically and declared: 'We are going…to *Mars!*'

A peel of lightning flashed across the sky. Since the garage door was still closed, no one paid it much attention.

'Why?' Anthony asked. 'What's so special about Mars?'

'Don't tell me you haven't heard about the race of super intelligent aliens who inhabit the planet? Their brains are immense, their thought process legendary. They're bound to have a solution to your problem.'

'Yes, I suppose they might,' Anthony said, 'had you not just made them up.'

'I swear to you Anthony, they exist.'

'Yeah, so you say,' Derek chuckled. 'Reckon you're more interested in the Martian brothels and nightlife, eh? You sly old dog.'

'There are no brothels!' the professor snapped. 'There is no nightlife.'

Derek sucked in his breath. 'Lucky I checked the small print there, Tone. Best steer clear of that one.' His engine rumbled into action. 'Stick with me, lad. I'll show you sights that'll make your hair curl.'

'If you have any interest in self preservation,' the professor said, as Derek's noxious fumes began to envelop them, 'you'll follow me to Mars.'

The vein in Anthony's forehead started to pulse again. 'Professor, the planet doesn't even have an atmosphere. All we'll get if we go to Mars is the chance to watch each other suffocate, which, given the circumstances, might not be such a bad thing.'

'I'll tell you one thing for sure,' the professor said, burying his head in his lab coat, 'we're certainly going to suffocate if we stay here any longer.'

Anthony folded his arms defiantly, and turned his back on the professor. The professor burrowed further into his coat.

A brooding silence descended – one which Derek's grumbling stomach immediately shattered.

'That's that sorted,' he grinned. 'Curry house it is, then.'

Ten

'Halt! Who goes there?'

Grison stepped from the lift, which led into the heart of the resistance's headquarters. A young, jumpy woman with cartridge belts full of spoons crisscrossing her pistolero outfit was stood blocking the corridor.

'Evening, Susan.' Grison glanced at the large wooden spoon she held at the ready. 'Battle going well, is it?'

Susan lowered her spoon and holstered it. 'I wouldn't know, sir. Stokes has got me covering this exit.'

'Just you and your spoons between the enemy and salvation, eh?'

'That's right, sir.'

'Remind me to commend old Stokesy on his masterful tactics.'

'He's just a few corridors down, if you want to have a word.'

'Unless his linguistics skills have improved since we last spoke,' Grison mumbled, 'one word's all I'm likely to get.' He marched off down the corridor, and squeezed his way through the large group of unlikely-looking recruits he found obstructing his path.

Crouched down before a door marked 'cloning' was a huge slab of meat masquerading as a man. He didn't look like he'd been born, he looked like he'd been constructed in a lab, possibly by a group of first year philosophy students attempting to find an answer to the age old question of 'who ate all the pies?' A tattoo on his forehead bore the name 'Scrote', a misspelling for which the tattoo artist would no doubt have suffered dearly, had anyone actually been brave enough to point it out.

'Okay lads,' the man-mountain rumbled in what he clearly thought of as a whisper, 'on the count of three…'

'Sounds a bit ambitious, Stokes,' Grison said, striding towards him. 'Best make it count of one, eh?'

'Grison.' The word rumbled out like an earthquake.

'Okay people, stand at ease.' Grison spread his hands out at the crowd of recruits. 'I'll take it from here.'

'Like hell you will.'

'Four words?' Grison whistled. 'Impressive.'

Stokes drew himself up to his full height. It took a considerable amount of time for him to complete the process. 'This is my show.'

'Well, I'm sure you've got everything under control. What's the situation?'

'Found the resistance base. Subtracted two. Got a third trapped in here.' He motioned to the door the recruits were crouching beside.

Grison inspected the sign upon it. 'Just the one of them, is there?'

'That's right.'

'In a room full of cloning equipment?' He waited a moment for his words to sink in. Judging by the vacant expression on Stokes' face, he could be waiting for some time.

Stokes waved a dismissive hand. 'Enough of these mind games!'

'You're right, you're right. War tactics never were my strong point. So, what's your plan, Stokesey?'

Stokes' rock-jaw split open to reveal some impressively large teeth. 'We're going to rush him.'

Grison looked back at the rabble of recruits wedged in the corridor. 'All of you?'

'That's right. All at once.'

'Through that door there?' Grison nodded at the single wooden door in front of them.

'Yes. I'll be leading the charge, of course.'

Grison looked up at Stokes, and then further up. 'If you don't mind me asking, Stokes, how tall are you exactly?'

'Seven foot four,' Stokes said proudly.

'And I'll bet about half as wide, eh?'

'What's your point?'

'No point.' Grison smiled. 'Mind if I watch?'

Stokes held out a hand that could've comfortably encompassed Grison's entire head. 'No civilians.'

'Stokes, you know full well I'm not a civilian.'

'You don't have a weapon,' Stokes said. 'Therefore, you're a civilian.'

'What about him?' Grison gestured to one of the recruits, who was brandishing a butterfly net. 'He doesn't have a weapon.'

'Yes he has. He's got his net.'

'And I bet he's a dab hand with it, too.' Grison patted the scrawny net-wielding recruit on the shoulder, loosening several ligaments. 'Chalked up many casualties, slugger?'

'Well, there was this Australian Longwing –'

'Shut up, Craig.'

'Yes, sir.'

'You really want to make yourself useful, Grison? Go back up that corridor and relieve Susan of her guard duty. I'd rather have her and her spoons at my side than you hanging around waiting to steal the subtraction bonus out from under us.'

'That's hurtful, Stokes. That's really hurtful.' Grison walked back up the corridor, grinning to himself.

'Halt! Who goes th–'

'Save it for the enemy, Susan. You're needed back there.'

'But who's going to guard the exit, sir?'

'I'll keep the exit covered whilst you provide much needed spoon support.'

'But you're unarmed,' Susan said.

'Just the way I like it.'

Susan pressed a spoon into the palm of Grison's hand, and closed his fingers around it. 'That'll give the enemy something to think about.'

Grison opened his hand, and stared at his puzzled reflection in the spoon. 'It certainly will.'

'Best of luck, sir.'

'You too, Susan. Oh, and before you go.' Grison waggled the spoon, his mouth cracking into a wide smile. 'Any chance I could have another one?'

Susan tossed a spoon over her shoulder and raced off down the corridor.

'Take your time, Susan,' Grison called after her. 'He's still got to count to three yet.'

'One!'

There was a pause.

'Two,' Grison prompted.

'Sod off, Grison,' an angry voice hollered back. 'I'm doing this. *Two!'*

Another long pause. The sound of whispered conferring.

'Seven! CHEEEAAAAAAAAARRRRRGE!'

The noise of wood splintering, followed by:

'Ah, crap! Help me someone – I'm stuck!'

'Oh dear. Er. Perhaps if we all push at once, sir?'

'Yes, that's a good – Argh! Jesus Christ, Craig! Get that butterfly net out my arse!'

'Sorry, sir. Thought I saw a butterfly.'

'Oh my god. Oh Jesus!'

'Do you see the enemy, sir?'

'Of course I see the goddamn enemy! There's…there's – what's more than three?'

'Four, sir.'

'Four of them! At least. And some more!'

'Can't get a clear shot, sir. Mind if I shoot through you?'

'Yes, I mind if you shoot through me. All together now. *Puuuuushhh!*'

A bone jarring *'Pop!'*

'I'm free! Sweet merciful lord, I'm free!'

'Good god, they're everywhere!'

BUDDA BUDDA BUDDA!

'That's considerably more than four, sir!'

BDOOM! BRAKKA! BRAKKA! BDOOM!

'There's too many of –'

FOOM! BLAM! BDAM!

'Arrrrgh!'

'Aiiiiiiiiiiiieeee!'

As gunfire ripped through the corridors, and the cries of the dying filled the air, Grison sat cross-legged on the ground with spoons in hand, rapping out a tinny metallic rendition of 'Ride Of The Valkyries'.

Derek pressed a button on the speaker system outside Rancid Larry's Float Through Curry House, and placed his order.

'One Hot Bastard, two Flaming Arses, and a triplet of Napalm Death's please, Larry. Make it lively.'

'Six lively curries, sir,' a distorted voice answered.

Anthony looked around at his surroundings; a takeaway parlour floating high up in the clouds, surrounded by a dozen or so more fast food joints. Occasionally, one would break off from the pack and swoop down towards densely populated areas, responding to a distress call. 'What are we doing here?'

'Refuelling. Got to keep the stomach juices churning over if you want me to take you all the way to Mars.

Though I still think Dirty Michael's Slagorama would've been far more your scene.'

'Derek, for the last time, we're not going to Mars.'

'Oh, come now Anthony –' the professor began.

'Aliens don't exist. They are but a figment of your overactive imagination. The idea that these super intelligent beings could've been up there all this time, without us noticing. It's preposterous.'

'Well, that's rich,' the professor countered, 'coming from a man with a planet in his head.'

'A planet which you put there, thank you so very much indeed.'

'The way I see it Anthony, you have two choices. You either choose to believe in these imaginary aliens of mine, or you choose to sit around and wait for your head to explode. Which is it to be?'

'All right then,' Anthony said. 'For arguments sake, let's say these aliens exist. How are we going to get to them? Eager as Derek may be, he's not equipped for space travel.'

'I could hold my breath for a bit,' Derek said keenly.

'Look, it really isn't a problem, Anthony. The spaceport isn't that far from here. They have expeditions launching all the time – rich, heroic foolhardy idiots desperate to discover and colonise brave new worlds. Seems rather fitting, don't you think, that we hijack one of those?'

'Hijack an entire space cruiser. Simple as that, eh?'

'I did tell you it was going to be risky,' the professor chided. 'You really ought to pay attention more often.'

A window in the side of the curry house slid open. 'Your order, sir.'

Derek pulled up alongside the window and took a dripping brown paper bag from the attendant. 'Pay the man, will you Tone? 'Fraid I've got my hands full.'

Anthony turned to the professor. 'Pay the man will you professor? I'm afraid I'm wearing your trousers.'

'Isn't there any money in them?'

Anthony plunged his hands deep into the pockets and rapidly withdrew them. 'No, just a couple of hankies.'

'That's all I've got in these ones as well.'

'Neither of you have any money on you?' Derek rolled his eyes. His onboard fare meter had been ticking away optimistically ever since he'd met Anthony, and was already beginning to forge new ground in the realm of experimental mathematics.

'We did leave in something of a hurry.'

'Derek,' Anthony said, 'ask the nice man if he accepts hankies.'

Derek sighed in resignation. 'Someone open my glove compartment. There's some loose change inside.'

Anthony glanced warily at the glove compartment. 'I'll, uh, leave that to you, professor. I've seen what else is inside.'

The professor strained forward and climbed into the front seat.

'With you in a tick,' said Anthony, as he leaned out the window and smiled at the frowning attendant. 'Just give us five more seconds.'

There came a scream from inside the car as the professor opened the glove compartment.

'Perhaps ten,' Anthony added.

The attendant pointed a trembling curry-stained finger at Anthony's face. 'T-t-t-t-t–' he stuttered.

'What?' Anthony said. 'What is it?' The attendant was staring at his head in a most peculiar fashion.

'T-t-t-t-the –'

'Ah, it's the branch sticking out of my ear, isn't it? It upsets you.'

'The planet!' the attendant cried, his body trembling in excitement. 'I've found it! It's mine! All mine!' He ran off, babbling to himself.

Anthony ducked his head back into the car, and wound the window up. 'Oh dear,' he said. 'This can't be good.'

A small crowd started to gather on the platform, drawn by the attendant's cries.

'He knew about the planet,' the professor said. 'How is that possible?'

'Oh, everyone knows about that.' Derek prised the lid off a curry, and sniffed its contents. 'They've been broadcasting it on the radio all day. Seem to have Tony pegged as the next Jesus. Don't see it myself, though; his beard's crap, for starters.'

The professor peered through the window at the crowd outside. It had already doubled in size. 'And you didn't think to tell us that the whole world knows?' he hissed.

Derek tipped the curry into the gaping hole in his dashboard. 'I thought you knew.'

The gathering mob surged forward. Several leering faces pressed up against Derek's windows. Their eyes scanned the interior within.

'You'd think the sight of Derek's innards would be enough to deter them,' Anthony said, crouching back in his seat.

'These are curry eaters, my friend,' Derek said, 'they're a very hardy breed.'

The car started to rock from side to side as the mob outside sought for a way in.

'If they think I'm their messiah, they've a funny way of paying their respects.'

'Well, there is a rather sizeable bounty on your head.' Derek's massive grey tongue snaked out around the curry container and dragged it into the vast depths of his mouth.

'Ten million creds to the person who locates you, and another fifty to the lucky individual who brings you in.'

'Just a thought,' the professor said, 'but perhaps we should be making tracks?'

'We won't be going anywhere until I've got a bit more fuel inside me.' Derek prised open another curry. 'Who's for a Flaming Arse?'

A brick bounced off Derek's rear window.

'Derek!' Anthony snapped. 'You *are* a flaming arse! Get us out of here, dammit!'

'Oh, please yourself.' Derek shook off the grasping hands of the mob. 'I guess I'll eat the rest on my way down.' He launched himself unsteadily from the landing platform.

'Down?' Anthony said. 'What do you mean by down?'

Derek's engine made a sad 'Phutt! Phutt!' noise and cut out.

'That,' he said between the huge mouthfuls of curry the professor was frantically shovelling into his dashboard, 'is what I meant by *down.*'

The spoon solo ended. The corridors fell deathly silent.

Grison stepped over the bodies of several people that he knew and hated, and edged into the cloning room.

The ground was thick with corpses, more than half of them the same grey skinned man, the rest the Administration. Though the clones were mostly unarmed they appeared to have defeated their attackers through sheer weight of numbers.

Grison found Stokes' corpse slumped over a contraption with a circular hole in its centre, head firmly wedged in the front, and a butterfly net jutting out his rear. Perhaps more surprisingly, it had a butterfly in it.

'Hello?' Grison called. 'Everyone dead?'

Nobody answered.

'Excellent!' He turned to leave.

From somewhere behind him there came a creak and a click.

'Reach for the sky, fat boy!'

Grison sighed. 'There's always one, isn't there?' He turned back. A gun was pointing up at him from under the lid of the cloning machine.

'Yes?' Grison said. 'Can I help you?'

'Drop your weapon and get down on the ground!' a voice commanded.

'What weapon? I'm unarmed.'

'No you're not,' the voice said accusingly. 'You've got spoons.'

'Hardly an offensive weapon now, is it?'

'Try telling that to her.' The gun rattled in the direction of a female corpse lying among the bodies, with a jagged metal spoon jutting out of her eye socket.

'I stand corrected,' said Grison. He threw the spoons aside. 'Happy now?'

'All right,' the voice said. 'Now, very slowly…hand me one of those guns.'

'What?'

The lid opened a fraction more. A grey arm gestured out of it. 'Just there, by your feet. That Reaper's Kiss ought to do. Come on, chop chop!'

'Ah.' Grison smiled. 'Out of bullets, are we?'

The voice cursed. 'Nooooo,' it brayed. 'Not at all. I just really want to take a look at that gun. Haven't seen one like it before. Hoo-ee, sure is a beauty. Could you pass it here, please?'

'Okay, whatever you say.' Grison picked up a bright red semi-automatic pistol with a picture of the grim reaper blowing a kiss etched crudely into its side, removed the magazine, and threw it to the clone. 'There you go.'

The clone stared at it a moment, cursed, and tossed it aside. 'All right smart arse, so I'm out of bullets. What's it to you?'

'Just tell me where Cresswell is.'

The clone sprang out from beneath the lid, and landed in a close approximation to a kung-fu pose. 'You'll have to kill me first!'

'Love to, given the time. Unfortunately I'm in a hurry. Where's Cresswell?'

'Right! Unarmed combat it is. Have at you, you dog!' The clone advanced, fists flailing.

'Forget it,' said Grison, turning to leave. 'I'll find him myself.'

The clone snatched up a spoon and tossed it rapidly from hand to hand. 'Haha! Now who's got the upper hand? Beg for mercy, fat boy!' He flung the spoon. It bounced off Grison's retreating back.

'Oi! Come back here!' The clone dashed after him. 'Don't you know who I am?'

'Yes,' said Grison, 'a nutter. Go away.' He strode off down the corridor.

'I'm the fearless resistance fighter, Chico Mantango!' the clone yelled after him. 'I'm not to be trifled with.'

'You're also a clone, and not worth a penny to me dead.'

'What? What's that you're saying?' The clone finally caught up to him. 'I demand to be worth a penny!'

'Well you're not, the bounty on you went years ago. That's the trouble with clones – technically, I'd be subtracting the same man twice.'

Chico grabbed Grison by the shoulder and attempted to spin him round. It took quite the effort. 'You've killed me before?'

'Only once, back when you were worth something.'

'Right! I'll have you for that, you slag!' The clone raised his fists and circled round Grison, ducking and weaving.

Grison shook his head, and walked off in the other direction.

'I bet you killed the original professor too, didn't you?' Chico hollered. 'Bastard!'

'No,' Grison said, 'that was you.' He strolled past the kitchen door. Inside, a small hairy chimp was sat drinking tea. He immediately dismissed the image from his mind.

'What's that supposed to mean?' Chico snarled. 'How dare you accuse me –'

Grison stopped walking and turned. 'You're a traitor, Chico. Or would you prefer it if I called you "Kevin"?'

'I most certainly would not!' Chico said. 'Hey, hold on. How do you know my true name?'

'Don't you think it odd, Kev,' Grison said, advancing on him, 'that you were the only one to survive the original massacre?'

'Not at all,' Chico said. 'That was thanks to my own resourcefulness and guile.'

'Was it now? Do tell.'

'It's far too long and complex a story –'

'Summarise it.'

'First,' Chico said, 'I brutally impaled one of the enemy with a water cone.'

'A water cone? You don't say.'

'Then I parachuted out the window using a collection of man-sized handkerchiefs.'

'From two hundred and fifty six floors up?' Grison's stare hardened.

'That's right. And there was this gunfight I had with some ninjas…' Chico's voice gradually trailed off. 'Oh no,' he said quietly. 'I betrayed him, didn't I?'

Grison nodded. 'Why do you think you change your name so often "Chico"? You're desperate to escape the past; avoid becoming the man you once were. But betrayal's built into your genes.'

'Lies!' Chico clamped his hands over his ears. 'All lies!'

'How do you think the Administration found this place so quickly? We received a signal from this very location.'

'Well I didn't send it. I'd have remembered.'

'In the same way that you remembered killing the professor the first time round?'

'I didn't kill him!' Chico screamed. 'I just –'

'Told us where he was and what he was up to, claimed the reward, and let us do the dirty work?'

'I've changed,' Chico sobbed. 'I'm a different person now.'

'Of course you are,' Grison said soothingly. 'Curious though, isn't it? That, once again, you seem to be the only survivor.'

'Ha!' Chico spat. 'That's where you're wrong. The professor and Tony are still very much alive. They escaped through the secret passage in the cloning room. Stick that in your pipe and smoke it!'

Grison smiled tightly. 'Cloning room back that way, is it?'

The victorious grin seeped off Chico's face. 'Oh bloody hell,' he whispered, 'I've done it again, haven't I?'

'I shouldn't feel so bad about it,' Grison said as he strolled back the way he'd come. 'First time around, you betrayed us as well.'

'I did?'

'Yes, by using stolen cloning equipment to resurrect the professor. Still, you got what was coming to you in the end.'

Chico nervously licked his grey lips. 'I did?'

'Whilst you were wracked with guilt over your past actions, some noble crusader convinced you to take your own life. Bullet to the brain, I believe.' Grison tossed Chico the magazine he'd taken from the Reaper's Kiss. 'Well, lovely chatting with you. Must do it again sometime.' He strolled back past the door to the kitchen.

'Wotcher, Mr Grison!' a voice called from within.

Grison's feet took root as the image of a monkey sat drinking tea settled uncomfortably at the front of his mind. 'No…' he whispered. 'Please, anything but that.' He poked his head around the kitchen door. A small semi-naked man looked up at him, mouth full of scone.

'No!' Grison screamed, his face reddening with rage. 'You're dead! I subtracted you! You're supposed to be dead, dammit!'

'Yeah.' Grott scratched his head. 'I thought that too. Any chance I could have another go at that jumping thing? I don't think I got it quite right the first time.'

'That,' Grison rumbled, 'is an excellent idea.' He marched out into the corridor with Grott trailing along behind. Chico was slumped against a wall, struggling to load the magazine into the wrong gun.

'You!' Grison snapped. 'Follow me.'

'Why? Where are we going?'

'To take a nice brisk stroll off a roof top.'

'Thought you said there's no profit in killing clones,' Chico muttered.

'Then thank your lucky stars,' Grison growled. 'I'm feeling in a real charitable mood.'

Anthony clawed his way out through Derek's buckled rear door, with a large paper curry bag wedged on his head. He'd put it there himself moments before the collision, under the mistaken impression that it might help him deal slightly better with the situation.

'Sorry about that, lads,' Derek said, rocking himself upright. 'Blacked out for a moment. Did we hit anything big?'

'Just a building,' the professor said, dragging his bruised and battered body out Derek's front passenger door. 'Nothing at all to concern yourself with.'

Anthony cautiously removed the bag from his head, and peered around at his surroundings. They were in an apartment, pitifully small in nature; there was barely enough room to swing a rat, though more than enough test subjects with which to practise. In the centre of this squat, dank, vermin infested hole sat a solitary piece of furniture; an ugly brown sofa that, by some cruel twist of fate, had somehow survived Derek's onslaught.

'At least the owner's not likely to sue.' Derek gestured to a sad pile of decomposing bones heaped in the corner of the room.

'I wouldn't be so sure about that,' Anthony said. He slid his hand down the back of the sofa, pulled out a device with the words 'Holographic Generator' written upon it, and pressed a button.

The room flickered and faded, replaced by something a lot more pleasing to the eye. The rats merged together to form a delicate rippling carpet. The sewage-brown colouring seeped out of the sofa, replaced by a silky sky blue. The skeletal remains of the previous tenant twisted and re-shaped to become a slightly macabre exhibit of Art Nouveau.

'That brightens up the place a bit.' The professor patted Anthony's shoulder and sat on the sofa. He wasn't surprised to discover it was far less comfortable than it looked. 'Handy little device that. How did you know it was there?'

Anthony slumped down onto the sofa beside the professor. 'Because this is my apartment.'

'Is it?' The professor forced a smile. 'Nice place. Love what you've done with it.'

'Break out the beers then, Tone,' Derek said, licking his lips. 'Don't be stingy now.'

'I don't have any beers,' Anthony said. 'I don't even have a fridge.'

'There's a fine display of hospitality, I must say,' Derek grumbled. A small blue flame streaked out his rear exhaust pipe, further devaluing Anthony's property. His stomach rumbled noisily back into action. 'Ah, there she blows! All fuelled up and ready to go. Next stop, the off-licence.'

'We won't be going anywhere, I'm afraid,' the professor said. 'The word is out. We'd be lucky to make it five yards before Anthony's recognised and turned in.'

'Fifty million creds is an awful lot of money,' Derek said.

'So that's it then?' Anthony said miserably. 'We just sit around here and wait until my head explodes?'

'Unless anyone has an idea to the contrary, I don't see what else we can do.'

They sat for a moment in silence.

'I've got an idea,' Derek said.

The silence resumed.

'I said I've –'

'We heard you, Derek.'

More silence.

'Don't you want to hear my idea then?'

Anthony sighed. 'Go on then.'

'Like I said,' Derek grinned, 'fifty million creds is an *awful* lot of money.' He let his words hang in the air, along with his smells.

'That's it, is it?' the professor said. 'That's your grand idea? Turn Anthony in and claim the reward?'

'It'd go a long way towards paying his fare. Probably even guarantee him lifts for life.'

'Another fine reason not to do it.' The professor tutted. 'It's disgraceful, it's sickening, it's…it's –'

'Ingenious!' Anthony cried, leaping to his feet.

'Exactly what I was… *What?'* The professor screeched.

'Don't you see?' Anthony said, striding purposefully towards Derek. 'This could be my only way out of the situation. The one way to turn it around to our advantage.'

'Uh, steady on, Tone.' Derek smiled sheepishly. 'I was just having a laugh.'

'You have to turn me in and claim that reward, before anyone else can.'

'They'll put you in a lab, Anthony,' the professor said, gesticulating wildly. 'They'll slice you up and run tests on you. In their eagerness to see what makes the planet tick, they'll most likely destroy mankind's only salvation. It's how these people work.'

'You're wrong,' Anthony said. 'Knowing our current government, they'd be far more likely to use me as a high profile tool to assist in Prime Minister Hardcastle's re-election campaign.'

The professor stormed up and down the carpet, ignoring its squeaks of protest. 'You'd still be a prisoner, Anthony. A pawn in their every devious scheme.'

'Yes, well, whilst they're using me, I'll be using them.' Anthony wrenched Derek's door open, grim determination glistening in his eyes. 'If the public want a new messiah so badly, then by god I'll give them one!'

Eleven

As second comings go, Anthony's would probably be considered, all in all, a bit of a let down.

It was a good turnout, that much could be said in its favour. The skyways were packed thick with pedestrians, and not just on the top. People stood out at all angles – diagonally, sideways, and upside down. Anti-grav boots had been selling like hotcakes.

Several new temporary skyways had been hastily erected, just to cater for the overwhelming demand. Although most of these collapsed the moment anyone set foot on them, this only added to the frivolity of the occasion.

The whole city ground to a halt as everyone turned out to see their fabled new messiah in all his glory. What they certainly hadn't expected was for him to arrive in a quivering mound of misshapen flesh, powered almost entirely by its own wind. Not quite the golden chariot the papers had led them to believe.

Still, they were here now, and they were going to make the most of it. They waved their 'I love Colin' banners aloft, and wore their 'Colin for messiah' T-shirts with pride. Some enterprising young ladies even threw their underwear down at the procession passing below, with phone numbers and local charge rates securely attached.

The procession slowed. The car stopped. The front passenger door slowly began to open.

A roar went up from the crowd as Anthony stepped out. 'Colin!' they cheered. 'Colin! Colin! Colin!'

Anthony held up his hand for silence.

After several minutes had passed, it became apparent that he wasn't going to get it.

'Colin! Colin! Colin! Colin!'

'Uh, I think there's been a mistake,' Anthony said, as loudly as he could. 'I'm not –'

'Coliiiiiiiiiiin!' A well-toned and well-groomed man who was all smarm and smiles strode down the red carpet towards him, with arms spread wide. 'Col! Coller, old son!' He gripped Anthony's hand and pumped it vigorously, skilfully turning him towards the entourage of news cameras and press photographers that lined the route.

The cameras flashed. The man's mouth widened to display an immaculate set of pearly whites that would've had ivory poachers the world over reaching instantly for their guns.

'Such a pleasure to meet you, Colin,' said the Prime Minister. 'If there's anything I can do for you Colin, anything at all, don't hesitate to ask.' He turned to the cameras again, pointed at Anthony and mouthed 'It's Colin! *Colin!'*

'Well,' Anthony said, 'you could stop calling me Colin for starters.'

The Prime Minister's perfect smile froze. 'What?'

'My name's Anthony.'

A frown valiantly attempted to work its way through the Prime Minister's false tan. 'Are you sure about that?'

Anthony laughed nervously. 'Pretty sure, yes.'

The cameras zoomed in for a close-up. The Prime Minister clicked his fingers, and an aide came rushing to his side. He took a clipboard from him, and flicked through the notes clipped to it.

The smile returned with renewed vigour.

'Ha! Says you're a bit of a joker on your profile, Col, but I never expected to encounter such raging mirth!' He slapped Anthony roughly on the back.

'The name's Anthony,' Anthony said slowly. 'Anthony Cresswell. It always has been Anthony, it always will be Anthony.'

'You were identified from the photos as Colin Frogfertler,' the Prime Minister growled, starting to lose his patience. 'Therefore, you must be Colin Frogfertler.'

'What photos?'

'The ones taken by the surgeon who discovered you.' The Prime Minister thrust the clipboard under Anthony's nose, and showed him the photos pinned to it. One of them involved Anthony and a sheep, neither of which were clothed.

'Good god!' Anthony exclaimed. He turned his head sideways and looked again. 'Is that even possible?'

'Fakes, obviously. Just your bog standard blackmail material. Dr Skrunk does it to all his favourite clients.' The Prime Minister made a fist. 'Damn him…'

'These haven't…leaked out have they?' Anthony said, staring wide-eyed at a particularly creative forgery involving himself and several nuns.

'But of course they have, our publicity department made sure of that. The public love a good scandal. They think you're the bee's knees, Colin.'

'Colin! Colin! Colin! Colin!'

Anthony looked up at his crowd of adoring fans. One of them was waving a blow-up sheep. Several were dressed like nuns.

'I wouldn't mind so much,' he sighed, 'if they at least got my name right.'

The Prime Minister leant in close to Anthony's ear. 'The entire world is watching, Colin,' he hissed, motioning to the cameras. 'So I'd appreciate it if you stop making me look like an arse.'

'I'm sorry, but you've made a mistake,' Anthony protested. 'My name really isn't Colin. You see, I had my appearance genetically al–'

The Prime Minister's fist lashed out and knocked Anthony to the ground. 'No, you're the one who's made a mistake!' he yelled. 'You've made a powerful enemy today, Colin. A powerful enemy!' He stormed off, followed by his grovelling aide.

The press cameras clicked away furiously.

A murmur rippled out through the crowd.

'What happened there?'

'Said his name wasn't Colin.'

'You *what?*'

'You're joking aren't you?'

'This T-shirt cost me a fortune!'

'Took me hours making this banner…'

'What about my tattoo? "Colin for Messiah", it says.'

'Ungrateful bastard!'

'Who does he think he is?'

'Not a Colin, that's for sure.'

Another pair of knickers was hurled at Anthony's head; this time, with a rock in it.

More rocks were quick to follow, and far less knickers.

'You're off to a great start, Anthony,' the professor hollered, as Anthony was whisked away under the cover of a blanket into a waiting security vehicle. 'A *great* start!'

'That went about as well as expected,' Derek said. 'Time for a swift half, I reckon.'

The professor stared out of Derek's rear window at the enraged mob they'd left behind. 'They hated him,' he said miserably. 'They absolutely hated him.'

'Oh, I'm sure the Prime Minister's spin-doctors will put a positive angle on things,' Derek said reassuringly. 'He'll be fine.'

'Even the Prime Minister hated him. He punched him in the face.'

'Well, the world loves a bastard.' Derek grinned. 'Let's get drunk.'

Professor Langerman withdrew his glum face from the window, and slumped in his seat. 'You don't seem to understand, Anthony's entire plan hinged around convincing the public that he's some sort of messiah figure. How's he supposed to achieve that now?'

'Never mind. At least they paid us our finder's fee up front before the fighting broke out. I reckon first we should start at the Plastered Pigeon – knock back a couple of Drambuie's. Next, onto the Arse Over Tit; flaming Sambuca's all round.'

'No,' the professor said firmly. 'We stick to the plan.'

'Nah, like you said – lost cause.' Derek licked his lips, his mind already on other matters. 'Flatulent Monkey, that's where we're going. They serve synthetic Banana Daiquiris there. You'll love it.'

'We'll need every penny to hire us a ship. Passage to Mars does not come cheap.'

'No point in hiring a ship now. Tony'll never get loose, and it'll take more than the two of us to break him free.'

'You're right.' The professor scrambled around in his pocket, and pulled out his communicator. 'We need help.'

'Terrific! Alcohol to the rescue.'

'Fortunately, I know the perfect man for this sort of job.' The professor flipped the communicator open. 'I just hope he's still alive.'

'Now,' Grison said, addressing the two dishevelled men who stood before him on the rooftop. 'You are both going to die.'

Grott tilted his head at a peculiar angle. 'You said that the last time.'

'Yes, but I really, really mean it this time. That's why I chose a much higher building.'

'It's just I'm not jumping if you're not sure. I might make a mess of it again.'

'Trust me,' Grison said, 'the only mess you're likely to make will be to the pavement.'

'Well, you're the expert I suppose.' Grott started to struggle out of his underwear.

'What the hell do you think you're doing?' Grison said, hurriedly averting his eyes.

'Don't you want me to get naked again?'

'Sweet lord, no.'

'If he's getting naked,' Chico said, edging away from Grott, 'I'm jumping now.'

'Seriously, it's not that sort of occasion.'

'No nudity?' The grating nasal whine that passed for Grott's voice radiated utter disappointment.

'Absolutely not. Under any circumstances.'

'I suppose you'll be telling us there isn't any cake next,' Grott huffed.

'There *isn't* any cake.'

'Aw, what! You said there'd be cake.'

'I only said that to stop you whining,' Grison sighed.

'Didn't bloody work, did it?' Chico muttered.

'A nice slice of Battenberg, that's what you said. I'm not jumping if there isn't any Battenberg.'

'I'm sure there'll be more than enough Battenberg in Heaven,' Grison said, massaging his eyelids.

'It was a lot better last time,' Grott whispered conspiratorially to Chico. 'There were scones and tea and nudity and everything.'

'Let's just get on with it, shall we?' Grison said through gritted teeth.

'And shoes,' Grott continued. 'Real shoes, with real laces. None of that fancy Velcro garbage.'

Both Chico and Grison exchanged glances. They slowly edged behind Grott.

'And the company,' Grott sighed. 'A finer group of lads and lasses you'll never be likely to meet. Bit depressed most of them, but still, great conversationalists. What was it old Mr Tessler used to say?'

As one, Chico and Grison shoved Grott roughly in his back.

'Aaaaaaaah!' said Grott, as he tumbled from the rooftop.

'Your turn next, I believe?' Grison said cheerily.

'Mind if I get a run up?' Chico asked.

'By all means.'

Chico put some distance between himself and the roof's edge, and then hurtled towards it, his legs a wrathful blur. 'Geronimo, you bastards!' he yelled.

'Chico?' a voice crackled suddenly.

The clone tripped, fell and skidded to a halt hanging by his fingers over the edge of the rooftop.

'Tsh!' Grison tutted. 'Isn't that always the way?'

'Chico?' the professor's voice hissed. 'Are you there?'

'Well?' Grison said, peering over the roof's edge at the moribund resistance fighter. 'Aren't you going to answer that?'

Chico glanced down at his pocket. It seemed an awful long way off. 'I might fall.'

'You were in the middle of jumping anyway.'

'Fair point.' Holding on with one hand, Chico carefully drew the communicator out of his pocket with the other. 'Yes? What is it?'

'Chico!' The professor's relieved voice crackled back. 'Damn good to hear your voice, man. I was beginning to fear the worst.'

A large shadow enveloped the clone as Grison leaned in towards him. 'Uh, this is a private call,' Chico said. 'Would you mind if –'

'Oh. Yes, yes, I'll leave you to it.' Grison beamed at him. 'I assume you know the way down?'

'Ha! Yes, good one.'

Grison walked off, chuckling to himself.

Chico waited until he was securely out of sight. 'Is this going to take long, sir? It's just I'm sort of in the middle of something.'

'Well, can't it wait?'

'Not really, sir,' Chico said. 'I'm killing myself.'

A pause of static.

'Must be a very bad line or something,' the professor's voice replied. 'Could've sworn you just said you're killing yourself.'

'That's right, sir.'

'Whatever for?'

'Because I killed you,' Chico sobbed.

Another pause of static.

'Did you?'

'Yes!'

'But I'm talking to you now,' the professor said. 'Can't you hear me? Hello?'

'The old you. The first you.'

'What are you blathering about, man?'

'The first me killed the first you.' Chico cast his eyes downwards in shame. It would be so easy to let go…if only his fingertips were in agreement.

'Did you take a knock to the head or something?'

'Kevin!' Chico wailed. 'Kevin betrayed you!'

'Oh, that. I'd always had my suspicions. Think nothing of it, happens to the best of us.'

'But…but…' Chico stammered. 'I did it *again*.'

'Killed me?' The professor said. 'Surely I'd have noticed?'

'Betrayed you. I told the Administration where you were.'

'No you didn't.'

'Yes I did! How else do you think they found us so quickly? I sent them a signal.'

'No you didn't,' the professor repeated.

'Sir, I appreciate your faith in me, but –'

'*I* sent them the signal.'

Chico's knuckles whitened. *'What?'*

'It was a calculated risk,' the professor said. 'Possibly a miscalculated one.'

'You…betrayed yourself?'

'It was the only way to keep Anthony's mind focused on other matters. Based on the deductions myself and the other professors made, after discovering a rogue planet in his head Anthony's most likely course of action would've been to kill himself.'

'Can't say I blame him,' Chico mumbled. He tried to pull himself up with his one free arm. The ledge creaked and groaned in protest.

'Naturally we couldn't allow that to happen, no matter what the cost. So we sent the Administration a signal, told Anthony the news and waited for the inevitable massacre, hoping it'd be enough to spur him onwards.'

'Hang about,' Chico said, instantly regretting the expression, 'why didn't you just knock Tony out and tie him up?'

'Chico,' the professor said, 'sometimes it pains me to try to think down to your level.'

'Timeless classic, that plan. Would've worked like a charm.'

'That's hardly the point. There's a certain etiquette that's required when dealing with such situations. A flair that you clearly don't –'

'Where's Tony now then?' Chico snapped. 'Got him all nice and safe, have you?'

'I'm afraid not. There's been a bit of a complication.'

'Oh there has, has there?' Chico would've folded his arms, had that not been a manoeuvre guaranteed to send him plummeting to his death. As it was, he settled for a really fearsome scowl.

'Yes. That's why –'

'You need me to set things right?'

'Uh, yes. The government have him. Chances are, we may have to break him out.'

'What's the plan, then? Or is it too highbrow for me?'

'Haven't got one, actually,' the professor admitted. 'Thought this was much more your area.'

'Ah. Sort of a "rush in guns blazing, shoot everyone in sight" kind of plan?'

'Such simplicity,' the professor marvelled. 'Such a blatant disregard for any logical thinking. I *envy* you.'

'What if Anthony doesn't want to be rescued? What then, eh?'

'He will. He knows we're his best chance of survival.'

'Yes,' Chico insisted, 'but what if he doesn't?'

The professor sighed. 'Then I guess we knock him out and tie him up. A plan which I'm faithfully assured is a timeless classic.'

'Now you're talking.' Chico grinned. 'Just one slight problem…'

'You're hanging by your fingertips from a rooftop several thousand feet up?'

'Yes, sir. How did you know?'

'Because we're floating just below you.'

Chico peered down at the dense smog, as Derek rose up through it like a chain-smoking inside-out angel.

Professor Langerman poked his head out the side window of the front passenger seat. 'We've been homing in on your signal as we spoke. Best get in before you do yourself a mischief.'

The clone nimbly dropped down onto Derek's bonnet, slithered across his roof, and swung himself in through the rear passenger door.

Another passenger was already sat inside, clad in a pair of Chico's Guns and Ammo undergarments.

'Oh no!' Chico said. 'What's *he* doing here?'

'Found him hanging onto a windowsill a couple of dozen feet below you,' the professor said. 'Seemed a bit rude to leave him there.'

'There's a time and a place for manners, sir,' Chico said sombrely, 'and that wasn't it.'

Grott looked around at his surroundings in growing dismay. 'Oh dear,' he said, chewing his bottom lip. 'I think I've gone and made a bit of a mess of things again. Mr Grison isn't going to be at all pleased.'

Twelve

Grison strolled in through the doors of the Administration reception, feeling incredibly pleased with himself. There was something about subtracting Grott that always brought a smile to his face. Job satisfaction, that was probably it.

Though he couldn't help but think that there was something he was forgetting.

'Afternoon, Jeff,' Grison called, nodding a greeting at the receptionist. 'Running a bit late. Sign me in will you, there's a good ch–'

He paused. The short, clean-shaven receptionist staring blankly at him most certainly wasn't Jeff.

'Sorry,' Grison said. 'Forgot Jeff had involuntarily made room.'

'Think nothing of it,' the receptionist beamed. 'Name's Macemby, and if there's anything I can do to make your journey through the foyer a more pleasurable experience, please don't hesitate to –'

'Macemby?' Grison stared hard at the plump little man. 'Macemby Pickler?'

The receptionist absently fondled his bare top lip. 'That's me, all right. Sorry, do I know you? My mind's a little, uh –'

'I work for you, sir,' said Grison stiffly.

The little man's eyes twinkled with amusement. 'Oh, shush,' he chuckled. 'If anything, I work for *you*. Though I'm sure that if I apply myself, perhaps one day –'

Grison gripped him firmly by the shoulders. 'Good god, man, what did they do to you? What happened to your moustache?'

'You won't catch me with one of those nasty unhygienic soup strainers, sir,' Mr Pickler said, grimacing in distaste. 'It's against company policy. Prime Minister Hardcastle demands that all his employees be clean-shaven, so as to reinforce the idea that his administration has nothing to hide – not even a top lip.'

'Hardcastle?' Grison slammed his fists down on the reception counter, making Mr Pickler judder up and down on his seat. 'So he's behind this. Right!' He marched off towards the lift.

'Excuse me, sir,' Mr Pickler called after him. 'Could I have your name before you go, if it's not too much trouble?'

'Oh sure, I mean, why not?' muttered Grison under his breath. 'You've only known me for twenty years.' He gave the lift call button a good thump, and hollered back, 'Grison, with a G.'

Mr Pickler's eyes scanned the employee register. 'I don't see it down here, sir.'

Grison stomped back to the reception desk. 'Try the other one.' He motioned impatiently to the desk's top drawer. 'The separate one, reserved for the Subtractions department.'

'Subtractions department?' Mr Pickler opened the drawer and rummaged inside. 'Never heard of it.'

'You used to run it,' Grison growled.

'Ah, here we go.' Mr Pickler drew a second register out of the drawer and placed it on the desk. A large red cross had been scrawled through it. 'Oh dear,' he said. 'Oh deary, deary, deary, dear.'

'Problem?' Grison enquired.

'Sorry to be the bearer of bad news, but I'm afraid that department has been downsized.'

'Downsized? What's that supposed to mean?'

'As in it has ceased to exist,' Mr Pickler clarified. 'The Prime Minister has deemed that it no longer serves a purpose.'

Grison snatched up the register and stared at it. Almost every name had been crossed through with a neat red line; next to Mr Pickler's was the word 'reassigned'. 'There must be some mistake.'

'Mr Hardcastle does not make mistakes.' Mr Pickler motioned to the door. 'If you'd care to pick up a campaign leaflet on your way out, I'm sure the current administration would be more than happy to fit you up with a new career. Plenty of room for everyone in this brave new world.'

Grison stared past the box of Hardcastle re-election pamphlets, to the wall it hung on. It was the Wall Of Shame, and someone had painted it pink. Where once was written the Administration's sacred mantra: 'Your sacrifice makes room for others', a new slogan now stated: 'Live long, vote wisely.' A picture of the Prime Minister's hopeful grinning maw accompanied it.

'They've got the bastard, haven't they?' Grison snarled, storming off towards the lift. 'Cresswell!'

'You can't go up there, sir!' Mr Pickler called after him. 'You don't work here any m—'

The lift door slid shut on his words.

It pinged open again a hundred and thirty-two floors later.

Grison stepped out into what, up until yesterday, had been the Subtractions department's base of operations. The Prime Minister's bleached white teeth beamed at him from every angle.

With each additional step, a new tagline launched itself out of the propaganda material that covered every inch of the corridor, and burrowed into Grison's subconscious.

'Vote for Hardcastle because *you're* worth it…'

'One man can make a difference – but only if *you* vote for him…'

'Your Prime Minister does not make mistakes. He corrects them…'

As Grison's pace quickened, the taglines bombarded him faster and faster.

'A different vote is a wasted vote…'

'The choice is yours, the candidate is ours…'

'Live long, vote Hardcastle…'

Vote Hardcastle…vote Hardcastle…vote Hardcastle.

The words repeated in Grison's mind, and he found himself starting to think that perhaps Hardcastle wasn't such a bad choice for re-election after all.

He forced his eyes shut, and with a strangulated cry, barrelled in through the Assignment Room's door, and tripped over a beanbag. The room was crammed with them, and various other creature comforts that Hardcastle's workforce would never have the time or courage to use. To hammer this home, a sign upon the wall stated: 'All play and no work makes Jack redundant.' As Grison stared up at the sign, the name 'Jack' slowly faded away to be replaced by the name 'Philip'.

'Efficient,' he muttered.

It still hadn't been enough to deter one particularly lazy individual, who'd clearly decided the area directly below the sign would make for a nice, inconspicuous place to get a bit of kip.

'You there!' Grison said, giving the beanbag the employee was resting on a vicious kick. 'Where's Noddy?'

The man yawned, stretched, and looked up. 'All right Smiler?'

Grison looked the clean-shaven smart suited employee up and down. 'Nigel? What happened to you?'

'Hostile takeover,' said Nigel grimly. 'Too bloody hostile for my liking. They forced me to wear this ridiculous clown suit. I tried to tell them I'm just going to get porridge all over it, but would they listen?' He glanced down at his tie, and grimaced. 'See? I warned them…'

'I'm surprised they didn't wipe your mind as well,' said Grison, over the hideous slurping noise of Nigel sucking his tie. 'It's the first one I'd have gone for.'

'Nah, they just stood me outside in that corridor for a coupla hours. Tried to do the same with Mr Pickler, but he was having none of it. Kept screaming "you can lead a horse to water, but you'll never make it shave its moustache".'

'He was wrong about that,' said Grison.

'Anyway, whatever they were up to with me, I guess it didn't work. All I felt was a bit shagged out after all that standing around.'

'What do you think of Hardcastle?' Grison asked casually.

Nigel's pupils dilated and he snapped bolt upright. 'He's a god amongst men, sir, whom I'd gladly let date my daughter if ever I had one.'

'Yes, well, thankfully there's little chance of that,' Grison said, making a mental note to thank someone down in the Sterilisation Statistics department for coming up with the holo-pet idea (providing the Sterilisation Statistics department hadn't been sterilised itself, of course). 'Now, where's Noddy?'

The glazed look faded from Nigel's eyes. 'Eh? Oh, early retirement, I think. Gone to the big scrapyard in the sky.' He reached for the comfort of his tool belt, pulled out a screwdriver, and subjected a kettle to a good stabbing. 'No need for those sort of cloak and dagger shenanigans any more. Plenty of room for everyone in this brave new world.'

'We'll soon see about that.' Grison stepped back into the corridor, and snagged the arm of a harassed-looking employee as he attempted to hurry by. 'Who's in charge around here?'

'Just follow the loudest voice,' the man sighed, before hurrying on.

From somewhere down the corridor a female voice roared: 'What the holy hell is going on?'

Grison made towards it, and was met by a tidal wave of employees heading the other way, like rats fleeing the site of an impending disaster. Pushing his way through them, he emerged at the doorway to the main office. In the centre of the room, twisting and turning on those around her with the unpredictability of a tornado, was Kate Carver, Campaign Manager; a fact that the hypno-badge on her lapel ensured nobody would be likely to forget in a hurry.

'You there!' An elongated finger with nails that could disembowel a man in one easy swipe, shot out towards an unfortunate employee who hadn't been quick or smart enough to vacate the room in time. 'Perhaps you'd care to explain to me why our candidate has slipped in the polls?'

'But, uh, that's not my job ma'am. I'm –'

'Damn right it's not your job!' Miss Carver screamed. 'You're fired!'

'Yes, ma'am.' The employee left his seat in a blur, and made gratefully for the exit.

'Anyone else?' Her piercing blue eyes rooted out another hapless piece of office cannon fodder.

'Well ma'am, it's, um, it's that whole Colin fiasco.'

'Go on?'

'Well, it did, uh, did make the Prime Minister look a little, well, uh, foolish.' The employee braced himself.

'Get onto the research department and tell them to fix it!' Miss Carver hissed.

'But, uh, you've already fired the research department ma'am.'

'Then I'll guess you'll have to fix it, won't you?'

'Yes, ma'am.' Sweat dribbled down the employee's forehead. 'Um, uh, er, how ma'am?'

Miss Carver ground her teeth; a sound like butcher's cleavers being sharpened for the chopping block. 'Find out who this Colin really is, where he comes from and how we can control him.'

One particularly brave employee decided to make a play for promotion. 'How about a brain wipe?' he suggested.

Miss Carver's baleful eyes settled on him, like a fly on a corpse. The employee held his breath.

'Excellent idea,' Miss Carver said.

The employee exhaled deeply.

Miss Carver pointed a finger at him. 'Put this man down for a brain wipe. That ought to raise the efficiency around here.'

A security guard gripped the distraught-looking employee underarm, and dragged him towards the door.

'Er, no, uh, I, er, meant for the man with the planet in his head.'

Miss Carver snapped her fingers. The guard released the employee and returned to his post.

'Hmm, worth a try, I suppose. Make sure it's done before the afternoon press conference.'

'Yes, ma'am. I'll go set up the equipment, ma'am.'

Miss Carver turned her attention to a thin, pasty-faced boy who was standing before her with a clanking tea tray gripped in his trembling hands.

'Yes? What the hell do you want?'

'Your tea, ma'am.'

'Well you can't have it!' Miss Carver screamed. 'It's *mine!*' She snatched the cup from the trembling tea boy and took a sip. Her face reddened. 'You call this a nice calming cup of Chamomile?'

'Well, uh –'

'You're fired, dammit! Fired!' She hurled the cup at the retreating tea boy. It shattered against the wall, next to Grison's head. Her gaze transferred to him. 'Who the hell are you?'

Grison snatched the empty tray out the tea boy's hands as he passed. 'New tea boy,' he said swiftly.

'Well don't just stand there. Get me a cup of tea. Now, dammit!'

'Very good, ma'am.' Grison moved off towards a tea machine.

'Not from a machine! Do I look like an android lover to you? Handmade tea, god damn it!'

'Yes, ma'am.'

Grison marched out the door, waited for Miss Carver to find someone else to shout at, and slunk back in again. Something on a monitor had caught his eye. He peered over the shoulder of a man sat at a console. The screen before him showed Anthony, sat on his own in a darkened room, unhappily munching his way through a packet of Rich Tea biscuits.

The monitor flicked off. 'Yes?' The man sat at the console glared at Grison. 'Did you want something?'

'New tea boy.' Grison raised his tray as evidence. 'Don't suppose you know where the tea making apparatus is kept?'

'You're out of luck there, my friend. Kettle's broken.' The man glanced warily in Miss Carver's direction. 'Over-use,' he mouthed.

'Any substitute?'

'Might be another in the supply room down on floor seventeen.'

Grison made to leave.

'But you can't go in there.' The man flicked the monitor back on, and pointed at Anthony. 'That's where they're keeping him.'

'Is it now?'

'Yes, but keep it between you and me.' The man tapped the side of his nose. 'Classified information.'

'Say no more.' Grison beamed pleasantly. 'I'll make sure it doesn't fall into the wrong hands.'

The lift door pinged open at floor seventeen.

Grison stepped out.

A dozen burly security guards greeted his arrival.

'Excuse me,' the guard with the least neck and most pectorals growled, 'could I see your security clear–'

Grison rattled his tea tray.

'It's all right, lads,' No-Neck said, 'it's only the tea boy.'

The guards stepped aside.

Grison entered the supply room, slamming the door shut behind him.

Anthony looked up into Grison's grinning face. 'Oh good,' he said glumly, 'it's you.'

'Yes,' Grison said, 'it's me.' He took a step back so he could properly appraise his trapped quarry.

Anthony's head had swollen like an overinflated balloon, and wasn't just green around the gills but a tad on the mossy side too. His hair had brambles sprouting from it, and a miniscule mountain range had begun to push its way out through the middle of his face, accentuating his nose in a less than flattering manner.

'You're looking well,' Grison added.

'If you're here to kill me, you'll have to wait in line,' Anthony said. 'The whole world's after my blood.'

'You've got me all wrong Tony,' Grison said, advancing. 'I want to *help* you.'

Anthony frowned at Grison over the top of his mountainous nose. 'That's what you said the last time you tried to kill me.'

'At the moment the entire world hates you, but I can change that. I can make you a man of the people.' Grison clutched a hand to his heart. 'Someone they love…' He threw his arms out as widely as the tiny supply room would allow. 'Cherish…adore…' He leant in close to Anthony's face, which didn't take much effort given its size. 'Worship.'

'Thanks, but I think I'll take my own chances.'

'They're going to wipe your brain, Tony,' Grison said slowly.

The vast sprawling topography that passed for Anthony's face shifted around to accommodate an expression of horror.

'Once they've finished with you, you won't be able to use the bathroom without the government first taking a vote on it.'

'They…they can't…'

'It's the only way for them to have complete control over you. You made the Prime Minister look like a fool, and they can't afford to let that happen again, not this close to an election.'

Anthony gripped Grison by the arm. 'Don't let them take my mind,' he whispered. 'It's all I've got left.'

'I won't,' Grison said, prising his fingers loose. 'But first, you must do something for me.'

'I knew there'd be a catch,' Anthony muttered.

Grison reached up to a storage shelf, and took down a kettle and a box of teabags. 'First,' he said, 'you must show me how to make tea.'

Anthony stared at the kettle in confusion. 'Seriously?'

'Yes.' Grison shuffled his feet in embarrassment. 'I'm a little inexperienced in that area.'

'You don't know how to make tea?' Anthony struggled to keep the mirth from his voice.

'Never needed to.' Grison made a face. 'Can't stand the stuff.'

'But I don't know how to make tea either,' Anthony admitted. 'Not a good cup, anyway. My personnel report said I couldn't make a decent cup of tea if my life depended upon it.'

'I've got news for you, Tony.' Grison handed him the kettle, and patted him firmly on the shoulder. 'It most probably does.'

Miss Carver was still firing people when Grison returned.

'You're fired, and you're fired! And you – guess what? Fired!' Her eyes scanned the room for someone else to victimise, and fell upon Grison. 'Yes? What the hell do you want?'

Grison approached her with the tea tray. 'Brought you some tea, ma'am.'

'Well, it's about goddamn time!' Miss Carver snatched up the cup and grudgingly took a sip.

Those few employees in the room who hadn't yet been fired cringed in their seats, awaiting the inevitable verbal dressing down and redundancy.

It didn't come.

A puzzled expression settled on Miss Carver's stern face, like she was experiencing some sort of emotion that she couldn't quite put her finger on. And then, much to the amazement of everyone watching, she took a second sip.

'It's good,' Miss Carver said, draining the dregs from the cup. 'Damn good.' She set the empty cup aside. A respectful silence descended on the room.

'What's your name, lad?'

'Grison, ma'am. Philip Grison.'

'With tea making skills like those, Grison, you're going to go far.'

Grison offered up a packet of hobnobs. Miss Carver hesitated a moment, then took one. Several employees let out involuntary gasps. To get to this stage was unheard of.

'It's about goddamn time someone showed some efficiency around here.' Miss Carver shook the biscuit emphatically at her workforce. 'You people could learn from this man.'

'In that case, do you think I could have his job, ma'am?' Grison gestured to the sweat-drenched employee who was struggling to single-handedly set up the mind control equipment. 'He doesn't seem to do much around here.'

Miss Carver snapped her fingers. 'You had your chance, Sampson. Out of Grison's seat.'

'You're *firing* me?' Sampson whimpered.

'Don't be ridiculous, Sampson.' Miss Carver smiled, which was even more unsettling than when she didn't. 'I'm promoting you.'

'Really?' Sampson raised an optimistic eyebrow.

'Yes. To "Man Who Fetches Tea and Biscuits".'

'*Tea*, ma'am?' Sampson wailed.

'Excellent idea, Sampson.' Miss Carver's shark-like grin widened. 'Two sugars. Make it something *calming.*'

Thirteen

'Mr Cresswell?' A government aide gently shook Anthony by the shoulder. 'The world is waiting.'

Anthony peered over the reception desk at the mass of TV, radio and press representatives that had been squeezed into the room. 'There's hundreds of them!' he hissed, pointing a trembling finger. 'Hundreds…'

'That's right,' the aide said cheerily, 'and they're all here for *you*, Mr Cresswell.'

'They'll pick my bones clean,' Anthony whimpered.

'Oh, they just want a bit of a chinwag, that's all. I'm sure they'll be gentle.'

'Then why's that man carrying a brick?' Anthony gestured to a shaven-haired thug from the local sleaze tabloid 'The Daily Crap.' In one hand he held a brick, and in the other a camera poised and ready to capture the moment.

'I shouldn't worry about that,' the aide said, beaming. 'Probably wants you to sign it or something.'

'Take me back to the supply room,' Anthony pleaded. 'There were biscuits there. I was happy.'

'Plenty of time for biscuits later. If you could just start with a brief statement, then it's straight on to the questions and answers session.'

'Statement? What sort of statement? I haven't prepared a statement!'

'Just say a few words about the Prime Minister and what a terribly marvellous chap he is. That sort of thing, y'know?'

'But he punched me in the face!'

'Yes,' the aide chuckled, 'he's such a kidder.'

Anthony wiped the back of his hand across his gargantuan sweat-drenched forehead. 'Uh, hello?' He tapped the microphone, deafening several people. 'I'd like to start by saying –' He yelped as a brick whizzed past overhead.

'And in conclusion,' Anthony added, 'thank you all for coming. Goodbye!' He ducked back down behind the desk.

The aide sighed heavily and leant in towards the microphone. 'Any questions?'

A hundred hands shot into the air.

'Yes?'

'Could I have my brick back, please?'

'No. Anyone else?' The aide stared pointedly at a man near the front of the crowd, who'd been paid rather handsomely to ask the right sort of question.

'Oh, right. Yes.' The man cleared his throat. 'Which candidate do you favour in the upcoming election?'

The aide helped Anthony back into his seat. 'A nice easy one there, Mr Cresswell.'

'Why?' Anthony said. 'What did he say?'

'Never mind what he said,' the aide hissed, 'just answer "Prime Minister Hardcastle."'

As Anthony opened his mouth to speak, a voice echoed inside his mind.

Testing, testing…is this thing on?

Anthony cocked his head to one side. 'Did you say something?'

'Hardcastle, Hardcastle, Hardcastle!' the aide hissed.

Are you receiving me? One two, one two.

Anthony looked around warily. 'Grison? Is that you?'

I'm beaming a signal directly to your brain. Took a while to penetrate the planet's crust, but I think I've got it sorted now.

'What the hell are you doing in there?' Anthony snapped.

'Are you talking to me, Mr Cresswell?' the aide said, looking puzzled.

'No, I'm talking to the voice in my head.'

'Oh dear. We're at that stage already are we?' The aide backed away slightly.

I can hear the thoughts of everyone in the building. The mind control technology they have up here is remarkable.

'I don't want you crawling around in my brain!' Anthony hissed. 'Get out of it, you sod!'

I've already saved your mind; now let me save your skin.

'Mr Cresswell?' the aide coaxed. 'They're still waiting for an answer.'

Anthony looked up at the crowd of journalists. 'What was the question again?'

The journalists sighed collectively.

'Which candidate do you favour in the upcoming election?'

The answer rolled off Anthony's tongue, before he'd even thought of one. 'Myself,' he said.

The journalists let out a gasp.

The government aide swooned.

'I'm sorry?' the journalist spluttered. 'Did you just say "yourself"?'

'Oh god, yes, I did didn't I? Hang on a moment.' Anthony turned away from the microphone. 'Grison?' he whispered. 'Why did I just say "myself"?'

Anthony searched his thoughts, and turned up static.

'Grison?'

'Well then, perhaps you'd care to tell us a little something about your policies?' A journalist hollered.

'Uh…' said Anthony.

'Or your views on immigration?'

'Well, er…'

'The election's less than a week away. Don't you think it's a little late to enter the running?'

'Grison?' Anthony whimpered, ducking down behind the desk. 'Help…'

The static relented. *Sorry about that, Tony. Had a few management issues to clear up. They were a little bit surprised by the answer you gave, so I had to wipe their minds a bit.*

'*They* were surprised?' Anthony screeched. 'How do you think *I* felt?'

Relax. With your trusty Campaign Manager on the case, you stand to make a fortune.

'My who?'

Me, you fool. Now stand up, and let me work my magic.

Anthony stood and faced a barrage of oncoming questions.

'What do you think about pollution?'

'Babies?'

'Cheese? How do you feel about cheese?'

Anthony held out his hand for silence. 'One at a time please, one at a time.' The noise abated. He selected a journalist at random. 'Yes?'

'What are your opinions on the other candidates running against you in the election?'

'As low as can be expected,' Anthony said.

'I hope you realise you're up against some stiff competition?'

'Incredibly stiff,' Anthony agreed. 'Dead, in one case.'

'Mr Katanga's death is no laughing matter,' the journalist snapped. 'He took his own life to display his dedication to the people. What have you done lately, eh?'

'Well, I do have this planet in my head.'

'But you have no policies and you have no experience,' the journalist persisted. 'Why would anyone in their right mind vote for you?'

Anthony shot the journalist his winning demented badger smile. 'Because I'll reserve them a plot of land on the planet in my mind, if they do.'

'But isn't that the Prime Minister's main policy?'

'That may be so, but the land in *my* mind is not *his* to offer.'

The journalist stared hard at the rolled-up parchment in his hands. 'You're saying the deeds Prime Minister Hardcastle's been offering his loyal voters aren't actually worth anything?'

'If you were to examine that deed, I believe you'd discover it's made out for land on the planet Colin. Which, as I'm sure you're aware, doesn't actually exist.'

The journalist unravelled the deed, inspected it silently, and then tossed it aside.

'As for land on the planet Tony,' Anthony tapped the side of his head, 'that's up for grabs to all loyal voters.'

'Well then,' the journalist said, 'I guess you get my vote.'

'And mine,' cried another eager journalist.

'Me too.'

A rotund journalist near the front row cleared his throat. 'If it's not too much trouble, I'd like to reserve a small villa in Tunisia.'

'My dear sir,' Anthony brayed, 'you can *have* Tunisia.'

'Ooh! That's very kind of you.'

'Just remember to vote for me.' Anthony turned to the cameras and gave the viewers at home a wink. 'That goes for everyone else. Now, if you'll excuse me, I have a campaign to build, and babies to kiss.'

As Anthony left the room, the roar of the crowd was deafening. He strode down the aisle between the cheering journalists, and stepped into the lift.

The moment the doors shut, his eyes glazed over and he slumped to the ground. 'What the hell just happened?' he whimpered.

You made a successful bid to become Prime Minister.

'But I don't want to be Prime Minister. You manipulated my mind!'

They loved you, Tony. You're a hit.

'But it isn't in the plan.'

Oh, yes, right – the plan…convince the world you're their new messiah, and then at the right moment tell them you're going to be ascending…in a spaceship? Grison's chuckle echoed through Anthony's mind.

'It might've worked,' Anthony muttered. 'Hey, wait a minute – how do you know what I was planning?'

I'm inside your mind. I know everything you know. Deep down, you know there is no cure and there are no Martians, other than that Reality TV colony that got abandoned the moment their ratings began to slide. I somehow doubt there's a brain surgeon in their midst. No, all that exists is one cold, hard fact; you have just a few days left to live. How you choose to spend them is down to you.

The lift door pinged open. Anthony was immediately swamped by a mass of overexcited office workers.

'Just wanted you to know you've got my support, Mr Cresswell,' an employee said, pumping Anthony's hand vigorously.

'I've been backing you since day one, Mr Cresswell,' said another man Anthony had never met in his life.

'We're behind you all the way, Mr Cresswell,' several more employees enthused. 'One hundred and ten percent.'

Grison pushed his way through the rabble. 'All right people, back to work, back to work.' He clapped his hands sharply. The rabble scurried off.

'Who were all those people?'

'Your loyal election campaigners, of course.'

'Then why were they wearing badges that said "Vote Hardcastle"?'

'Because they used to be his loyal election campaigners, until I wiped their minds and reprogrammed them.'

A stern-featured woman with nails like spikes tapped Grison gingerly on the shoulder. 'Uh, excuse me?'

'Yes, Kate?' he said, without turning.

'Why is my name on that door?' She gestured to a sign on the office door that stated 'Kate Carver. Campaign Manager.'

'To give you something to aspire to, of course,' Grison beamed. 'Now, how about a nice cup of coffee, Kate?'

'Ooh, yes,' Miss Carver said, 'that'd be lovely.'

Grison stared at her. 'You were getting *my* coffee, Kate?'

'Was I?'

'That's right. Two sugars.'

Miss Carver staggered off in confusion.

'Just can't get the staff these days,' Grison tutted. 'So, how about it, Tony? Ready to take on the world?'

'Well, I –'

'No, no, don't answer yet. *Sampson!*' Grison clicked his fingers.

A harassed-looking man drenched in perpetual sweat bounded towards them. 'Yes, sir?'

'Show Tony the campaign poster.'

'Well, I've only been working on it a few minutes. It's not really –'

'Sampson!'

'Yes, sir.' Sampson unravelled a poster and showed it to Anthony. 'It's not quite finished, but you get the general idea.'

Anthony's thick mossy eyebrows made a break for the ceiling. The poster depicted him in designer robes, being nailed to a cross by his political opposition. A housing deed was clutched valiantly in his hand. 'He's back,' the tagline at the bottom read, 'and this time when he dies for your sins, he's leaving you a bungalow!'

'What do you think then, Tony?' Grison asked. 'Too much?'

'I think I'm going to be sick.'

'Maybe it does need toning down a bit,' Grison admitted. 'Put bedsit instead of bungalow.'

'Very good, sir.' Sampson scurried off.

Grison led Anthony into his newly acquired office, and closed the door.

'I don't think I'm cut out for this,' Anthony said, as Grison helped him into a seat.

'Pull yourself together, Tony. This is your one chance to make something of your life, your one chance to make a difference.' Grison reached into a desk drawer and produced a tin of sweets. 'Fruity bon-bon?'

Anthony shook his head.

'You see? Typical Cresswell. Always passing up the great opportunities in life.' Grison popped a sweet into his mouth and put the tin away. 'Seize control, Tony. Turn things around to your advantage. Follow my counsel. Live rich, die happy, and when you go they'll build statues in your likeness.'

'But it won't be my likeness, will it?' Anthony said. 'This isn't even my own face. It's the face of a murderer who died in a sewer.'

'You want a new face?' Grison shrugged. 'Fine, I can get you a new face. I know people, I have connections.' He reached for the holo-phone.

'I don't want a new face, I want my old face back.'

Grison gave him a sympathetic look. 'Let's be honest Tony, your face wasn't much cop to start with.'

'Yes, but it was *mine*.'

'Oh, very well.' Grison sighed. 'If that's what it takes to get you on board, I can get you your face back.'

'You know who has it?' Anthony narrowed his eyes. 'I was right, wasn't I? It was you who took it!'

Grison sucked his sweet noisily. 'Not me, no.'

'Then who?'

'The same man who gave you that one.'

Fourteen

Rakembalo's new business wasn't going at all well. He was a hat maker; he designed and made hats for every shape of head. Fat, thin, small, large, moderately to hugely deformed. 'If you have a head,' the sign outside the door stated, 'I have a hat.' Which wasn't, strictly speaking, true. Not if you had a normal-shaped head. The great Rakembalo – or 'Thin Tony' as he now preferred to be known, didn't do normal. He was an artiste, he was a creator…he was going about successfully bankrupting himself for the second time in a row.

'Helena!' he called to his attractive blonde misshapen hat-wearing assistant. 'My paraffin oil, if you please.'

Helena tugged in frustration at her golden locks. 'We only set up shop last week.'

'I appear to have once again misjudged the market,' Rakembalo sobbed. 'I have no customers, I have no money; all I have is hats and a vision. But sometimes, no matter how grand the vision, that just isn't enough.'

'So you're going to burn the place down and have me claim on the insurance again?' Helena sighed.

'Yes, and I must find myself a new identity with which to start afresh. Something female this time, perhaps.' Rakembalo stared thoughtfully at his assistant. 'Helena! How would you feel about me being you for a while?'

'That's it, I quit,' said Helena.

'Share the vision, Helena! Encompass the dream!'

Rakembalo's assistant threw her hat down at his feet and stormed out of the shop.

'The dream has died,' he wept. 'The vision has fled.'

The door opened again.

'Helena?' Rakembalo looked up.

A man was stood in the doorway, his head blocking out the sunlight.

'A customer!' Rakembalo squealed with delight.

'Ex-customer,' Anthony growled.

'Now don't be like that, sir,' Rakembalo said, dashing towards the nearest hat stand. 'If ever there was a head badly in need of a hat, it's yours.'

'You made me this way, you bastard.'

'You must be mistaking me for someone else,' Rakembalo said, scrabbling around in his hat collection. 'I'm nothing but a humble hat maker, though these are far from humble hats.' He turned, clutching something large and furry that looked like it had dropped off a neutered Wookie. 'Don't be timid now. Try it on.'

Anthony knocked the hat out of his hands. 'I don't want a hat. I want my body back!'

'Not quite your style eh, sir? I understand completely. Let's see what else we have in stock.' Rakembalo turned back towards the hat stand.

'Cut the crap Rakembalo,' Anthony said. 'I know it's you.'

'I don't know what you mean, sir,' Rakembalo brayed. 'Thin Tony's the name, and selling hats is my –'

Anthony spun him round, scattering misshapen hats in every direction. '*I'm* Tony, and that's *my* body! The face of the crowd look, you said.'

'If we'd met before, I'm sure I'd have remembered. I never forget a face, especially one as expansive as yours.'

'You sold me contaminated DNA!' Anthony screamed. 'Thanks to you, my head's going to explode.'

'Well, we've all got to explode sometime, sir. At least when you do, people will say "now there goes a man who knew how to wear his hat".' Rakembalo deposited a large black beret on top of Anthony's head and tilted it at a rakish angle. 'Et voila!'

Anthony threw the beret down on the ground and stamped on it. 'Give me back my body!'

The warm smile on Rakembalo's face began to grow tepid. 'I'm afraid it's occupied at the moment.'

'Then I suggest you unoccupy it before I start telling people who you really are.'

'Let's not be hasty,' Rakembalo soothed. 'I'm sure we can work out some sort of hat-related deal.'

'There's got to be a reason you're hiding out in my body. Owed people a lot of money, did you? Thought I'd be the last place anyone would look?'

'Well, who'd think of looking for one as great as I, in a shell as dismal as this?'

'I did,' Anthony said. 'And if I can find you, anyone can.'

'Anyone who knows what you look like,' said Rakembalo, 'and believe me, they must be few and far between. You have a face so dull in appearance that people immediately dismiss it from their minds; that's why I chose it. Unfortunately, since all my equipment perished in the fire, I appear to be stuck with it.'

'There's no way you'd trap yourself in my body without leaving open an escape route.' Anthony's eyes fell upon a door marked 'Staff Only'. 'Mind if I take a look back there?'

'It's off limits,' Rakembalo said, blocking Anthony's path to the door. 'Lots of top secret hat technology. Very dangerous if it fell into the wrong hands.'

'If it's money you want, I can pay you.'

Rakembalo chuckled. 'I may not remember your face, but I certainly remember your credit rating.'

'Yes, well it's changed quite a lot since I got this planet in my head. Everyone's lining up to give me sponsorship deals.'

Rakembalo's eyes widened. 'That's *you?*'

'Why else do you think my head's this size?'

The smile returned to Rakembalo's face, with a rein-forcement of extra teeth. 'Oh, I say! A genuine celebrity in my midst. You're the toast of the town, dear boy. Why, you must permit me to furbish your head with a hat – free of charge.'

'Yes, you'd like that wouldn't you? And all the free publicity your hat business would gain as a result.'

'Can't say it had even crossed my mind, sir.' Rakembalo scrambled frantically around in his hat pile. 'Ah…how about this one, with the extra-large picture of me on it.'

'Picture of *me,*' Anthony corrected. 'I'll wear your hat, on one condition. I think you know what it is.'

The hat salesman sighed. 'Oh, very well, Mr Cresswell. Let's get you back into that ghastly body of yours.'

'You remember my name now, eh?' Anthony mumbled.

Rakembalo threw open the Staff Only door. It came as little surprise to Anthony that the entire genetics parlour was contained within.

'Everything perished in the fire, did it?' Anthony said.

'As far as the insurance company knows, it most certainly did.' Rakembalo strode up to a freezer marked 'nobodies and has-beens' and retrieved a small vial of Anthony's DNA. 'I trust you remember the procedure?'

'Disrobe, then step into the booth.' Anthony fumbled with his belt.

'Other way around. The last thing I want is to catch a glimpse of your naked body. It's been a traumatic enough experience having to put up with this one.'

Anthony stepped into the booth and disrobed. 'And you'll change yourself back once you're finished with me?'

'Naturally, sir. Can't have two of you running around; we'd run into all sorts of identity theft issues.' Rakembalo inserted the DNA into a hole in the booth.

'No cock ups this time,' Anthony said.

'You already have a planet in your head. What else could possibly go wrong?'

'I could have *two* planets in my head. Just be careful, that's all.'

The hat salesman keyed in the genetic structure. The booth flashed, and Anthony emerged. He raced over to a mirror, inspected his reflection, and screamed. It was his face all right, but three times its usual size.

'Congratulations, sir,' Rakembalo said, 'you're as ugly as ever.'

'I don't understand,' Anthony whimpered. 'The planet's still in there.'

'Of course it is. The procedure's specifically designed not to alter the client's brain. The planet seems to have formed a symbiotic relationship with it. You cannot remove one without destroying the other.'

'But that was the whole point of getting my DNA back. My brain's going to explode.'

'Is that all?' Rakembalo shrugged. 'Don't fret, I can re-place it if you like.'

'With what?'

'Somebody else's brain.' Rakembalo swung open a chest freezer, which was full of delicately packed brains; they had all been carefully labelled with their previous owners occupations.

'How would you like to be a scuba diver, or an ex-marine? Or perhaps something more in-keeping with your present appearance, like a stable-hand, or a donkey herder?'

'But it wouldn't be me. It'd be someone else's brain, in my body.'

'Let's try to look on the bright side – if, indeed, that isn't the bright side. Before I selected your DNA as my own, I had it analysed thoroughly. That body of yours is in perfect physical condition. Sure, it rates rather heavily on the "drab and dreary" scale, but with a new brain in that shell you could comfortably exist for a good few decades, until it's time to make way.'

'As a donkey herder?'

The hat salesman looked Anthony up and down. 'Perhaps donkey herder is a little above your station. Let's see what else we have.' He opened another freezer, and rummaged inside. 'Ah, here we go.' He offered up a brain to Anthony, in a jar marked 'last resort'.

'Mr Cresswell – how would you like to spend the next twenty years as a *Junior Accountant?*'

Grison sat in a limo-pod outside Thin Tony's Hat Emporium, listening with glee to the cries of anguish emanating from within.

Eventually, Anthony emerged, wearing a hat and a very glum expression.

'Hello, Tony. Like the new hat.' Grison stared at his oversized head. 'Not so sure about the new face though.'

'At least it's my own.'

'Still got a planet in it then?'

Anthony nodded, and almost toppled under the planet's weight.

'Now we've got your physical appearance sorted, let's see what we can do about the rest of your attire.' Grison opened the passenger door, and beckoned Anthony inside.

'This is…this is…'

Professor Langerman squinted through the descending alcoholic haze at the badly lit room that surrounded him. Since he couldn't work out what it was, he decided to work out what it wasn't.

'This is not a spaceport.' He slumped back in his seat, mentally exhausted.

'Correct,' Chico said.

'And this...' The professor turned his attention to the half-empty pint glass on the table before him. 'This is not mineral water.'

'Also correct.'

The professor frowned. One of the two statements he'd just made was of vital importance. After much deliberation, he decided it was the second one, and downed the rest of his pint. By the time he'd reached the bottom of the glass, he'd already forgotten what it was he was trying to remember.

'My tea tastes funny,' Grott said, staring suspiciously at his drink.

'That's whiskey for you,' said Chico.

'Ah. An Irish tea.' Grott grinned lopsidedly, and fell off his stool.

A conga-line of drunken astronauts in full spacesuits danced past in slow motion.

The professor watched them thoughtfully for a moment. 'Oh dear,' he said, once they'd passed. 'I didn't realise I'd had quite that much to –' As he reached for his glass, the realisation suddenly hit him. 'Good heavens!' he cried. 'This is a *pub!*'

'So it is, sir.'

'But...but...but...we were supposed to be going to the spaceport!'

'We've already been, sir. Don't you remember?'

'Have we?' The professor clutched tightly at the sides of his head, and attempted to rally the small band of brain cells that had somehow managed to survive his alcoholic onslaught. 'Wait a minute...I think...I think, yes, it's all coming back to me. We successfully hired a ship, and then came here to celebrate, right?'

'Not quite,' Chico said stiffly. 'I think I'd best refill your glass.'

'Why? What is it? Tell me!'

Chico pushed back his stool and rose unsteadily to his feet. 'Not until you've had another –'

'Damn it, man, just tell me!'

'Oh, very well.' Chico sat down, and took a deep breath. 'It was closed.'

'What was closed?'

'The spaceport, sir.'

The professor's eyes widened. 'All of it?'

'Yes, the entire spaceport.'

'They closed off an entire spaceport?'

'All commercial space travel has been temporarily suspended. You said it yourself, sir; no point in launching expensive expeditions into space when there's a fully habitable planet right here on our doorstep.'

'But we need to get Anthony off the planet. If we don't, he could destroy this one!'

'Yes, so you said, sir. In fact, you were getting quite het up about it, until Derek revealed he had a back-up plan.'

'We followed one of Derek's plans?'

'Ingenious it was, sir, and a great comfort to us all.'

'Then tell me it again,' the professor said, panic rising in his voice. 'I could do with some more comfort.'

'I don't think it'll work quite so well this time round, sir.'

'Why not?'

Chico motioned to the pub. 'Because this was it.'

'Going to the pub? That was his plan?'

'That's right.' Chico took another swig from his glass. 'A master strategist, sir.'

The professor's eyes scanned the dark recesses of the drinking hole. 'Where is that good for nothing curry shovelling –'

'Bouncers wouldn't let him in. Said he didn't meet up to the required dress code.'

'Probably because he didn't have a tie,' said Grott, from somewhere beneath the table.

'That or the fact that most of his innards are on the outside,' said Chico. 'Anyway, he went off to change into something more respectable.'

'So we're marooned here until further notice?'

'You haven't heard the worst of it yet.' Chico stared dismally into his near-empty pint glass. 'Technically speaking, it's *your* round.'

'Don't the government's technical experts realise Anthony's going to explode in a couple of days, and no doubt take this planet with him?'

'I don't think the government have technical experts,' Chico said. 'Mostly just marketing men.' He motioned to a gigantic viewscreen opposite the bar, which displayed Anthony on it, engaged in idle banter with a perpetually grinning talk show host. He was clad in a holo-suit, which altered every few seconds to match the outfits of his chosen sponsors; one moment Anthony was wearing a fashionable designer suit, the next trendy sportswear. The considerable breadth of his forehead had been rented out as advertising space for a variety of brand name products. At this present moment, an advert was flashing across it that proclaimed coke to be 'the choice of a planet.'

'At least Anthony doesn't appear to be in any immediate danger,' the professor said. 'Except perhaps of selling out.'

Chico's grey forehead creased. 'You mean we won't get to use that corker of a plan I came up with?'

'No point rescuing Anthony if we don't have the means to get him off planet. What we need's a private shuttle.'

'That's why we came here, sir,' Chico said. 'It's an astro-bar.'

The conga line of drunken astronauts, now led by a man in a dress, danced past again.

'One small step for man,' the transvestite hollered, 'one giant conga for mankind!'

'You mean that conga line there's real?' Professor Langerman rubbed his eyes and looked again.

'It would appear so, sir.'

The professor snagged the arm of a passing astronaut. 'Excuse me, my good man. Do you have a spaceship?'

'Oh yes,' the astronaut drawled. 'Five of them. All bright and shiny and made out of tinfoil.' He danced off to rejoin the conga line.

'Perhaps we should ask someone a little less inebriated?' Chico suggested.

At that moment, the man in the dress broke off from the group and heel-kicked his way towards them. There was barely an inch of exposed skin which hadn't been smothered with glitter, and his sequin-studded dress had been strategically torn to show a little of this and far too much of that.

'Hey there sweet-cheeks, is this seat taken?' he said in a thick Texan accent.

Chico's eyes followed where his finger was pointing. 'Yes,' he growled. 'I'm sitting in it.'

'Then mind if ah sit on *you?*' The Texan waggled his narrow eyebrows suggestively.

'Professor Langerman,' Chico said weakly. *'Help...'*

The Texan grabbed a spare seat, swivelled it around and sat. 'Langerman?' he mused. 'Where have ah heard that name before?'

Under the table, Chico slowly reached for one of five poorly concealed weapons. Even though the professor had taken the precaution of covering up his expiration tattoo with one of Chico's spare bandanas, there was still a risk of exposure.

The Texan transvestite clicked his fingers so sharply that one of his false nails flew off. 'Langerman's Lovers!' he cried. 'You're the guy who invented the sex clone!'

'Among other things,' the professor grumbled.

Chico relaxed the grip on his gun, and turned his attention to the more pressing issue of retrieving a glitter-coated nail from his pint.

'Hey everybody,' the Texan announced to the rest of the room in general. 'Y'all never gonna believe who this is. It's Professor Langerman!'

A few glances were exchanged, followed by disinterested shrugs.

'Inventor of the sex clone.'

Within minutes, everyone in the bar was keen to shake the professor's hand and buy him a drink.

'We're starting to draw a lot of unwanted attention,' warned Chico.

'Not entirely unwanted,' said the professor, downing another free pint, 'but I get your point. Perhaps we should see if we can hire a spaceship elsewhere.'

'Well hey, ah'll take y'all,' said the Texan. 'Where yuh heading?'

The professor gave him a look of doubt and dread. 'You have a spaceship?'

'It'd be a bit difficult to be a famous space adventurer without one, don't yuh think?' The transvestite gave him a grin full of lip-gloss.

'You're famous?'

'You better believe it, baby. Does the name "Wendigo Malfortune" mean anything to you?'

'It does now,' Chico said. 'It means "avoid".'

'Now don't pretend ya haven't heard of me. Mah exploits are legendary. Surely the fifteen mile Venus boogie must ring a bell?'

'Wasn't that when a lot of people burnt to death doing a fifteen mile conga?' said the professor.

'Yeah.' Wendigo bowed his head. 'Tragic waste of life. It said on the leaflet "wear asbestos disco-suits", but those poor brave fools had to try an' be fashionable. But don't let that fool ya. Ah'm not just famous for failures, baby.'

'What else are you famous for then?' Chico asked. 'Pissing people off in pubs?'

'A little trivia for ya. Who was the first man to set foot on the moon?'

'Neil Armstrong,' the professor said automatically.

Wendigo hoisted his high-heeled shoe up onto the table, and struck up a heroic pose. 'In *stilettos?* Ah don't think so.'

'Let me guess,' Chico said. 'Wendigo Malfortune again, was it?'

'You got it, baby. Admit it,' Wendigo grinned, 'you're impressed.'

'I'm impressed you've managed to hold our attention for this long.' Chico turned to the professor. 'Can we stop talking to him now, sir?'

'Do you have a ship or not?' asked the professor.

'Of course ah've got a ship. You don't get famous for hitchhiking, baby.' Wendigo slipped a hand into the folds of his dress, produced a leopard-skin wallet and displayed a photo of a ridiculously sparkly spaceship. 'Her name's Chastity,' he breathed, giving the photo a loving stroke. 'She's mah bitch, and one helluva ride.'

Chico leant in close to the professor's ear. 'What's the plan then, sir? Kill him and steal his ship? Or just simply kill him. I'm willing to go with either option.'

'Nothing quite that drastic, Chico.' The professor cleared his throat. 'We'd like to procure your services, Mr Malfortune. I assure you, money is no object. If you'd be so good as to take us to Mars.'

'Why? What's on Mars?'

'Aliens,' said the professor grandly, 'with intelligence beyond the ken of mortal men.'

'Never mind that,' said Wendigo. 'Are they *hot?*'

'Uh…sure. Why not?' said the professor, with considerably less grandeur.

'Then buddy, you got yerself a deal! It's long been a dream of mine to make first contact with an alien species – and bone the livin' hell out of it.' Wendigo spat in the palm of his hand and thrust it at the professor.

'Shake his hand then, Chico.'

Over the sound of some reluctant yet squelchy hand shaking, the professor added: 'Would tomorrow afternoon be okay for you? We've still got to pick up one of our companions.'

'Got a little business to take care of mahself first, so yeah, that oughta be perfect. Just the three of you, is it?'

'And me,' said Grott, from beneath the table.

'Yes,' the professor whispered, 'just the three of us.'

'Then let's drink a toast, for tomorrow we fly to Mars!'

'Oh, what the heck?' the professor said. 'One more drink's not going to hurt.'

Grison paced back and forth in his office, glancing impatiently at his watch. The door behind him began to open. 'Knock first, Kate,' he commanded.

'Sorry, sir.' The door closed again.

There came a polite knock, which Grison ignored.

This was followed by another polite knock, then a less polite knock, then an absolutely downright urgent knock.

Grison casually took a seat at Kate's desk and helped himself to one of her biscuits. He flicked a few crumbs off his suit, and hollered: *'Enter!'*

Kate entered, looking troubled.

'Working late, Kate?'

'Yes, sir,' she said tiredly. 'I couldn't remember where I lived.'

'Ah,' Grison murmured, 'that explains why I found Sampson sleeping in the storage cupboard. Now, what's bothering you?'

'To be perfectly frank, it's the war situation.'

'War?' Grison raised an eyebrow.

'Haven't you been following the news?'

Grison gestured to the broken viewscreen.

'You really ought to get that fixed,' Kate said.

'I'll have Nigel take a look at it in the morning. You were saying something about a war?'

'Yes, sir,' Kate said. 'The foreign heads of state are a little concerned that the land inside our candidate's head is only up for grabs to British people. If the problem isn't addressed soon, their next logical step would be to declare a major land war against England.'

'Fantastic news!' Grison beamed. 'I was starting to think they'd forgotten us.'

'This is no laughing matter,' Kate said sternly. 'Prime Minister Hardcastle has already taken to referring to our candidate as "The Harbinger of Doom". This is hardly the image we wish to project before an election. It could pose a major setback for us.'

Grison entwined his fingers. 'Not if we throw the election open to the entire world.'

'Not sure I follow you, sir.'

'It's quite simple, Kate,' said Grison, offering her one of her own biscuits. 'The other countries can hardly wage war on us if they're offered the opportunity to vote for Tony.'

'Prime Minister of the world?' Kate's brow wrinkled. 'You really think they'll go for it?'

'They'll have no choice, not if they want access to the land in Tony's mind.'

'And Hardcastle?'

'He's an over confident, power hungry mental case. He'll be keener than anyone for a shot at the grand title.'

Fifteen

'Uuuuuuuuuuuuuuuurrrrrrrgh!' groaned the professor.

'Uuuuuuuuuuuuuuuurrrrrrrrggggghhhh!' replied Chico.

'Mornin' lads!' Derek trundled across the garage floor with a breakfast tray balanced on his bonnet. 'Didn't have much in, so I threw a few leftovers together. Who fancies a black pudding?'

'*Uuuuuuuuuuuuuurrrrrghhhhh!*' the professor and Chico groaned in unison.

'Well, I *say* black pudding...' Derek added, glancing down at the tray. 'It's more a sort of grey-green pudding, really.'

The porta-loo cubicle in the garage's far corner let out a groan of protest as someone attempted to flush the toilet several times, and then gave up. Grott emerged, smiling sheepishly. 'Toilet's clogged,' he announced.

'Oh no...you brought him too?' The professor sighed.

'No choice. You were all practically unconscious when I returned. Except for lover boy there,' Derek gestured to Chico. 'Who was busy tryna chat up some bloke in a dress.'

'I wasn't chatting him up,' Chico muttered. 'I was trying to help secure us all a ride.'

'That's what you call it, is it?' Derek sniggered. 'Reckon your beer goggles were operating at maximum capacity there, mate.'

'As a matter of fact that dress-clad gentleman is our pilot. He's very kindly agreed to take us all to Mars.'

'What d'ya need him for?' Derek said, shovelling plate-fuls of food into the hole in his dashboard. 'I've already said I'll do it.'

'And we've already established you can't,' the professor countered.

'Ah, that's where you're wrong. Take a look at *this.*' Derek popped open his bonnet, revealing something wet, slimy and tube-like inside. 'Lung extensions. Got 'em whilst you were down the pub. With these little babies operating at full whack, I could hold my breath for hours.'

'I certainly wish I could,' the professor said, turning green.

Chico clutched a hand to his mouth. 'Back in a moment,' he mumbled, dashing off towards the toilet.

'I'd leave it a good ten minutes if I were you,' Grott called after him.

'Plus everything's airtight now,' Derek continued, 'so you'll be all nice and safely sealed inside with my gases. Then, of course, there's the brand new curry to rocket fuel converter. Go have a peek round the back, I think you'll be impressed.'

The professor averted his eyes until Derek's bonnet had safely snapped shut. 'I appreciate your enthusiasm,' he lied, 'but I think we'd all much rather travel with the transvestite.'

''S right,' Grott said, settling down onto the sofa. 'You know where you are with a bloke in a dress.'

'Besides, we won't be going anywhere if Anthony doesn't succeed in convincing the people of the world he's their new messiah.'

'He's certainly making a good go of it,' Derek said. 'Last I heard, he was running for Prime Minister.'

The professor sat bolt upright. His stomach protested, but his brain ignored it. 'But that's not part of the plan.'

'I guess he's got a new one. Seems to have backfired a bit, especially with all this annoying World War Five business.'

'*World War?*' the professor shrieked.

'It's all over the radio. Seems everyone wants a slice of that planet in Tony's mind. Harbinger of Doom they're calling him now. But I shouldn't concern yourself – I'm sure Tony's spin doctors will put a positive angle on things before today's election.'

The professor buried his head in his hands. 'I think you'd best put on the radio, Derek,' he said quietly.

'I can go one better than that.' Derek pointed a remote control at the wall opposite the sofa and pressed a button. Every flat surface in the garage – walls, floor tiles, ceiling, discarded curry containers – lit up with a different projected TV image. 'I call it Bachelor Vision,' he said proudly. 'One hundred channels of pure mindless round the clock entertainment.'

'Just the one channel will do for now,' the professor said. 'Find me that election!'

Anthony's massive face towered over the bright red plastic podium several fussing studio assistants had carefully positioned him behind. On the blue podium to his far right rested the urn of recently deceased electoral candidate Darren Katanga. In the centre of the stage a large solid gold podium stood vacant.

'Okay, loves.' An immaculately dressed floor manager clapped his hands together. 'We're going live in five.'

'Seconds?' Anthony whimpered.

'Minutes,' the floor manager said. 'So let's run through the –' He did a double-take at Anthony's face. 'Good heavens!' he cried. '*Makeup!*'

A makeup girl scurried onto the stage.

'See what you can do with that,' the man said, pointing at Anthony's head.

'I don't think there's enough time, sir,' the girl said, reaching into her makeup bag.

'Just do your best, love. I don't expect you to work miracles.'

The makeup girl started tentatively applying blusher to Anthony's face.

'Right, then. Rules and –' The floor manager's voice trailed off. He frowned at Anthony. 'Is that a holo-suit?'

Anthony looked down at his designer suit as it cycled through Jean-Paul Necrosis' summer, autumn and atomic winter range. 'I'd be lying if I said it wasn't.'

'No, no, no! That won't do at all.' The floor manager shook his head. 'No product placement on this show, they're very strict about that sort of thing. You're going to have to wear something else.'

'But I haven't brought anything else.'

'That won't do either. Can't have a naked man running for Prime Minister, not after what happened last time.'

'Why?' Anthony asked. 'What happened last time?'

'He almost won. For a few perilous moments the entire of England was poised on the brink of becoming the world's largest nudist colony.'

'Well, if it helps get voters…'

'Fortunately there is another option. Put your finger in your left armpit, please.'

'Excuse me?' Anthony scowled at the man.

'There should be a button there that restores your suit to its factory settings.'

Anthony gingerly probed his armpit, and located the button. His designer suit melted away into a drab grey object that even the lowliest of tramps would've been quick to reject.

'Better.' The floor manager smiled. 'Much, much better.'

'We're out of blusher!' the makeup girl declared.

The floor manager inspected Anthony critically. 'Worse,' he said, shaking his head. 'Much, much worse! We're just going to have to be very creative with the lighting.'

The makeup girl scampered off.

'Now, rules and regulations.' He began to pace up and down, but stopped when he noticed the vacant podium. 'Hold on, are we all here?'

'No, Hardcastle's missing,' Anthony said. 'Does this mean I win by default?'

'Dream on, sunshine!' Prime Minister Hardcastle strode up to the gold podium, flanked by two burly bodyguards, and flashed the floor manager a cosmetically enhanced grin. 'Sorry I'm late. Couple of foreign bods wanted a bit of a chinwag, but I think I managed to steer the conversation in a mutually beneficial direction.'

'They said yes?' The floor manager smiled hopefully.

Prime Minister Hardcastle nodded. 'Did they have a choice?'

'An audience of fifty billion…' The floor manager rubbed his hands together. The scent of promotion was in the air. 'Jack will be ecstatic. I'd best make sure the satellite feeds are set up and ready to roll.'

The Prime Minister snapped his fingers, and his bodyguards departed.

'Fifty billion viewers?' Anthony flicked a bead of sweat off the end of his mountainous nose.

'That's right,' Hardcastle said, casually checking his teeth in a pocket mirror. 'This election has just gone global. To the winner, absolute power and dominion over the entire world's population.'

'And to the loser?'

Hardcastle smiled nastily. 'Let's just say our android host has a very unusual taste in clothing…'

Grison chuckled to himself as the screen of the Psychic Autocue displayed a whole string of expletives, mostly directed at him.

'Yes,' he said into the headset that was connected to Anthony's thoughts, 'it is good news isn't it?'

Everyone in the world's going to be watching me, Anthony's panicked thoughts said across the screen. *Waiting for me to screw up!*

'No need to get in a tizzy,' Grison said. 'I'll be with you, every step of the way.'

Yes, laughing as I screw up.

'Program's starting,' Sampson hollered, his eyes fixed on the gigantic viewscreen that Anthony's entire force of campaign workers were huddled around.

'Just keep calm, stay focused, and the world will be ours for the taking,' Grison said.

Ours?

Grison cursed at his slip up. 'Well, Prime Minister of the world is hardly a one-man job, you know. You'll need loyal advisers; people with your best interests at heart. Now hush up – your host's about to make his grand entrance.'

On the viewscreen, a skin-clad android in a loud chequered shirt pranced his way down a staircase, to the delight of the studio audience. The android reached the bottom of the stairs and clanked across the stage towards a microphone stand. 'Grrrreeeeetings, fellow humans!' he cried, winking at the audience. An eye popped out. Someone in the audience caught it and threw it back.

Jack! Jack! Jack! Jack! the audience chanted.

Haranguer Jack held his hands out for silence. 'Welcome to another glorious episode of Haranguer Jack's Election Day Derby, and boy have we got a show for you! Firstly, I'd just like to say massive thanks to the previous election's runner-up, Dennis Riley, for having made such a generous donation to my wardrobe.' Jack did a little twirl, showing off his latest flesh-suit. 'I'm sure you'll agree that his sacrifice wasn't in vain. Don't I look dapper, ladies and gentlemen?'

A chorus of yeses erupted from the audience.

Another string of expletives scrolled down the screen in front of Grison.

'Relax,' Grison soothed, 'you're not going to lose, I'm on the case. I'll see you through this – all the way to the end. *Trust me!*'

'Whilst I'm at it,' Jack continued, 'I'd like to extend a hearty "Howdy-doo" or whatever the continental equivalent is, to all those viewers tuning in across the globe. Thank you for joining us for what promises to be the first ever world wide election!'

A loud fanfare erupted from Haranguer Jack's lips.

The audience cheered.

'And now, the main event!' Jack cried. 'In centre place, going for his twenty fifth consecutive year in office – it's Prime Minister Hardcastle!'

The camera cut to a close-up of Prime Minister Hardcastle's grinning maw. 'Vote for me,' he mouthed hurriedly. 'It's tradition.'

His score immediately rose.

'And to his right – dead, but still very much putting up a fight, it's Darren Katanga.'

The camera cut to a close-up of the urn. A jaunty, upbeat funeral dirge played out over the image.

'And finally, to Hardcastle's left we have Anthony "Don't call me Colin" Cresswell.'

The camera cut to a close-up of Anthony, and then zoomed out a bit so it could fit him all in.

'An ex-accountant with a planet in his head,' Haranguer Jack enthused. 'Let's hear it for that massive melon, ladies and gentlemen!'

The audience applauded Anthony's sizeable head.

'And now let's hear it for his lovely hat!' cried a voice from somewhere near the back of the audience.

The audience ignored it.

Rakembalo sat back down again, grumbling to himself.

'Don't forget, viewers, you can vote anytime at home using the buttons on your remote. Press red for Cresswell, yellow for Hardcastle, or blue for Katanga. Follow your selection up with the green button if you wish to deduct a vote.' Haranguer Jack glanced at the scoreboards on the front of the podiums. 'And as I see by Tony's score, you've already *found* that button.'

Chico and the professor glared at Grott as he very slowly put the remote control back down.

'Whoopsadaisy,' said Grott.

Professor Langerman cuffed him round the back of his head, and then hurriedly looked around for something to wipe his hand on. 'Excellent going. The first round hasn't even started, and thanks to you Anthony's already losing.'

'To a dead man, and a moron,' Chico added.

'It's not my fault I've got podgy fingers,' Grott whined. 'And the buttons are all too close together.'

'Don't you see what you've done?' the professor seethed. 'You've made Anthony look a complete fool. Now everyone else is going to follow your fine example and vote against him.'

'What's it matter?' Derek said, trying to be diplomatic. 'You've already made it perfectly clear that becoming Prime Minister isn't part of the plan.'

'Yes, but I've had time to think about it. If Anthony wins the election, no one's going to be able to stop him from leaving the planet. He'll be Prime Minister of the world, and able to do whatever he bloody well wants.'

'Fat chance of that happening.' Chico gestured to the image projected onto the wall opposite. 'He's on minus fifty points now.'

'Can't we just vote again?' Grott asked.

'Nope,' Derek said. 'One vote per TV licence. Since I'm the only one here licenced to use Bachelor Vision, we've already used it.'

'Then I guess there's only one thing for it.' The professor dislodged himself from the sofa and stood. 'There must be thousands of loyal licence payers living practically on our doorstep. All we need do is influence their votes, and Anthony might be in with a chance.' He glanced at the back door to the garage. 'How many people occupy this building, Derek?'

'I dunno, I keep myself to myself, mate. The neighbours insist on it.'

'Take a guess.'

Derek shrugged. 'One, maybe two hundred thousand. It's quite a small block, really.'

'Even if we got three hundred thousand people to vote for Tony, it still wouldn't be enough to beat Hardcastle's score,' Chico said.

'No, but it may be enough to turn the tide. Once the viewers realise that a lot of people are voting for Anthony, they might be more inclined to vote for him themselves. They'll start thinking he's popular. They might even start thinking his policies make sense.'

'So what's the plan?' Chico asked.

'The three of us are going to go door to door canvassing.'

'Three?' Derek looked around, and did a quick bit of mental arithmetic. 'There's four of us.'

'Your job, Derek, will be to keep us appraised of the situation with this communication device.' The professor tossed Derek his homemade walkie-talkie.

'So basically my part in this great plan of yours is to stay at home, drink beer, and watch the telly?' Derek said.

'In a nutshell.'

Derek lumbered keenly towards his industrial sized beer cooler. 'And you call yourself a genius? I could've thought of that!'

'How long does this show go on for?'

'About an hour, I think.'

'Then we haven't a moment to lose. *Grott!*' The professor said in his most commanding voice. 'You'll take the top floors. Chico, you'll take the middle floors. And I'll take the ground floor, because there's less stairs involved and it's furthest away from Grott.'

'How do you feel about the use of necessary violence in this particular endeavour, sir?' Chico asked innocently.

'Whatever it takes to get those votes, Chico.'

'And unnecessary violence?'

'Use your better judgement.'

Chico removed a full clip of ammo from his gun, and slammed in another fresh clip for dramatic effect. 'Let's go canvassing!'

Grison tapped in frustration at the Psychic Autocue's keyboard, and was greeted by another incomprehensible error message.

'Sampson!' he hollered.

Sampson tore his eyes from the viewscreen and rushed to his side. 'Yes, sir?'

'Why does that keep happening?'

Sampson peered at the error message. 'Depends. What are you trying to do?'

'I thought I'd have a quick peek inside Hardcastle's mind, and see what he's got planned.'

'Oh you won't be able to get in there. Not without the proper authorisation code.'

'You mean he's hacker proof?'

'That's right, sir. He had the security measures installed after that group of international Brain-Jack terrorists took him on a joyride through Newcastle.'

'Well, someone around this office must have the code.'

'Why?' Sampson asked, looking baffled. 'We're Cresswell's campaign workers, not Hardcastle's.'

Grison coughed. 'Uh, yes, right, of course. Just send Kate over, will you?' He glanced at the viewscreen. 'Scratch that, it'll have to wait. Looks like the first round's about to start.'

On the viewscreen, Prime Minister Hardcastle adjusted the comical naked lady tie which his chief advisers had assured him would guarantee a few extra votes from the youth sector, and leant towards the microphone on his podium.

'On this historic occasion –' he began.

A siren immediately sounded.

He cursed and tried again. 'In this time of change –'

The siren sounded once more.

'I…have a dream –' Hardcastle said cautiously.

The siren went into overdrive.

'Oh, what rotten luck,' Haranguer Jack cried, hanging his head theatrically. 'Let's have a round of applause for Prime Minister Hardcastle.'

The applause from the audience drowned out the vulgarities spewing forth from the Prime Minister's lips. Gradually the noise abated.

'Anthony, are you ready to take centre stage?'

Anthony fiddled nervously with the rim of his hat. 'Uh, I'm not quite sure I understand what I'm meant to do here.'

'It's quite simple, Anthony. In this first round each contestant is granted sixty seconds to make their opening statement, without saying the hidden sound bytes.'

'Just sixty seconds?'

'Beginning…*now!*'

A timer in the corner of the viewscreen started to count down.

'Uh, well, I, er…'

'Mind if I cut in?' Grison said into the P.A's headset. He tapped a key on the computer. On the viewscreen, Anthony straightened suddenly. Words began to tumble out his mouth as Grison dictated them. 'Prime Minister Hardcastle speaks of change, he speaks of peace, but he knows nothing of either. Indeed, if you were to ask him how to spell them he would find it a challenge at best.'

The audience sniggered.

'I mean, what has Hardcastle actually done to solve the population crisis? We've seen great sacrifices made by other nations, many of whom have joined us on this fine morning; Japan surrendered its independence by genetically amalgamating their entire population into one great super being. China shrunk everyone down to the size of an amoeba and have proceeded to lead a perfectly happy existence on the diet of a single grain of rice –'

'And let's not forget America,' Hardcastle interrupted. 'Who legalised cannibalism, and *ate* its surplus population. Or France, who outlawed sex, and then became so depressed about the situation that the entire nation committed suicide.'

Haranguer Jack held up a hand for silence. 'You've already had your say, Mr Hardcastle. Any more outbursts and I'll have to deduct votes.'

Anthony continued. 'My point being, up until now there have been many ways of dealing with the population crisis. But none of them have been quite as ridiculous as DON'T FORGET TO REGISTER! As ridiculous as DON'T FORGET TO REGISTER!'

Haranguer Jack stared at Anthony with suspicion radiating from his artificial eyes.

Grison ripped the P.A's headset off his ears, and snagged Sampson's arm. 'What the hell is going on?'

Sampson squinted at the monitor. 'Oh dear…I, er…'

'DON'T FORGET TO REGISTER! DON'T FORGET TO REGISTER!' Anthony's voice chanted from the viewscreen. The electoral staff watched in dismay as Anthony's rising score started to trail off and drop again.

Grison thumped the keyboard. 'What's wrong with this damned machine?'

'I – I – I must've installed the evaluation copy of the P.A. software by mistake!' Sampson blurted.

'– FORGET TO REGISTER! DON'T FORGET TO –'

Grison glanced up at the viewscreen. Minus two hundred votes…minus three hundred…minus four hundred…'It's going to lose Tony the election if you don't show me how to get rid of it.'

'Just, er, click the pop-up box in the corner.'

'– REGISTER! DON'T FORGET TO REGISTER! DON'T FORGET –'

'I've already tried that!'

Click! Click! Click!

'Try it some more. It'll get the hint eventually.'

Click! Click! Click! Click! Click! Click! Click!

'DON'T FORGET TO REGISTER! DON'T FORGET TO –' On the viewscreen, Anthony suddenly fell silent. The studio audience looked at him expectantly.

'Uh…technical difficulties.' Anthony tapped the side of his head. 'Grison?' he whispered. 'Are you there? Hello?'

'Ten seconds left,' Kate said, staring at the timer in the bottom corner of the viewscreen.

Grison grabbed the headset and thrust it over his ears. 'Let's hope it's enough time to undo the dama–' A wave of mental feedback ripped through the headset and burrowed into his brain. Piercing static ricocheted around his mind, threatening to split his skull open like an egg.

From the viewscreen, a gong sounded as the counter hit zero.

'Oh! Time's up!' Jack cried. 'Didn't he do well, ladies and gentlemen?' As the audience applauded, Jack glanced at the scores, and rapidly revised his last statement. 'No, it would appear he did not. Tony is now on minus five thou-sand points. Let's hope Darren Katanga fares slightly better.'

Grison slowly got to his feet. Steam was rising from him.

'You okay, sir?' Sampson asked.

'Mouth…tastes like…battery acid…' Grison spat on the floor and wiped the back of his trembling hand across his lips.

'I'll go put the kettle on, then,' Kate said cheerily.

Grison's vision slowly cleared. The computer containing the Psychic Autocue software was a smoking wreck. 'What just happened?'

'I guess Haranguer Jack doesn't like cheaters, sir,' Sampson said.

'How was he able to do that?'

'He's an android; probably using the same package we are. You're lucky he didn't melt your synapses.'

'Sure as hell felt like he did,' Grison said hoarsely. 'Can you fix it?' He motioned to the twisted molten mess that had once been a computer.

'Not a chance. I'll have to set up a new computer system, and reinstall the package.'

'How long will it take?'

'Half an hour. Forty five minutes, max.'

'You've got twenty,' Grison said. 'And make sure it's a licenced copy this time.'

'With respect, sir, what's the point? You can't influence our candidate's responses. Jack's onto you now. Tony would be disqualified, or worse yet, you'd be lobotomised.'

'Just get that P.A. back online,' Grison snapped, heading out the door. 'Everything depends upon it.'

The professor rapped gently on the first door he encountered.

It opened, with reluctance.

'Ah, hello.' The professor smiled warmly at the wary-looking occupant. 'Sorry to bother you. I stand representing the Cresswell party, and I was wondering –' The door slammed shut in his face. 'Okay, fine, never mind.'

He approached the next door and knocked, slightly more firmly. The door creaked open and two suspicious eyes peered out.

'Ah, hello.' The professor's warm smile heated up a few notches. 'A hearty good morning to –' The door creaked shut. 'No, no, you're quite right,' the professor said. 'Thanks for your time.'

He knocked on a third door. After a few moments, it opened.

'Ah, hello! It's national help a bearded stranger day, and boy are you going to do a good deed for me…'

'Bugger off!' cried a voice. The door closed again.

The professor stared at it. 'Right, that's it! I tried to be nice…' He began to disrobe. 'I didn't want to do this,' he said, raising his voice at the closed door, 'but you've really left me no alternative.'

He finished undressing, and knocked again.

The door swung open. 'Look, pal, I've already told you –' The angry tenant froze as his eyes settled on the naked elderly man standing outside his front door.

'Now that I've got your attention,' the professor said, 'what say you let me inside so we can have a bit of a political tête-à-tête, eh?'

'You're…you're…naked,' the tenant observed.

'That's right,' the professor agreed, 'and if you don't let me inside in five seconds flat, I'll knock on all your neighbours doors and tell them I'm your *dad.*'

'You wouldn't dare!'

'This is politics, son,' the professor said, smiling. 'Anything goes.'

Jack pranced back to the centre of the stage, accompanied by a loud fanfare. 'Round four!' he cried. 'The evasive answers round.'

The lights dimmed. A spotlight surrounded Anthony.

Haranguer Jack approached his podium. 'Anthony Tobias Cresswell. That is your name, correct?'

'That is correct, Jack,' Anthony said.

A buzzer sounded.

'Oh dear.' Haranguer Jack shook his head. 'You really haven't quite grasped the aim of this round, have you? Let's see how a pro handles it.'

The spotlight moved to highlight Prime Minister Hardcastle. Haranguer Jack followed it. 'Prime Minister Hardcastle. Feeling confident?'

'Well, I think that raises a valid point there, Jack,' the Prime Minister replied smoothly. 'I mean, in today's modern society is it still possible for a man to feel? Is it possible for a man to love? Is love just an abstract concept thrown together by greetings card manufacturers in order to turn a profit? And, if this proves to be the case, does this indicate that love can indeed be bought, from all participating retail outlets?'

Jack eyes shone with admiration. 'Excellent avoidance technique!' he cried. 'Completely failed to answer the question, threw up some irrelevant new ones, and went off on a wild tangent that ultimately led nowhere. All the hallmarks of a true politician.'

Hardcastle's score rose considerably.

The spotlight settled on Darren Katanga's urn. Jack approached it. 'Darren Katanga...still dead?'

Darren Katanga remained silent.

'Fantastic!' Jack enthused. 'Sometimes silence is the best response to an uncomfortable question. And, as your rapidly rising score seems to suggest, this was one such occasion. Anthony, back to you.'

Jack approached Anthony's podium. 'So, Anthony...do you like cake?'

'Love it,' Anthony said, smiling.

That familiar buzzer noise again.

Haranguer Jack grinned sardonically. 'You're not doing very well at all, are you?'

The spotlight returned to Hardcastle. 'Prime Minister Hardcastle. What's your opinion on the policies of your political opponents?'

'Well, Jack, when it comes down to it, are we not all trapped together in this harsh encumbering realm?' Hardcastle clutched a hand to his bosom. 'And is that not what life is truly all about? My father, god rest his soul, had a saying which I believe bears particular relevance to this situation. Is black *black?* Is white *white?* Could up be comfortably mistaken for down if there was but one true path through life? And, when it comes down to it, is that not what life is truly all about?'

Haranguer Jack shook his head in wonder. 'The "up the garden path" technique! A true professional indeed.'

Darren Katanga's urn lit up in the spotlight.

'Darren, there's been a lot of talk in the press that you may not be fit to compete in this election. Any comments?'

Darren Katanga remained silent.

The audience murmured disapprovingly.

'Oh dear. Looks like you milked the silent technique a little too much there, Darren.'

A buzzer sounded, signalling an end to the round.

'As we can see after that round, Hardcastle's storming into the lead with a cool fifty million votes. And chugging along behind with a laughable ten million votes, it's Anthony Cress...' Haranguer Jack's voice trailed off. He blinked in astonishment at the scoreboard. 'That can't be right.' He poked a finger in his ear. 'Are those scores correct, Hal?'

'I'm afraid so, Jack,' said a voice in his earpiece.

'Well!' Jack said. 'It appears we've underestimated young Tony. Not bad, not bad at all. But, before we make any assumptions, let's see how he fares in the popularity vote round.'

Grott's grubby little fist soiled the outside of a pristine white door.

It was answered by an upper class gentleman with a nose so severely upturned he could've drowned in a light drizzle.

'Morning, guv,' Grott said, grinning amiably.

'Whatever you're selling we've already got.' The wealthily-dressed tenant looked Grott up and down. 'And whatever you've got, we most certainly don't want.' He attempted to close the door, but found Grott's head wedged in it.

'Any tea?' Grott asked. His face was slowly turning blue, but it didn't seem to bother him.

'What?' the tenant said, releasing his pressure on the door.

'Got any tea?'

'Yes, plenty,' the man snapped. 'Now clear orf!'

Grott ducked under the tenant's arm, and pushed past him into the apartment.

'Now hang on a moment!' By the time the tenant had turned around, Grott had already made himself comfortable on the sofa.

'Any biscuits?' Grott asked, sipping from a tepid cup of tea he'd found on the coffee table.

'No, there aren't any ruddy biscuits! Now, what's all this –'

'Those look like biscuits.' Grott pointed a grubby digit at a plate of Rich Tea biscuits.

'Well you're not having one!'

'Can I have four then?' Grott shovelled the biscuits into his mouth without waiting for an answer.

The tenant glared at him. 'Is this going to take long?' he said through gritted teeth. 'I'm in the middle of watching something.'

On the TV screen opposite the sofa, Prime Minister Hardcastle was riding a unicycle whilst attempting to juggle. He was proving to be not particularly good at either.

'About as long as it takes to finish this biscuit,' Grott said, polishing off another biscuit. 'And that one,' he said, reaching for another.

'Dammit, man! Will you stop eating my food and drinking my drink, and tell me what you're selling?'

Grott looked confused; it was something he did remarkably well. 'Selling?'

'I assume you're here because you're selling something?'

'Nope.' Grott casually took another sip of tea.

'Ah, a charity worker is it?' The man looked Grott up and down again. 'Or a charity case, maybe?'

'Nope. Just going door to door.'

The tenant frowned at him. 'Doing what, may I ask?'

Grott leant forwards and pressed the little red button on the remote. 'That,' he said.

Anthony's score went up a point.

'Oh, you annoying little man! I was going to vote for Hardcastle.'

'Lucky I came along when I did then, isn't it?' Grott wandered back out of the door. 'Thanks for all the tea and biscuits.'

The gong sounded.

Prime Minister Hardcastle dismounted his unicycle, and took a bow.

'Well!' Haranguer Jack beamed. 'You're going to find that a tough act to follow. What talent will you be swaying the audience's affection with today, Anthony?'

'Uh, talent?' said Anthony.

'That's right. This is the popularity vote round, after all.'

'Well, I, uh, do have this planet in my head.'

'Yes, so you keep saying Mr One Trick Pony,' Hardcastle heckled. 'But can you juggle, sir? Can you juggle?'

'Well, no,' Anthony said. 'But neither could you. You were rubbish.'

'That's up to the audience to decide,' Jack said. 'And unless you put on a good show, they're not going to have much to judge it against. So...do you have any talents?'

Anthony racked his brain for a moment. 'I can count.'

'You can count?' Jack monotoned.

'Oh, and I can make tea.'

Jack tilted his head. 'Do you have a kettle on you?'

'Er, no.'

'Then you can't make tea, can you?'

'Well, er...'

Jack turned to the audience. 'Let's have a big round of applause for Anthony Cresswell, ladies and gentlemen, who will now *count* for your entertainment!'

Anthony cleared his throat. 'One,' he began. 'Two. Three. Four. Five...'

The program cut to an extended ad break, in which a much more suave and sophisticated Anthony attempted to sell the world a variety of different products that were guaranteed to bring the owners unimaginable wealth, or improve their sex lives in some inconceivable fashion. The break ended and the program returned to Anthony, still counting.

'Seven thousand four hundred and sixty eight,' he continued. 'Seven thousand four hundred and sixty nine –'

Prime Minister Hardcastle held up a card and coughed for attention. A gong sounded.

'Oh, I'm afraid I'm going to have to stop you there, Anthony,' Jack said, unsuccessfully feigning disappointment. 'Prime Minister Hardcastle's played the joker. Which, as I'm sure you're aware, means your last five thousand votes are automatically awarded to him.'

'That's not fair!' Anthony cried. 'How come I don't get a joker card?'

'Because you're not Prime Minister.' Hardcastle grinned.

'In that case,' Anthony said, holding up an imaginary card, 'I'm playing my "cheating bastard" card.'

'Oh dear,' Jack tutted. 'Another five thousand votes deducted from Anthony for swearing on live TV. And now, as we look at the scores, I'm sure we'll see no surprises…' Jack's voice trailed off as he looked at the scores. 'Well! It appears the ability to count is still highly prized in this society. Both Hardcastle and Cresswell are neck and neck with five billion votes apiece.' Jack shook his head in amazement. 'How the hell did *that* happen?'

Chico kicked in his eighteen thousand three hundred and seventy fifth door. 'Vote Cresswell,' he yelled, 'or I'll blow your friggin' head off!'

The occupant hurriedly obliged.

The trigger happy clone kicked in another door and commando rolled inside. 'Vote Cresswell!' he yelled, waving his gun at the startled occupants. Another few votes winged their way towards Anthony's scoreboard.

Chico commando rolled out the door, kicked in another, and commando rolled in. 'Vote Cressw–' He froze as he caught sight of the TV screen.

On it Anthony was kissing realistic baby dolls as they rolled towards him along a conveyer belt. As he picked one up and lifted it to his lips, the head dropped off and clattered to the ground.

Anthony back heeled it under the conveyer belt, and grinned hopelessly at the camera. 'Uh, this isn't going to count against me is it?'

The tenant's finger slowly crept towards the remote's yellow button.

Chico pressed a gun against the side of his head. 'I understand where you're coming from,' he sympathised, 'truly I do. But I'm afraid I just can't let you do that.' He grabbed the remote, sighed deeply, and pressed the red button.

Grison strolled back into the office. A Champaign cork whizzed by overhead. 'Sampson! Have you got that P.A. operational yet?'

'I most certainly have, but I don't think you're going to need it,' Sampson said, offering Grison an overflowing glass of bubbly. 'Our candidate's storming into the lead.'

Grison waved the glass away. 'You mean Cresswell's actually winning?'

'That's right, sir.'

'Without me? *Impossible.*' Grison looked to the viewscreen for confirmation.

Anthony was ten votes ahead.

'It's going to be a close one, sir.'

'Not if I can help it.' Grison sat down in front of the newly installed P.A. system. 'Whilst Jack's keeping an eye on Tony's mind, let's see if we can sneak into Hardcastle's.'

'I've already told you, we don't have the access code.'

Grison handed Sampson a piece of paper. 'We do now.'

He uncrumpled it, and read it through. 'The code to Hardcastle's mind! Where did you get it?'

'Kate's office.'

'I have an office?' Kate said.

'You did have until I wiped your mind.' Grison's finger casually stroked the delete key. 'Whoops! There it goes again.'

Kate stared at him blankly.

Grison slipped a tea tray into her hands. 'Two sugars, Kate.'

She wandered off in a daze.

'Okay, Sampson,' Grison snatched the piece of paper back from Sampson's unresisting fingers. 'Show me how to input this code.'

Sampson dribbled at him.

'Oh come off it! I only erased your short-term memory,' Grison snapped. 'Hop to it, you lazy bastard.'

'Well!' Haranguer Jack said, spinning round to face the Prime Minister. 'I'd certainly like to hear what Hardcastle has to say about *that*.'

Hardcastle stared blankly at the ceiling. A thin thread of drool trickled from the corner of his mouth.

'Prime Minister?' Jack waved a hand in front of his face. 'Hello…?'

Hardcastle blinked. 'Hm? What?'

'It's your turn, Prime Minister.'

Hardcastle looked around himself in confusion. 'My turn at what?'

'To build a sleaze campaign.'

'Oh, right. It's that round already is it?'

'That's right, the final round. Your last chance to slag off your competitors and narrow that gap in the scores.'

'Gap?' Hardcastle said. 'There's a gap?' He bent over the podium to get a better look at the scoreboard. Anthony was eighteen votes ahead. 'Oh no. Oh no, no, no, no, no,' He tutted. 'That won't do at all. Cresswell should be much further ahead by now. What's wrong with you people?' He shook his head at the audience.

'Are you sure you're all right, Mr Hardcastle?'

'What? Yes, never felt better. Apart from this tie, of course.' Hardcastle loosened his naked lady tie and thrust it at the camera. 'I mean, come on people! Doesn't that tell you everything you need to know? I can barely dress myself with any degree of success, let alone run an entire planet.'

'A word of caution, Mr Hardcastle,' Jack interjected. 'The objective here is to insult the opposition, not yourself.'

'Face it folks, you'd be much better off with someone else in charge.' Hardcastle strode over to Anthony, and dangled a comradely arm over his shoulder. 'And I'm nominating Cressface here for the job.'

Anthony raised a quizzical eyebrow. *'Cressface?'*

Hardcastle winked at him.

'Mr Prime Minister, are you trying to throw this election?' Jack said sternly.

'I hardly think I need try,' Hardcastle said. 'Not with someone as courageous and charismatic as young Cresswell here to go up against.'

'That's me, all right,' Anthony said, grinning.

'Foregone conclusion, if you want my opinion. This election has Cresswell written all over it.'

'How kind of you to say so.' Jack stared closely at Hardcastle. 'And deeply suspicious. Are you sure these words are your own?'

'Look at it this way,' Hardcastle said, 'if I lose you'll have a new outfit to add to your collection, and boy is it a handsome-looking number.' He did a little twirl.

Jack stroked his chin thoughtfully. 'That's a good point.'

'And how many people in this world can say they own a genuine Hardcastle original?' Hardcastle said, laying his sales pitch on thick. 'An outfit for all occasions. Be the envy of your friends, the life of the party, the catch of the day.'

'Keep talking,' Jack said.

'Are you seriously telling me you'd even contemplate wearing this sorry-looking item here?' He tugged roughly at Anthony's swollen cheek. 'I mean look at it. Damaged goods, if you want my opinion. You'd have to wrap the head around ten times just to make it fit.'

Jack inspected Anthony with a sneer on his face. 'Oh god, yes, you're right,' he said. 'I'd be a laughing stock.'

Anthony pressed his buzzer in objection. 'Hey, steady on!'

'So I guess there's only one thing for it, isn't there?' Hardcastle beamed.

Jack signalled to the floor manager, who approached with a golden TV remote held upon a velvet cushion. A drum roll sounded. Jack took hold of the remote and, as the drum roll reached the crescendo, pressed a red button.

Anthony's score went up a point.

'Anthony Cresswell for Prime Minister!' Jack cried.

The audience cheered.

Anthony took a bow.

'People of the world I urge you…no, beg you.' Hardcastle dropped to his knees. 'Vote for Tony, the man who dares to care. Change the world, make a difference, put meaning back into your lives. In fact, here –' Hardcastle got to his feet, and handed Anthony his joker card. 'Have a few of my votes, lad. It's not like they count for anything.'

Anthony raised the card. A gong sounded, and five thousand votes were instantly transferred from Hardcastle's score to his own. As the rest of the world followed suit, Anthony's score doubled, tripled, and then crashed under the sheer weight of numbers passing through it.

'Thirty billion votes!' Jack cried, once the scoreboard had been fixed and finalised. 'That's more than two thirds of the planet's population.'

'Then it's unanimous,' Hardcastle said. 'Planet Earth has a new Prime Minister. A man who will bring peace and freedom to all.'

The studio audience whooped and cheered enthusiastically.

'And my wardrobe has a new outfit!' Jack proclaimed.

The studio audience whooped and cheered again.

'And now, as my final act as Prime Minister I can think of no greater way to usher in this new age of peace –' Hardcastle's arm constricted around Anthony's shoulders. '– than by declaring *war* on planet Tony!'

More whooping and cheering from the studio audience. And then silence. Deathly silence.

'Er, what?' said Anthony.

'And since this is a war situation, voting for the enemy is an act of treason, punishable by death.' Hardcastle pointed an accusing finger at the camera. 'Those of you who have already voted – we know who you are, we know where you live. Your treachery will be dealt with!'

Sixteen

'Vote Cresswell!' Chico yelled as he kicked in Derek's door, and commando rolled inside.

'Little late for that, chief.' Derek's eyes were glued to the 'please stand by' message projected onto the wall.

'What's the verdict?' asked the professor, as he stepped over the splintered door and made for the sofa.

'First things first,' Derek said, looking the professor up and down, 'why are you naked?'

Professor Langerman waved a dismissive hand. 'Oh, a couple of people wouldn't play ball, so I had to scare them a little.'

'Well, you're scaring *me* now.' Derek attempted to tear his eyes away, but morbid curiosity kept dragging them back. 'Any chance you could put some clothes on, chief?'

'Oh, if I must,' the professor grumbled.

Grott trailed in, munching on a scone. 'Did we win?'

'It's sort of a good news/bad news scenario,' said Derek. 'Except mostly without the good news.'

'What's that noise?' Chico asked, straining his ears. In the distance it sounded like a herd of angry wildebeests were migrating purposefully towards them.

'At a guess, I'd say it's a gathering mob of enraged tenants, furious at the fact that you've just more or less convinced them all to commit suicide,' said Derek casually.

The noise grew louder, to the point where they could make out individual expletives and death threats.

'Tell you what, Derek,' the professor said, hurriedly buttoning his lab coat, 'why don't you tell us all about it whilst we flee for our lives?'

Etnor Buckwhistle, 69th President of the United States, pilfered a cigar from the Columbian delegate sat next to him at the Virtual Counsel table, bit off the end, spat it at the President of Russia, struck a match on the Indian Prime Minister's forehead, and exhaled a thick plume of holographic smoke in Prime Minister Hardcastle's face. 'Let's get diplomatic here,' he said. 'Hardcastle, I've known you for quite some years now, and in that time I've always considered you to be a bit of an ass. But you're the sort of ass that I *admire*.'

Hardcastle raised a questioning eyebrow.

'The kind of ass that doesn't take any crap from other people's asses.'

A second inquisitive eyebrow rose to join the first.

'But if your ass is gonna persist in taking hostile actions against my ass, it's gonna find itself out there on the firing line, being shot at by all these other asses.' Etnor swept an arm out to take in the room full of baffled-looking delegates. 'Are we clear?'

The delegates exchanged glances.

Several translators made swiftly for the virtual exit.

'I don't think so, no,' Hardcastle said.

'I think what the President's trying to say,' the Indian Prime Minister, Vihaan Kapoor, cut in, 'is we believe you may have acted a little overzealously.'

The world leaders bobbed their heads up and down in agreement.

'Well, I think my ass analogy was better,' Etnor grumbled.

'This isn't a popularity contest,' Prime Minister Kapoor said sharply. 'We're here to address a very serious matter. Hardcastle has threatened to cull the people of our lands.

He has stolen a planet, and robbed humanity of its one chance for a new start in life.'

'Yes, so let's have no more of this silliness, eh?' Etnor stubbed out his cigar in Prime Minister Kapoor's coffee. 'Hand over Cresswell to us and we'll say no more about it.'

'By "us",' Hardcastle said, 'I take it you mean you?'

'Well, hey, can you think of anyone more deserving?' The American president grinned.

The hands of all assembled waved in the air.

Etnor let out a snort of derision. 'Oh please, you guys don't even have proper countries.' He hoisted a fat digit at the President of Iraq. 'Yours is full of *sand* for starters; it's basically just one giant children's play pit. No, I'm definitely the man most qualified for the job. I've got plans, people. Ideas…visions. In my hands this brave new world, or "Big Mac" as a couple of our sponsors prefer to call it, is gonna be a five-star tourist paradise. Just imagine yourself traipsing through the Coca-Cola continent, or taking a magical journey through a Disneyland the size of Russia –'

'And just where would that be built?' the President of Russia asked, fixing Etnor with her steely gaze.

'Ooh, could be anywhere,' Etnor said swiftly, 'anywhere at all. The point I'm trying to make is this: I'm bigger than you, and I've got all the nukes.' The President of America settled back in his chair. 'Any objections?'

'Not all of them,' the President of Iraq said fiercely.

'Yes,' the President of Russia agreed. 'Not all of them.'

'In fact, you sold me five only last Thursday,' said the President of Italy.

'All right, okay…' Etnor rolled his eyes. 'I've got all the nukes that I didn't sell to other countries.'

'So,' Hardcastle said, 'round about none of them?'

The world leaders chuckled collectively.

Etnor's face reddened. 'I've still got more than enough to turn your country into a tea stain on the map!'

'You'd have to find it on the map first,' Hardcastle said. 'And that, I believe, would be half the challenge.'

'Oh! Right! It's like *that* is it?' Etnor rolled his sleeves up, and clenched both podgy fists. 'That's a reason, that is. That's a reason! You're history, pal!'

'Go ahead, fire away. Just one slight problem – you might hit Cresswell.'

'Ha! I'll just aim where he *isn't*.'

'To do that you'd first need to know where he *is*,' Hardcastle countered.

Etnor folded his arms defiantly. 'What makes you think we don't already have him?'

'Because you keep asking me to hand him over,' said Hardcastle simply.

'Ah. Right.' Etnor unfolded his arms again, and went in for a spot of stern finger waggling. 'But it won't be long before we *do* have him. We've got some of our best undercover agents scouring the English megascape as we speak. They're masters of disguise, trained in the art of English etiquette. You won't even know they're among you before it's too late.'

Hardcastle casually stirred his tea. 'One of these agents wouldn't happen to be a strapping six foot tall Texan transvestite, by any chance?'

Both of Etnor's eyes competed with each other over which could be the twitchiest. 'I can neither confirm nor deny that rumour,' he said through gritted teeth.

'It's just we recently apprehended one as he attempted to land a giant glitter ball on the Administration building's rooftop. Once he'd finished signing autographs and making a pass at anything with a pulse, we made him an offer that he could not refuse.' Hardcastle smiled tightly. 'He works for us now.'

'You *turned* my agent?' Etnor lurched violently to his feet. 'Gimme one good reason why I shouldn't just reach over this table and crush your neck with my bare hands!'

'Aside from the fact that this is a holographic virtual environment, you'd have to lose some weight first,' said Hardcastle coolly. 'And we certainly don't have time for *that*. Still, if it makes you feel any better, I swear to you on pain of death that I won't execute a single one of your countrymen.'

'You won't?' said Prime Minister Kapoor.

'No.' Hardcastle's grin widened. 'It'll be much more fun to have *you* do it.'

The presidents and dignitaries exchanged confused glances.

'Um,' said Prime Minister Kapoor. 'You, uh, want us to kill our own people?'

'Not just kill, I'm talking full-on nuclear Armageddon here. After all, we're on a tight schedule, people. We have a birth rate to contend with.'

'You want us to *nuke* our own countries?' Etnor screamed.

'Oh, heavens, no,' Hardcastle chuckled. 'I want you to nuke each others.'

'Pal, you're out of your mind,' rumbled Etnor. 'Why the hell would we do such a thing?'

'Because I'll give you and your loved ones safe passage off this planet if you do. I already have a spaceship, of sorts, all fuelled up and ready to go.'

'I'm president of the freakin' USA, boy,' Etnor snarled. 'If I wanted passage off this sorry-ass planet I'd arrange it myself. We invented space travel.'

'I think you'll find that was us, comrade,' said the President of Russia.

'Ha! Shooting monkeys at the moon hardly counts.'

'You did the monkeys, we did the dogs. Use an education booth!'

'Don't have them in America.' Etnor sniffed. 'We favour the Hollywood movie education system.'

Hardcastle settled back in his seat. 'How about if, to sweeten the deal, I also give you Cresswell?'

A cacophony of scheming whispers filled the room. Gradually the noise abated as caution overcame greed.

'Just like that?' said the President of Russia. 'You'll hand over the planet?'

'That's right, I'm offering you a way out of this predicament – a planet all of your own to evenly divide among yourselves. A younger, sexier Earth, not this middle-aged sagging mess we've been lumbered with.' Hardcastle shook his head sadly, laying on the theatrics. 'Face facts, people, this world has fallen into disrepair. It is little more than a sick, ageing arthritic old nag that's had its day. Show the poor creature some mercy, and do what you know in your hearts to be right; inject it with your nuclear needles of justice. End the suffering.'

'Never!' Etnor bellowed, banging his fists on the table. 'United we stand, divided we fall. You will *never* get us to turn against each other!'

The President of Turkey swiftly raised his hand. 'Bags I get to nuke America.'

'Awww...I wanted America,' grumbled the President of Russia.

'I've got dibs on Russia.'

'Why pick on us, comrade?'

'Went there for a holiday once. Bloody cold, and full of foreigners.'

'I'll show you cold! I call Iraq.'

'Right, well in that case I'm taking Egypt.'

'But you're the President of Egypt.'

'That's right.' The President of Egypt folded his arms defiantly. 'And if anyone's gonna nuke it, it's gonna be me.'

'Brothers...sisters...heyyy, surely there must be a *peaceful* solution?'

'Oh, I am *so* nuking India...'

A huge misshapen mass covered in thousands of tiny mouths slunk in through the virtual door, and took a seat. 'Excuse please the lateness of our arrival,' said the amalgamated population of Japan. 'Did we miss anything?'

The presidents and dignitaries exchanged glances.

'*Dibs!*'

Seventeen

Derek weaved erratically down a one-way air lane, tooting in protest at those vehicles brazen enough to be travelling up it the right way.

''Ere, we're just like the dirty dozen or something,' Grott piped up from the back seat.

'Except there's only four of us,' the professor observed.

'All right then. The dirty...the dirty...'

'Bastards?' volunteered Chico.

'Pants?' suggested Derek.

Professor Langerman massaged his eyelids with his fingertips. 'Can you please stop trying to think of a name for our little outfit, and let me concentrate on the task at hand?'

'Certainly, sir,' said Chico. 'Have you got a fix on Tony yet?' He craned forward from the rear passenger seat, and attempted to get a look at the juddering image on the navigation console.

'It would help if our course remained a little more steady,' snapped the professor.

'I'll straighten up once I've shaken off these clingy sods.' Derek zigzagged through the oncoming traffic, whilst a small horde of angry tenants clung desperately to his rooftop, screaming obscenities. 'What is it with you and enraged mobs?'

'Just ignore them, Derek,' the professor said, 'you'll only encourage them.'

'Well you sort of encouraged them,' Derek replied, 'by forcing them to vote for Tony.'

'Even so, I still think they're overreacting.'

'Good thing one of us had the common sense to vote against him, eh?' said Grott smugly.

'This is all your fault,' Chico snapped.

'How is it my fault?'

'I haven't quite figured that part out yet,' Chico admitted. 'But I will. I'm onto you!'

The professor wound his window down and poked his head out at the raging rabble of disenchanted voters. 'Come on, chaps. A joke's a joke.'

'You bastards!' a voice hollered back from outside. 'You've murdered us all!'

'That sounded like Miss Dempson from number thirty two,' Derek said, listening keenly.

'And give me back my bloody toenail clippers!' the voice added.

Derek did a loop the loop, sending the mob tumbling down towards the huge pink sea of writhing limbs that lay a short distance below. 'Mine now,' he said.

'What the hell is all that?' the professor said, looking down.

'Human jam,' said Derek. 'That's what you get when everyone in the city tries to flee at once.' He moved in for closer inspection.

Hundreds of vehicles had already become embedded in the half-mile high mass, being swept slowly along with its treacherous tide. Occasionally, a Population Control catch wagon would swoop in and scrape off easy pickings from the crowd with one of their giant catch nets, to be 'processed' up against the wall of the local station.

'Don't let those fingers touch you!' Chico warned. 'If we get caught in this, we'll never get out again.'

Derek pulled up at the last minute to avoid scores of desperate grasping hands. 'How are we supposed to find Tony in this?'

'Just look for the person with the hugest head, who everybody's punching,' suggested Chico.

'Administration Headquarters,' said the professor, staring at the blip on the navigation console.

'You want us to fly straight into the heart of the gazelle's den?' said Derek.

'Something like that, yes,' said the professor. 'According to the tracking beacon I placed in Anthony's cranium, that's where they're keeping him. The only question is whether we go in stealthily via the roof, or noisily via the front door. Chico, I'll leave it to you to decide.'

There came a triumphant cry from the back seat, followed by the deafening noise of eight guns somehow being cocked simultaneously.

'Front door it is, then,' Professor Langerman sighed.

Grison stood at the bottom of the landing ramp of the good ship Chastity, watching the world leaders arrive in a staggering assortment of city hoppers, supersonic gliders, bullet-planes, cloud shifters, pulse rockets and air limos.

'Thank you all for coming ladies, gentleman and...' His eyes fell upon the small crowd of buxom women and well-tanned men with improbably proportioned appendages, who were carrying the world leaders' luggage. 'Oh for cryin' out loud, who brought the sex clones?'

As one, the world leaders timidly raised their hands.

'You do realise they're engineered to have a twenty-four hour life cycle, yes?'

'But boy what a ride,' leered Etnor Buckwhistle.

'When Hardcastle said you could bring your loved ones, I doubt this is what he had in mind,' Grison said. 'I rather think he meant husbands...wives...families.'

'I brought a pig,' volunteered a voice from somewhere near the back of the group.

The President of America heaved his vast bulk up the ramp, and stood nose-to-nose with Grison. 'Who the hell are you, anyway? Where's Hardcastle?'

'Sorry, forgot we hadn't met in the flesh. I'm Philip Grison, Campaign Manager, and representative of Cresswell Planets Incorporated.' Grison held out a hand, and then withdrew it before Etnor could shake it. 'Unfortunately Hardcastle's unable to attend in person, though he will be with us in spirit.'

Right on cue, a loud fanfare erupted from the top of the landing ramp, and a skin-clad android pranced towards them, clanking and grinning.

'I believe you're all familiar with the popular game show host, Haranguer Jack?'

'Good god! What, or perhaps more accurately, who is he wearing?' Etnor's lip curled up in distaste. 'Is that Hardcastle?'

'Thank you for noticing, my good man.' Haranguer Jack did a pirouette in his brand new skin suit. 'I feel fab-u-lous!'

'I *knew* it!' cried Prime Minister Kapoor. 'The election was rigged. No wonder Hardcastle threw in the towel when he was so close to winning. You brain-jacked him during his speech!'

'What of it?' Grison shrugged. 'Our deal remains the same, and as you can see I am a man of my word. Harangeur Jack was promised a brand new skin suit for his cooperation, and doesn't he look dapper?'

Harangeur Jack gave a curtsey, making his new face slide around in a distinctly unsettling fashion.

'Now, if you'll be so good as to write down your nuclear launch codes on the scraps of paper that Mr Jack will be distributing among you, we'll get this apocalypse rolling.'

'No way, pal,' Etnor said fiercely. 'Not until we've seen Cresswell. A deal's a deal.'

'Very well.' Grison beckoned them aboard the ship. 'Follow me, everybody.'

The world leaders stood there, shuffling their feet, glancing impatiently at the door that led to the stairwell.

'Oh, and if you're waiting for your agents and assassins to converge upon this location and wrestle Cresswell from my dastardly clutches, I feel it's only fair to warn you that they've been delayed…in a most terminal sense of the word.' Grison gave the headset of his Psychic Autocue a meaningful tap. 'Just thank your lucky stars you're all hacker-proof, which is more than can be said for the amalgamated population of Japan.'

He gestured to a megascraper opposite, which had a colossal enraged blob slowly oozing its way up the outside, swiping its amorphous limbs at passing hover cars.

'Shall we?' Grison beamed.

Muttering and grumbling, the world leaders reluctantly mounted the spaceship's ramp.

They walked across mirrored floors, past countless minibars and beauty salons. Intricate glass tubes packed with brightly-coloured tropical fish criss-crossed the corridors overhead, and a selection of increasingly unpopular musical hits menaced their ears from a concealed tannoy system.

'What's with all the karaoke booths?' asked Etnor as they passed another small, distastefully decorated cubicle.

'Escape pods, actually,' said Grison.

'They have disco balls in them,' said the President of Russia stiffly.

'More a case of style over practicality, I fear.'

Colourful floor tiles lit up beneath their feet as they moonwalked across the Disco Deck, and then schmoozed their way through the Lava Lamp Lounge.

'Hey there!' called a voice, as they passed beauty salon number sixteen. 'With you fellas in two shakes of a steer's tuchus. Just getting the ol' stars and stripes waxed.'

'Don't rush on our account,' said Grison, moving hastily on.

'*Traitor!*' Etnor Buckwhistle hollered as he passed.

The President of Italy knocked back something luminous and alcoholic he'd snagged from one of the bars. 'Wasn't that Wendigo Malfortune?'

'Yes, he's the pilot,' said Grison. 'Heard of him, have you?'

'The guy's a living legend,' the President of Italy breathed. 'According to several well-respected tabloids, he's singlehandedly responsible for spreading venereal diseases to all four corners of the known galaxy.'

'Since the known galaxy extends about as far afield as Essex,' Grison said, 'I find that surprisingly easy to believe.'

'Um,' said the President of Egypt, glancing back down the corridor and scratching the tip of his nose. 'Where'd all our, uh, recreation clones go?'

From a little further down the corridor, there came the familiar 'pop' of a Champaign cork, and giggling.

'I believe Wendigo may have diverted them,' Grison smirked. 'Right, we're there.' He stopped at the door to a supply closet, unbolted it, and took a step back as Anthony barrelled out, screaming at the top of his lungs, swinging a mop handle.

He barely made it two steps before his oversized head wedged in the doorframe, whipping him off his feet and suspending him in the air like a marionette puppet.

'So, this is Anthony Cresswell,' Grison said, gesturing to the fat-headed man who was wriggling pitifully away in an attempt to free himself, 'saviour of the human race.'

Without waiting for further introductions, Etnor brandished a permanent marker and advanced.

'Right, here's what I propose we do. We split the planet down the middle, fifty-fifty.'

'Hey,' cried Anthony indignantly, his pinprick eyes glaring out from deep within the vast mass of rippling facial topography, 'that's my face!'

'Don't talk – you'll make my line go wiggly,' commanded the President, scrawling away. 'So, I'll take this half and you lot can take that half. All even-steven, yeah?'

The President of Egypt stepped forward and critically appraised Anthony's ink-stained features. 'Our half looks considerably smaller,' he grumbled. 'More like an eighth, in fact.'

'It's hardly my fault his head's all wonky.'

Anthony cast a sidelong glance at Grison. 'What's going on?' he demanded. 'Where am I? Who are these jokers? Did you declare war on me?'

'Certainly did,' Grison beamed. 'And then you had a panic attack like this one, and I was forced to administer a mild sedative to calm you down.'

'You punched me in the face!' Anthony snapped.

'That's right, I chose to administer the sedative in the form of a fist.' Grison drew his knuckles back. 'Observe.'

The fist ploughed into Anthony's face, making his limp body swing back and forth in the doorway like a pendulum.

Etnor Buckwhistle grinned in admiration. 'Hey fella, did you just punch out a planet?'

'It's quicker this way,' said Grison, picking a tiny splinter of Mount Kilimanjaro out of his knuckles. 'He does tend to whinge on a bit.'

Harangeur Jack retrieved Anthony's hat from the floor, brushed it off, and upturned it. 'Okay everyone, please place your country's name and launch code in Tony's massive hat and we'll get this nuclear tombola rolling.'

'Ooh, ooh, will there be prizes?' asked Prime Minister Kapoor.

'Yes,' said Grison. 'If you pull out a launch code belonging to someone else, you get to nuke their country.'

'Doesn't sound like much of a prize,' the Prime Minister of India sniffed.

'And you get a lovely badge,' added Harangeur Jack, 'which states: "end nuclear testing now".'

'Ooh, ironic. I like it.' Prime Minister Kapoor cheerily scribbled on a piece of paper, popped it in the hat, and offered it round.

Grison flicked a switch on the ship's internal visi-com, making sure to mute the picture first. 'Wendigo, if you've quite finished violating those sex clone's warranties, any chance you could get this neon nightmare moving? The party's just about to get started.'

'Party never stopped rolling at my end, baby,' Wendigo Malfortune's bourbon-soaked voice crackled back over the visi-com. 'Though y'all gonna have to put yer own party on hold. Got a few other passengers to meet an' greet first.'

The President of Russia deposited the last of the nuclear codes into Anthony's hat, gave it a vigorous shake, and handed it to Etnor. 'Others?' she said. 'I thought our ride was exclusive.'

'Never let it be said that Wendigo Malfortune was an exclusive ride, baby. Got a prior commitment to a coupla rodeo Joe's ah picked up in a bar last night. Nice fellas, ah'm sure you'll get on famously.'

Etnor pulled out a scrap of paper from the hat, read it, grunted, put it back, pulled out another one, frowned at it, put it back, pulled out a third one, grinned widely and shook it at Grison. 'Yes! I got England! In your *face*, you Limey loser!' He lifted up his sweat-stained 'Make America Freakin' Awesome' t-shirt and performed a celebratory Truffle Shuffle. 'Someone get me a holo-phone, I've got a call to make.'

'Unless you want to be sat slap-bang in the middle of a nuclear explosion,' Grison said back into the visi-com, 'you might want to give those other fares a miss.'

Chico charged in through the door to the Administration building, performed an impressive array of cartwheels, somersaults and flips, and tumbled over a mound of corpses.

'Congratulations! You're our hundredth gun-toting customer of the day,' said the receptionist, eagerly rattling a tin of sweets. 'Have a boiled sweetie.'

'Got any balloons?' asked Grott, as he and the professor edged in through the door with considerably less flair than Chico.

The unhinged clone scrambled to his feet, stormed over to the reception desk, and thrust the barrel of his P74 Argument Settler under the receptionist's nose. 'Did *you* do this?'

'Oh shush, no, I'm just a humble receptionist,' Mr Pickler beamed. 'It was the darnedest thing, actually. Their faces went blank, their eyes crossed, and then they just sort of started murdering each other. I tried to encourage them to hold hands and sing songs of spiritual unity, but there's just no helping some people.'

Chico threw his gun down on the floor in disgust. 'An honest-to-god continental gun battle, and I missed it!'

'On the plus side,' said the professor, 'at least you're still alive. Come on, let's go see if we can locate Anthony.'

After hijacking the sweets tin and going floor by floor, they finally made it to the roof, just in time to see a spaceship depart in an impressive cloud of rainbows and glitter. 'And there he goes,' said the professor. 'Along with our ride, if I'm not mistaken.'

'What makes you so sure that's our ride?' asked Chico.

'Oh, just call it a hunch,' said the professor, combing glitter out of his beard.

'So, now what?' asked Grott, rubbing his hairy hands keenly together. 'Pub?'

A smile crept stealthily across the professor's wrinkled face. 'Indeed, this calls for a celebration.'

'Celebration of what?' said Chico.

'Getting Anthony off the planet before he exploded and took the entire human race with him, of course.'

Chico's eyes narrowed. 'I thought the plan was to take him to Mars and convince the aliens there to remove the planet from his head before that happened?'

Professor Langerman shrugged. 'I made them up. No such thing as aliens, every rational man knows that.'

'I didn't,' said Grott.

'Which rather proves my point,' said the professor. 'At least this way we don't have to explode alongside Anthony. All's well that ends –'

A high-pitched wail, like a million cats suddenly suffering an existential crisis, tore through the city, making buildings judder, teeth grind, and giant amorphous blobs scream in rage and punch helicopters. Those still caught in the human-jam below surged forwards in renewed panic, swarming like ants over everything in their path.

'What's that noise?' Chico yelled over the din.

'Air raid siren,' said the professor stiffly. He was old enough to remember its ear-piercing din from the I.Q. Wars of 2197, in which six of the biggest, smartest countries sent their least intelligent populace out to fight each other for no apparent reason, just to see if they'd do it. Needless to say, it was a resounding success, and came with the added bonus that the reality TV industry was practically wiped out overnight.

The stench of curry and cheap cologne assaulted their noses, as Derek touched shakily down on the rooftop. 'You might want to listen to the radio, lads,' he said, squelching his doors open.

They reluctantly clambered inside, as Derek skimmed through the channels. All of them were playing the same sombre tune.

'– imminent nuclear attack,' said the newscaster. 'Repeat! Missiles have been launched at England, seemingly by our allies in the USA. Someone clearly got out of the wrong side of the bed in the Black and White House this morning.' The newscaster chuckled nervously. 'But don't fret, I have just been informed that we have already launched our own retaliatory nuclear strike, er, apparently against Bulgaria. Not quite sure what Bulgaria has to do with this, but they'll certainly think twice before invading our fair shores, yes indeed.'

'So, Derek, these lung extensions of yours,' the professor said casually. 'Reckon they're up for a road test?'

Derek hurriedly shovelled an emergency extra-hot chilli and bean curry into the hole in his dashboard, and ignited the noxious fumes. 'Please fasten your seatbelts and make sure your seats are in an upright position,' he said. 'Oh yeah, and you might want to wind those windows up a bit,' he added as an afterthought.

With a leap and a fart, he rocketed into the stratosphere.

Eighteen

Aboard the good ship Chastity there was music, laughter, finger foods and party hats. Whilst recreation clones strutted their improbably proportioned stuff on the dance floor, the world leaders stood upon the observation deck, sipping Martinis and squinting through extra-long lens opera glasses at the drab blue planet below. Any moment now, they promised to be treated to an absolute belter of a fireworks display.

'Ten, nine, eight, seven…'

The President of Columbia gave his maracas a vigorous shake, building up the tension.

'Six, five, four…'

The world leaders put down their drinks, and joined hands.

'Three, two, one…'

Paff!

The first nuclear missile hit its target, triggering a veritable Mexican wave of explosions. All over the world, ugly fat mushroom clouds blossomed like vengeful flowers.

'Oooooh!' said the world leaders, as the magnificent floating cities of Stockholm evaporated in a whiff of napalm.

'Ahhhhhh!' they breathed, as the colossal ice sculpture known as Greenland melted into nothingness.

'Eeeeeeee!' they squealed, as one of the missiles went vastly astray and annihilated the International Space Station and Starbucks.

Down at ground level, people were running, screaming, crying, vomiting and dying. It was, in many ways, just like any other Friday night, except in this case a bit more final.

Upon the rooftop of the Administration building, Nigel, Mr Pickler, and a handful of other dishevelled-looking employees stood watching the nuclear sunrise.

'Turned out nice again,' Nigel observed, incorrectly.

'Hang on a bally moment!' Mr Pickler exclaimed, fondling his top lip. 'I used to have a moustache!'

The blast hit. Acid rain rolled across England's black and burning shores, giving those few survivors who weren't carrying their melted eyeballs in a knotted handkerchief one last brief opportunity to have a bit of a grumble about the weather.

And then silence.

Up aboard the good ship Chastity, Etnor Buckwhistle hummed the few bars of the Star-Spangled Banner that he could actually remember and saluted the red, white and blue mushroom cloud which hung over the charred remains of his once proud nation. 'There goes America, god bless her.'

Behind his back, the presidents of Iraq and Russia gave each other a high-five.

'You, er, really think we've done the right thing here?' asked Prime Minister Kapoor.

'It was bound to happen sooner or later,' said the President of Egypt.

The others nodded in agreement.

'Out with the old, in with the new.' Grison beamed.

Anthony sidled in through the door, cradling his enormous head in his hands, like Atlas with a hangover.

'Here he is,' said Grison, 'the man of the hour.'

The world leaders raised their glasses and cheered.

'You punched me in the face...*again!*'

'Well, you were going on a bit. Samosa?' Grison rattled a food tray under Anthony's mountainous nose.

He pushed past, and squinted through the observation window. 'What's everyone staring at?' His sunken eyes focused on the glowing mass of nuclear rubble a little out from the moon. 'Why are there two suns all of a sudden?'

The world leaders shuffled their feet and coughed.

'One of them's Earth.'

'Oh,' said Anthony. He stared unblinking at the colossal lump of charcoal he'd called home for the past twenty-five years. 'Don't you think that was perhaps just a little bit excessive?'

'Don't worry, there's bound to be a few rough-and-tumble types who make it through the holocaust,' said Grison. 'All those preppers, burrowers and basement brewers, not to mention any cocky sods who happened to be off planet at the time.'

'Hear-hear!' yelled the President of America, raising his glass boisterously in the air, and spilling its contents over everyone else.

'The important thing to note is I've certainly done more than enough to meet my lifetime subtraction quota.' A serene smile settled on Grison's face. 'Now I can retire in peace with the knowledge of a job well done.'

Anthony looked around the room at all the powerful people wearing party hats and sipping cocktails, completely oblivious to the planet burning behind them. 'Fruit-loops, the lot of you,' he said, before staggering to the bar to help himself to a little of everything.

'No alcohol,' Grison commanded, snatching his drinks away. 'Not in your condition.'

'What does it matter?' Anthony grumbled. 'I expect I'll be exploding in a moment anyway.'

'Yes, but no need to poison the planet beforehand. Fresh start, and all that.'

'Uh, hang on there fella,' Etnor interjected. 'Did he just say he's gonna *explode?*'

'How else did you think we'd be getting the planet out of him?' asked Grison, giving a tumbler a vigorous shake.

'I thought it would be like giving birth or something,' said Prime Minister Kapoor. 'You know, bit of a scream and then "pop!"'

'Yes, if you like,' said Grison, 'except in this case it's going to be rather a loud pop with the sort of force equal to all those nuclear explosions combined.'

One by one, the world leaders began to edge away from Anthony.

'But, hey, uh, aren't we in a bit close proximity for that sort of thing?'

'So use the escape pods then, you big cowardy custards. I'd make it snappy if I were you – Tony's looking a bit peaky there.'

'Ugh,' said Anthony, as tectonic plates slid around inside his skull, making a crunch so audible that it set everyone else's teeth on edge. 'My head's killing me.'

'Abandon ship!' wailed Haranguer Jack. 'Women and androids first!' He fled off down a corridor, making 'awooga!' noises, with the world leaders following in hot pursuit.

Grison looked around at the overturned chairs, discarded drinks and scattered finger foods. 'Thank goodness for that, I thought they'd never leave.' He popped an olive in a Martini, took a long sip, and flicked a switch on the visi-com.

'Okay, Wendigo, the lunatics have left the hangar, repeat; the lunatics have left the hangar. Have you got the executive escape pod down in your quarters primed and ready?'

'The executive escape pod *is* mah quarters,' Wendigo's voice crackled back. 'And ah'd prefer if you call it by its proper name, if yuh don't mind.'

Grison sighed, and said through gritted teeth: 'I do beg your pardon. Have you got the Last Waltz Mobile Party Pad prepared, as instructed?'

'That's a big roger right there,' Wendigo chirped back. 'The L.W.M.P.P. is stocked with beer, stacked with porn and ready fuh action.' The enthusiasm momentarily drained from his voice. 'Fat lot of good it'll do us though, since the Earth just blew up.'

'Oh, don't you worry about that.' Grison clamped a hand on Anthony's shoulder, and squeezed. 'It's not for us.'

Out of breath, time, and options the freethinking leaders of a nuclear-ravaged world squeezed themselves awkwardly into an escape pod and prepared for launch.

'Any chance you could suck in your gut, Mr President?' asked the President of Russia, who was stood opposite Etnor and seriously in danger of being crushed.

'If you don't like it, get your own escape pod,' sniffed Etnor.

'Can't. This is the only one left.'

'Oh merciful Allah,' muttered the President of Iraq, glancing around at their leopard-print and velour-clad surroundings.

'No time to be choosy,' said Harangeur Jack, reaching past him and flicking a switch.

A hatch opened beneath them, and the pod dropped into outer space.

The President of Russia wrinkled her nose at the over-powering stench of Power Trip cologne. 'This is most irregular! There should be one pod per five registered passengers. What happened to all the others?'

'I think I can guess,' said Prime Minister Kapoor, face pressed against the porthole. An escape pod floated past, with several randy clones copulating in it.

'Damn! The sex clones beat us to it. Told you we shouldn't have stopped at that hair salon to get a New World Restyle.' The President of Italy ran his fingers through his mohawk.

'It was your idea, as I recall.'

Their tiny escape capsule tumbled onwards through the inky blackness, like a sardine can stuffed to the brim with overdressed salmon.

'Hey, I've just had a real hum-dinger of an idea,' said Etnor. 'We could put that Cresswell fella in the escape pod and blast him away from us. That way, we get to stay aboard the ship all nice and safe until he explodes.'

'Mr President, that is indeed a brilliant idea.' Harangeur Jack glanced back at the distant speck that was the good ship Chastity. 'Bit late though.'

As one, the collection of presidents frantically flicked every switch, twisted every dial and jabbed every button in sight, which only served to engage the mood lighting and shower them in confetti. 'Where's the reverse button?'

'Escape capsules don't have a reverse function,' Harangeur Jack observed dryly, 'as they rarely have call to dock with the ship they've just escaped from.'

'Bit of a design flaw, if you ask me,' said Prime Minister Kapoor.

'Nobody asked you.'

'Er, hey, yeah,' said Etnor, craning to get a look out the porthole. 'Any idea where this escape capsule's heading?'

Below them, a fiery planetary inferno drew ever closer...

After much grunting and heaving, Grison finally managed to squeeze Anthony's ever-expanding cranium in through the executive escape pod's door.

'Once again, lubricant to the rescue,' said Wendigo. 'You're lucky ah had some left – those sex clones practically ran me dry.'

Grison and Anthony shuddered in unison at the unwelcome mental image.

'Who's for the grand tour?'

Before either of them could raise an objection, Wendigo was already dragging Anthony across the mirrored tiles. 'Right, let's skip the foreplay and move straight to the main attraction – the sensomatic zero-g vibro bed.' Wendigo took a running jump, let the anti-gravity waves catch him, and skilfully rolled over in the air until he was lying face down on a hovering heart-shaped duvet. 'So comfortable it's like you're sleeping on thin air, which, in fact, you are.' He patted the duvet beside him. 'Come on up, an' take the weight off yer face. There's room enough fuh two, or four if y'all feeling ambitious.'

'No thanks, I've got a headache,' said Anthony.

'Ah've got just the thing for that.' Wendigo glided down, snagged Anthony's arm and guided him towards a wall unit composed of metallic arms of varying sizes. 'The micro-massage pleasure unit. Soothes away your aches and pains, on a subatomic level.' He moved Anthony into position, twisted a dial, and took a step back as the hands began to pinch, pound and knead his flesh at supersonic speeds. Pistons clanked, gears ground and skin wobbled. 'The deep massage setting is to die for,' said Wendigo, as Anthony juddered away. 'Quite literally; there've been at least seventeen reported cases of users being accidentally liquefied.' He switched the machine off again, and waited a moment for Anthony's body to stop vibrating. 'Well worth the risk, as ah'm sure y'all be first to agree.'

'F-f-f-f-f–' said Anthony.

'You're right, it *is* fun isn't it?' Wendigo skipped across the room, making the bunny ears on his pink slippers bob playfully up and down. 'Ah! Mah personal favourite – the Boozi Jacuzzi.' He twisted a flamingo-shaped tap, scooped a jug through the waters, and took a swig of bubbling pink froth. 'And who wouldn't want to take a nice relaxing dip in bubbling pink Champaign?'

'Could we move things along before one of us dies?' said Grison, staring pointedly at Anthony.

'Hold on to yer teabags, son, ah'm almost done. And over here we have the emergency karaoke machine.' Wendigo gestured to a red metal box sprinkled liberally with orange flashing lights, which was sat in front of a display screen so large that it put Derek's Bachelor Vision to shame. 'It was formerly a boring old emergency radio system, before ah had it converted. Now it'll automatically broadcast your interpretation of the musical classics on all known emergency radio frequencies. On a day like today y'all guaranteed to have a record number of listeners, so make sure yuh get straight in there with some "Disco Inferno" to let them burning earthers know you care.'

Wendigo casually reached for the microphone stand, but a sharp look from Grison made him hastily reconsider.

'Last on the agenda, yet first port of call in a crisis – the unisex bathroom.' Wendigo approached a cubicle door, which displayed a silhouette of a man and a woman locked together in sexual embrace. 'As a treat for our celebrity guest,' he said, aiming a wink at Anthony, 'ah've squirreled away a couple of feisty sex clones, to help you while away those long and lonely hours. Now, ah wasn't sure of your preference so ah saved you one male, one female, and one pig.' He swung open the door, and gestured inside. 'Quite the lookers, there's no doubt ab–'

The colour drained from Wendigo's face. He hurriedly slammed the bathroom door, and stepped backwards to avoid the puddle oozing underneath. 'Looks like their twenty-four hour life cycle has just run its course. Ah'd avoid using the bathroom for a while, if ah were you. Here's hoping the pig'll dispose of the icky bits once he's finished doing his ablutions in the shower. Any questions?'

'Yes,' said Grison. 'How do you make it go?'

'Just press the eject button on the wall over there, and it's bon voyage.'

'And the guidance systems?'

'Disabled, as requested. This little baby's goin' nowhere.'

'Well, I guess this is it then Tony.' Grison gave Anthony a sharp slap on the back. 'I'd like to say it's been a pleasure,' he said, 'but we both know that's not true. If you'd kindly do us the courtesy of waiting until our ship's a safe distance away before you explode, we'd be much obliged.'

He span on his heel, and marched out.

Ten minutes later, he marched back in again.

Anthony was half way down his third jug of Jacuzzi booze. His head had increased in size, and begun to develop its own weather system; a miniscule electric storm was currently raging above his left ear.

'You're still here,' Grison observed.

'Yup.' Anthony took another swig of pink bubbly.

'It's a mobile party pad, Tony. I expect you probably have to be on the move to get the full benefit. So slap that button over there, and get the party rolling.'

'I'm good, thanks.'

'But if you don't leave, I'll die,' Grison said, as if the very idea hadn't occurred to him. 'Then who's going to name the planet after you? Who's going to sing out your praises in the hallowed temple of Tony? You're not thinking clearly – too much primordial soup sloshing around in the brain.'

Anthony closed his eyes, clenched his fists, and strained until he was red in the face.

'What are you doing now?' Grison asked.

'Exploding,' said Anthony. *'Hnnnggggh!'*

'Is that all the thanks I get?' Grison tutted. 'After all I've done for you.'

The red flush momentarily faded from Anthony's cheeks. 'Like what?'

'I made you president of the world, for one thing.'

'And then destroyed it.'

'Offered you my hand in friendship.'

'And punched me in the face.'

Grison folded his arms. 'You asked for your body back. I delivered.'

'It's still going to explode.'

'Try not to think of it as exploding,' said Grison, 'more as transcending to a higher plain of consciousness. Throwing off the shackles of this feeble shell to spread your mighty spirit across the cosmos, immortalised in the stars for future generations to –'

'What future generations?' Anthony said, gesturing at the porthole to the burning planet that lay beyond. 'You've subtracted everyone.'

'There you go again, always focusing on the *negative*.' Grison laid a hand on Anthony's shoulder. 'I'm doing this for your own good, you know.'

'How is exploding in an escape pod going to benefit me, exactly?' Anthony snapped.

'All right, it's for my own good,' Grison admitted. 'Getting blown up alongside you is not part of my retirement plan. That involves a rather lovely plot of land inside your head, that goes by the name of "Hawaii". Four thousand square miles across, and a trillion light years from the nearest neighbours.'

'Except for me,' said Wendigo, poking his head around the door. 'Ah'm coming too, remember? Y'all promised me ah could be the first person to set foot on the planet. One bold step, an' all that.'

'Of course you're coming, Wendigo,' Grison soothed. 'Of course you are. How's that cocktail I made you?'

Wendigo stirred his finger through the powdery white lumps floating around in his Ladyboy. 'Tastes a bit hinky, now you mention it.'

'And your mood?'

'Bit depressed.'

'Excellent! Now get over there and press that eject button. I'll pilot the damned ship myself.' Grison pushed past Wendigo, and marched towards the door.

'Ah made an extra special effort today,' said Wendigo, sipping dejectedly at his cocktail. 'Put on mah best Jean-Paul Necrosis Day-Glo disco suit, and did anyone bother to pass comment?' He wandered over to the porthole, gazed out at the stars and sighed.

'Yes, yes, nobody loves you,' muttered Grison. 'Just press the button, Wendigo.'

Anthony's head began to vibrate ominously, like an egg that was ready to hatch. 'If you want to live,' he said through gritted teeth, 'I'd suggest you get this planet out of me.'

'Sure, what do you want me to try first,' Grison said, glancing around the room, 'curling tongs, or the shoehorn?'

'That ain't a shoehorn,' said Wendigo. 'Anyhow, we could just ask those aliens.'

'For the last time,' Grison said, rolling his eyes, 'we are not going to Mars. There's nothing there but dust and death. Aliens do not exist.'

'Oh yeah?' said Wendigo, pointing a well-manicured finger at the colossal slithering space squid attempting to rather clumsily parallel park alongside them. 'Then who the hell are *they?*'

Nineteen

The ship's interior lit up like a discotheque, bathed in red, yellow and green alert lights.

'Intruders on the bridge,' squealed Wendigo, sprinting for the nearest beauty salon. 'Stall them until ah'm gorgeous!'

'Not enough time in the world,' Grison muttered. 'Come on, Tony. Let's go see what these bug-eyed bastards want.' He dragged Anthony towards the nearest lift, and then after a lot of futile pushing and shoving, dragged him towards the stairs instead.

A trio of sloppy green squidgy things awaited them on the bridge, scanning the buffet table, dipping tentacles in the foie gras, and grumbling about the lack of napkins and lemon fresh wipes.

'There goes mah dream about becomin' the world's first trisexual transvestite astronaut,' muttered Wendigo, as he edged in the door.

Grison coughed politely for the aliens' attention. When he didn't get it, he grabbed a bread roll from the table and threw it at the largest one's head.

This was immediately misinterpreted as a customary human greeting, and before anyone knew what was happening, there were carrot and cucumber batons, and sausage sarnies soaring through the air like culinary missiles.

After a few inhuman squeals (which turned out to be Wendigo, who'd taken a vicious egg roll to the eye), the alien leader snapped a commanding tentacle in the air, ordering a ceasefire.

'Now that we've got the formalities over with,' the alien said in its wet, rasping voice as it slithered up to Grison, and looked him squarely in the croissant. 'I am Captain Braktalian of the great Sp'tetshee Empire. And I demand an *apology!*'

Grison elbowed Wendigo in the ribs.

'Ah surely do apologise for the distinct lack of napkins,' said Wendigo. 'Had ah known ah'd be having guests from quite so far afield, ah assure you ah'd have made more of an effort.'

'Not for the napkins!' the alien snapped. 'You should be apologising for blowing up the planet.'

'What, Earth?'

'No, Uxtroloflax. Our home planet.' Captain Braktalian's eyeball stalks jutted out to stare accusingly at Grison. 'As if you didn't know!'

'Never heard of it,' said Grison. 'Perhaps you're mistaking us for some other bipedal life form?'

'Oh no, it was definitely you. I'd recognise those low-slung foreheads and ever so showy opposable thumbs anywhere. You're the ones, oh yes, you're the ones.'

'Doubtful,' said Wendigo. 'We barely made it past Pluto before the funding ran out.'

'It was a while ago, I'll admit,' the alien said, 'and you were all a little hairier back then, looking not dissimilar to that gentleman there.' Captain Braktalian turned, and hoisted a suction-cupped tentacle at Grott as he casually ambled in through the door.

'You!' Grison spluttered, choking on his croissant. 'Why aren't you dead?'

'Lack of motivation?' Grott scooped up a sausage roll from the floor, ignoring the perfectly clean ones on the table, wiped it on his crotch and wolfed it down. 'None for you,' he said, waggling a stern finger at the aliens, ''cause you don't exist.'

'I've already killed you *twice*,' Grison screamed. 'Three times if you count the nuclear explosion. You're like a human cockroach!'

'Sorry, my fault.' Professor Langerman made for the buffet before Grott could get his grubby little mitts on everything. 'We snuck in past one of the escape pods whilst it was ejecting. Didn't have time to jettison excess baggage as it were, as our own space vessel was having difficulty breathing.'

'Brrr! Bit nippy outside,' said Derek, shivering.

Chico grabbed a tablecloth and started to wrap it around Derek's frozen chassis, then had a change of heart and wrapped it around himself instead.

'May I continue?' Captain Braktalian said, clicking her throat pouch in irritation. 'I have come rather a long way, you know.'

'Oh yes, don't mind us – just pretend we're not here,' said the professor. 'Free bar is it?' He swiftly altered his trajectory.

'So, as I was saying,' said Captain Braktalian loudly, over the clattering of ice cubes, 'a short while ago we took a few of your less evolved relatives back to our homeworld as a gift for our children. They seemed harmless enough, grunting away, banging rocks together. Rather sweet, really. So we taught them a few tricks, much like you would your basic earth bruugle hound. You know, quantum physics, bio-chemistry, that sort of thing. Nothing complex. Anyway, we left them playing for a few moments whilst we went off to return the lawnmower to Mr Kaspl'xx of the Frantlefroot star system, and when we got back the little sods had blown up the entire planet.'

Chico wiped away a small tear of pride. 'It's in our nature.'

'Well it's not in ours – we used to be pacifists. Now look at us.' The alien captain swept out a tentacle to indicate her gun-toting alien cronies, and malevolent space squid. 'Armed to the teeth, and hell bent on revenge and the destruction of your whole sorry race.'

'Been there, done that,' said Grison.

'Yes, thanks for that, we noticed,' Captain Braktalian fumed. 'We travelled half way across the galaxy, only to discover you've already beat us to the punch. Poor Trevaaar over there was up all night drawing up invasion plans.'

'I used all me best Sharpies,' mumbled Trevaaar, his green face-fronds wobbling uncontrollably.

'Used all his best Sharpies,' Captain Braktalian reiterated. 'That's commitment, that it. And Borysz there was forced to endure every Jason Statham movie in preparation for his infiltration mission.'

'Shove it up yer gluuurk hole, you Muppet,' said a grizzled-looking blob, who had painted parts of himself pink and squeezed into a bald cap.

'You see this?' Captain Braktalian hefted her impressive-looking ray gun. 'I haven't a clue what this weapon does, but I was really looking forward to finding out. Guess I won't need it now, since there's nothing left to invade. You absolute bunch of uncouth jinny-cockers!'

At that moment, another wave of pain exploded in Anthony's skull as the immense crushing weight of planet Tony bore down on him with the full sum of its force. He could feel his skin stretching, expanding, and attempting to split asunder. For a few brief, terrifying seconds he thought his neck was going to snap like a twig, so he was actually quite relieved when his knees gave way instead. He fell to the ground, screaming in agony.

The alien leader oozed over to him, and looked him up and down. 'What's up with this fathead?'

'He has a planet in his cranium, which should be exploding out of him any moment,' said Grison. 'So if you don't mind…'

'Oh, does he now?' said Captain Braktalian, as Anthony crawled past like a top-heavy caterpillar, pushing his face first; part rolling, part crawling. 'How interesting. How very –' In one swift motion, the alien twisted Anthony's arm behind his back, whipped out a small green flag, and rammed it in his ear. 'Dibs!' she cried victoriously.

'Worst alien conquest *ever*,' Chico sighed.

'If you want it so badly, can't you just remove it from his head?' suggested the professor.

'Absolutely, but where would be the fun in that? No, I think we'll just retire to a safe distance and watch you all explode in glorious slo-mo on the ol' 6D widescreen. Then we'll claim what's rightfully ours.' The look of self-righteous smugness seeped off the alien's ugly face. She stared at her empty tentacles and frowned. 'Where the gruuxfar did I put my gun?'

Anthony dragged himself unsteadily to his feet, branch in one ear, flag poking out the other, and Captain Braktalian's ray gun pressed against his forehead. 'Remove…the planet,' he said, 'or I'll…pull the trigger.'

The trio of aliens gurgled collectively.

'You wouldn't dare!'

'He would,' said Grison, backing away. 'He's done it before.'

'Which only goes to prove that he's bluffing,' said the alien captain, 'otherwise he wouldn't still be alive.'

'That's only because he's a very poor shot,' Grison observed. 'Look at the size of his head – he can't miss this time.'

Captain Braktalian appraised Anthony's gargantuan bonce. It had developed its own gravitational pull, and several spring rolls had already gone into orbit around it. 'I'll admit,' she said, snagging a hors d'oeuvre as it floated past, 'it is a bit of a whopper.'

'I'll do it!' Anthony shrieked, blinking back tears of pain. 'I'll pull the trigger. Then who knows what might happen?'

'He's right,' said Captain Braktalian, licking her face-fronds nervously. 'Even I don't know what that gun does. Literally *anything* could happen.'

'He might turn into a duck,' said Grott.

'I find that extremely doubtful,' countered the alien. 'We're a highly advanced race of super-intelligent beings. Seems unlikely we'd create avian-based changeling weaponry.'

'A squirrel then,' said Grott, who was rarely one to let an idea go, especially a bad one.

'Very well, earthling, you leave us no choice.' Captain Braktalian gave a commanding flick of the tentacle, and her two companions begrudgingly lowered their weapons. 'We will concede to your will, and remove the planet from your head.'

Anthony slowly relaxed his trigger finger. 'Without removing my brain?'

'Why would we want your brain?' The alien captain wrinkled her set of noses in distaste. 'Horrid sticky smelly thing! No, you can definitely keep hold of that.'

'And without destroying the planet?' said the professor.

'That goes without saying. We'll be needing it to conquer later.' Captain Braktalian pulled out her communicator and barked: 'K'viin? Lock the Matter Transporter onto the planet at these coordinates, and beam it up.'

A blinding white light engulfed the room, and slowly narrowed its focus until it was hovering purposefully over a plateful of chocolate éclairs. After an angrily barked course correction from Captain Braktalian, the Matter Transporter beam reluctantly switched targets, hovered over Anthony, and began to pulse.

At first, it started to tickle, and then to itch. The itch turned into a burn, and before Anthony knew it every single atom in his body was screaming. He could feel the planet squirming around inside his head like a trapped animal, searching for an escape route. His brain started to unravel and trickled out his ears, and then his eyes melted away under his nose. His nose and chin went off to form a search party, leaving just his lips quivering in the air.

For a brief moment, Anthony felt what it was like to be one with the universe, and then, for an even briefer moment, what it was like to be a chocolate éclair.

The light faded.

Anthony's hands leapt to his face. His nose and chin were back, and they'd brought reinforcements; excess skin dangled from his head like some sort of reverse face-lift operation. He poked tenderly at its folds. He was under there somewhere, without a single tree, hill or mountain range to be found. Gently, he probed his ears. No branches, no flags, no bananas, nothing. He was himself again; plain old ordinary, unremarkable Anthony.

The planet had gone.

'How are you feeling, Anthony?' the professor asked.

'A little…light headed,' he managed.

Captain Braktálian snatched up her ray gun from the floor and rattled it menacingly. 'Now all that unpleasantness is over, I suppose we ought to get back to annihilating your race,' she said. 'But first, an éclair!'

She slithered towards the buffet table, humming a cheery alien death anthem, and stopped at an empty plate. 'Hmm…could've sworn there was an entire plateful here a moment ago.' Her eyes flitted to the observation window, as a cream-filled tube of pastry floated past.

She lowered her weapon, and raised her communicator. 'K'viin…small matter, but why did you beam all the chocolate éclairs into outer space?'

'Did I?' replied K'viin in alarm. 'Oh fanglefroop! Er, that wasn't supposed to happen.'

'You know I always enjoy a good éclair when I'm on the cusp of victory,' she said, drumming her tentacles on the table. 'This sort of behaviour just isn't on!'

'Sorry. Must've pressed the wrong button.'

Captain Braktalian slowly tilted her head, staring out at the giant space squid as it began to list dangerously to one side. 'Where did you beam the planet to exactly?' she said into the communicator in as steady a voice as she could muster.

'Um,' said K'viin, somewhat sheepishly, 'possibly the pantry.'

'It's just I'd rather hoped you might rematerialise it out among the stars or something,' Captain Braktalian brayed manically. 'You know, where planets are traditionally kept.'

'Uh-oh,' said K'viin, 'it seems to be expanding at an exponential –'

Captain Braktalian watched helplessly as the colossal space squid burst open, spilling its crew out into the cold, unforgiving depths of space.

'Oh, absolutely fantastic,' she seethed, rounding on Anthony. 'You've destroyed our entire race. I hope you're happy.'

'Well I can't speak for anyone else,' Chico said, chuckling away, 'but I'm having a whale of a time.'

''Ere, shouldn't that be squid?' said Grott.

The professor stared out the observation window, and pointed a trembling finger. A brand spanking new leaner and meaner planet earth was rushing eagerly forth to greet them. 'It's not stopping.'

'Well, you fellows have clearly got this in hand,' said Grison, making for the lift in a wild sprint. 'If you'll excuse me, I've just got to go inspect the unisex bathroom.'

'If I might make an observation,' said Derek, as the ship began to violently rumble, and the glass in the windows began to crack. 'I *am* fitted with airbags.' He squelched his doors open, and waggled them enticingly. 'Just sayin'.'

Twenty

The sun rose over planet Tony for the very first time, sending its golden rays spiralling down to investigate the strange new orb which had appeared out of thin air mere moments ago in an impressive burst of squid entrails. They filtered through the thick layer of purple clouds that hung above the planet's surface, skimmed over purple mountaintops, rolled across deep oceans of purest purple and settled upon a vast woodland canopy, distinctly mauve in nature.

A few seconds later, a gigantic space meatball crashed through it, carving out a deep groove in the earth and completely ruining the sun's majestic effect.

Whether the steam rising up from it was from heat or stench, it was impossible to tell; all Anthony Cresswell knew was he'd much rather be on the outside.

He clawed frantically at the sticky wet membrane that surrounded him, gouging a hole in its side. His lips pressed up against it, sucked in great greedy lungfuls of air, and then reluctantly withdrew. He tore again at the hole, gumming up his fingernails with sickly red ichor.

Anthony's head pushed through, shuddering in relief as the scent of fresh air and freedom washed over him.

With a grunt and a heave, he wriggled through the gap, slopped onto the singed grass that surrounded Derek's impact crater, and lay on his back, gurgling miserably to himself.

'Don't you like my airbag then?' Derek's muffled voice asked from inside the skin sack.

'Bit…biological…for my tastes,' said Anthony, between retches.

Another hideous squelch, and the professor plopped out next to him. He was up on his feet in an instant, giggling like a schoolboy. 'I did it,' he enthused, sweeping out his slime-encrusted arms to take in the majestic mauve scenery. 'I ruddy well did it. A perfect replica of planet Earth!'

Anthony wiped his face with a handful of purple leaves, spat out a purple bug, and gazed around at the purple trees, grass, flowers and shrubs that surrounded them. 'Shame about the colour.'

'Yes, well, can't be expected to get every detail absolutely spot on the first time round,' the professor grumbled.

With a squelch, splat, and a groan another unlucky passenger plopped down to join them.

'*Kill me,*' said Chico.

'Everyone's a critic,' Derek muttered. His long grey tongue wrapped around the pulsating placenta that surrounded his chassis, and began to noisily suck it back in.

'No need to panic, everyone, ah'm fine,' announced Wendigo, as he pranced out of Derek's rear passenger door, looking annoyingly immaculate. His outfit had clearly been designed to repel even the most persistent of stains, and the juices cascading through his hair made it shimmer and glisten like something out of a shampoo commercial. 'Which is more than can be said for mah ship.'

Smouldering fragments lay strewn around the clearing, demonstrating once and for all that coating the underside of a spaceship in glitter was no real substitute for good old-fashioned shielding. 'Chastity, sweet Chastity!' he howled. 'Gone, but not forgotten. Ah'll name a continent after you, of this ah swear, my love.'

'Virgin Isles is probably your best bet,' said Derek.

'I'm fine too,' said Grott, though nobody paid him any attention.

'Any idea what happened to Grison?' Anthony asked, as they waded through three sad green puddles, of distinctly alien origin.

The twisted remains of an escape capsule loomed out of the bushes.

'Not mah Mobile Party Pad as well,' Wendigo bawled, aiming a frustrated kick at a dazed-looking pig that was snuffling around outside.

Fortunately, Wendigo's alcohol and pornography collection had survived intact. The escape capsule's sole occupant had not been so lucky; a battered, broken body lay slumped in the Jacuzzi, clutching a jug of mostly red Champaign.

As they drew closer, his eyes flickered open, and focused on Wendigo. 'Perhaps next time,' said Grison, wincing with every word, 'you might want to think about adding some safety features, like shock absorbers for example.'

Wendigo shrugged. 'That's what the bed's there for.'

'You know, that honestly hadn't occurred to me whilst I was bouncing off the floor and ceiling.'

'On the plus side, the pig survived.'

'My innards have turned to soup,' Grison rasped. 'And I don't mean the thick, chunky kind.'

'Ah warned you the micro-massager was not to be trifled with.'

'It was the karaoke machine falling on me that did it. After that, my singing days were numbered.'

Wendigo scowled at him in distaste. 'You broke mah karaoke machine?'

'He's *dying*, Wendigo,' Anthony said softly.

Grison's arm flailed around. 'Cressface…? Is that you?'

'I'm here,' said Anthony, leaning forwards and gently taking hold of Grison's hand.

The hand constricted and pulled him in close. 'My one regret,' Grison hissed, as his last breath wheezed out of his broken body, 'is that I never got to subtract *you.*'

'Cooee!' said Grott, poking his head around the door.

'Oh, for the love of f–' Grison's features stiffened, and he slumped to one side.

Wendigo poked him with a loofa. 'Snuffed it. Shame, seemed like such a nice guy.'

'Anyone want to say a few words?' asked the professor.

'Not polite ones,' muttered Anthony.

Grott cleared his throat, clenched his fists and declared: 'He was a *man…*'

After a short amount of time had elapsed, it became apparent that was all Grott had to say about the subject.

'Right, off we go then,' said the professor, rubbing his hands keenly together. 'Let's explore this magnificent new planet of ours.'

They walked onwards through the ruthlessly purple landscape, with the professor stopping to sniff every flower he passed, and get stung by every bee. 'Isn't it glorious?' he enthused. 'A pristine paradise untouched by the foetid fingers of civilised society.'

'Which time period are we in, do you think?' Anthony asked, glancing around warily, on the off chance there might be dinosaurs.

'Quite far back, I suspect,' said the professor. 'Certainly don't recognise any of the flora.'

'Perhaps that's because it's purple?'

The sound of twigs snapping underfoot drew their attention to a squat, hairy form lolloping through the trees, grunting and a hooting.

'Ah,' said the professor, nodding sagely, 'the Palaeolithic era. At last, an opportunity to set Neanderthal man on the straight and narrow.'

'Are you sure that was a Neanderthal?' said Anthony, squinting through the sun-dappled wood glade. 'He was wearing unicorn motif undergarments.'

'Yeah,' said Derek, 'and trainers.'

Chico looked from Grott to the departing hairy form, and back again. 'Oh no,' he groaned, 'not another one…'

Grott clicked his fingers sharply. *'That's* where I knew him from.'

'Just a trick of the light, I suspect,' the professor said, sounding a little uncertain. 'We're seeing double – yes, that's it. We all took a bit of a knock in the crash, so it's perfectly logical to deduce –'

'There's a souvenir stand over there,' said Anthony.

'What?' the professor shrieked.

'Next to the plaque.'

They pushed through the undergrowth, stalked up to an impressively large bronze plaque, and subjected it to a barrage of irate scowls.

'Hyde Park Reservation,' it stated, in bold fanciful letters. 'England's number one suicide spot since 2156!' Below it, a fun fact had been written about the history of Hyde Park; how the first megascraper had been built on top of it, and the park's remains moved to the top of said megascraper to keep the environmentalists happy. Clearly this hadn't worked, as they'd all flung themselves off the building in protest, starting a trend that had led to the park's prestigious status as it was today.

At the bottom there were various endorsements written by the recently bereaved, claiming their dearly departed loved ones had either had a 'wonderful time' or a 'life affirming experience'.

As one, the companions turned towards the professor. He was tugging so roughly at his beard that clumps of grey hair tumbled out.

'It appears I may have made another miscalculation,' he said hoarsely. 'Rather a big one, I suspect.'

''Ere, does anyone else smell that?' said Grott, perking up.

'What, Derek?'

'No – scones!'

The park's treeline gave way to the megascraper's edge, upon which a grand English tea party was beginning to wind down.

Blankets were spread across the lawn, with discarded Styrofoam cups and plates of half-eaten savouries whipping around playfully in the breeze.

A dozen purple-tinged people balanced precariously on the lip of the roof, gathered before a bullet-headed man who was preparing to give what appeared to be some sort of motivational seminar.

He cleared his throat noisily, and began.

'Now,' said Grison, addressing the small group of naked people who stood before him on the rooftop, 'you are all going to *die.*'

Raucous cheering erupted from the group, along with many an approving nod.

'Your bodies will be spread like a magnificent purple pâté across the pavement thousand of feet bel–'

'Cooeee!' called a voice.

Grison's sentence juddered to a halt. He took a deep breath, centred himself, and turned towards the small group of unlikely looking no-hopers knuckling towards him from the trees. He sighed, and turned back towards his own sorry-looking group. 'Excuse me a moment folks, looks like we've got a double booking.'

He strode towards Anthony's group as they approached, and waved a clipboard. 'Hold it right there, gentlemen,' he barked. 'I'm afraid this time slot's already fully booked. The only no-show on my list is a Miss Knudson, and none of you look like a Miss Knudson.' He scanned the group, eyes resting momentarily on Wendigo. 'Well, perhaps one of you – but it's a stretch.'

Anthony pointed a trembling finger, mouth stammering open and shut.

'Oh no, you're not Gawpers are you?' Grison shook his head. 'That's all I need. Bunch of slack-jawed suicide spotters ticking boxes in their nerdy little notepads, and awarding each other merit badges.'

'We're not Gawpers, no,' said the professor.

'You sure about that?' Grison hoisted a thumb at Anthony, whose facial expressions were going on a rampage. 'This one certainly looks the part.'

'He's just a little surprised to see you, that's all.'

'Why? I've as much right to be up here as anyone else. More than some, in fact, since I had the foresight to book in advance.' Grison narrowed his eyes at Grott. 'You look very familiar. Have I subtracted you before?'

'Oh gosh yes, lots of times,' said Grott.

Grison raised a disapproving eyebrow. 'And yet you're still here.'

'And over there,' said Grott, pointing to his likeness, who was nose-diving his way through a stack of scones.

'Cooeee!' said Grott's likeness, favouring them with a grin full of crumbs.

Grison looked from one Grott to the other. His mind boggled and his stomach heaved. 'Clones,' he said grimly. 'That's illegal! You're in a lot of trouble, mister.'

'You don't know the half of it…' mumbled the professor.

Grison reached into his backpack, drew out a pair of Adios trainers and thrust them into Grott's hands. 'Since I don't have time to report you, put these on and fall in with the others. The rest of you can wait your turn…at a distance. Though if I catch any of you taking photos on your phones, I'm calling the Pervert Police.' He frog-marched Grott towards the waiting rabble of snuff streakers. 'Right, where was I? Ah, yes – pâté.'

Chico and Wendigo followed after him.

'Where are you going?' the professor said sharply.

'To have a good gawp,' said Chico.

'Nudity *and* scones?' Wendigo whistled in appreciation. 'Ah must've died and gone to heaven.'

'Professor,' Anthony said, once he'd finally managed to wrestle his emotions under control. 'What's going on? Why's Grison still alive? Why are there two Grotts?'

The professor massaged his growing army of frown lines with the tips of his wrinkled fingers. 'I think the answer's obvious, don't you?'

They shuffled closer to the edge of the building, and looked down.

Stretched out before them was a nightmarish vista of megascrapers, recyke factories and smog as far as the eye could see. In its centre, the huge grey slab-like exterior of the Ministry for the Administration of Necessary Reductions towered high into the city's polluted atmosphere, a massive holographic sign at its top radiating out the Ministry's sacred mantra: 'Your sacrifice makes room for others.'

'You cloned all the people as well, didn't you?' Anthony said glumly.

The professor nodded. 'Along with everything else, for that matter.' He expelled a long, drawn-out sigh, born from years of failure. 'Oh well, can't be helped. After all, it took Edison ten thousand goes to get the light bulb right, and I'm working on a much grander scale here.'

'No wonder Noddy wanted me dead, with all these people rattling around in my mind. How's this supposed to help solve the population crisis?'

'It doesn't,' the professor said. 'Sorry about that.'

'You mean I went through all that misery for nothing?' Anthony's legs almost went out from under him, and for a moment he teetered perilously on the building's edge. Even though there was no longer a planet inside his head, it still felt like he could explode at any moment. The mother of all migraines was rampaging around inside his skull, kicking over the furniture, and generally making its presence known. 'I've been stripped, shot, punched, clamped, insulted, had my DNA fiddled with, molecules disassembled, and almost had a poker inserted in a very uncomfortable area. For what?'

'Look, if you're going to jump, could you give it ten minutes?' hollered Grison from a little way along the roof-top. 'Wouldn't want people thinking you're part of my group – it could invalidate my contract.'

'It's all right, we're just working through some issues,' said the professor, giving Grison a reassuring wave.

'Come on, cheer up you daft sod,' said Derek. 'At least you've still got your health.'

'Health?' Anthony tugged in irritation at the lank folds of skin dangling from his scalp. 'I have a face like a deflated beach ball. Does that sound like the prime definition of good health?'

'Well, no,' admitted Derek. 'But I know a guy who could sort that out for you, at a very reasonable price. I'll give you a lift if you like, it's no bother.'

'Derek, I am never setting foot inside you or another genetics parlour as long as I live. Which might not be that long, considering how things turned out the last time.'

They stood a moment in silence, which was punctuated by the death cries of the occasional snuff streaker.

'You never know, perhaps events will transpire differently this time around,' said the professor, forcing a smile. 'They're all clones, after all.' He watched the thronging mass of people below as they went about the daily business of living, dying and killing time in-between. 'Every single one of them is slightly different to how they were before. It's a long shot, granted, but it just might be enough.'

'Enough for what?' said Anthony.

Professor Langerman laid a gentle hand on his shoulder. 'Hope, my dear boy. Hope.'

Several thousand feet below, a slightly more mauve shade of Anthony stood staring in disbelief at his brand new company hover car.

A small naked dead man jutted from the punctured roof, legs spread upwards in a wide V-shape, like a two-finger message sent by the gods.

Anthony looked to the sky for an answer. A leaflet drifted towards him. He snatched it out of the air and examined it.

'Adios trainers,' it read. 'Go out in style.'

About The Author

David Hailwood used to write whilst hanging upside-down by his legs, from a tree. Now he's an adult he's apparently not allowed to do that sort of thing any more, so instead he sits at home in his office, cackling manically at his computer (occasionally he remembers to switch it on).

He has written comedy material for the BBC, ITV and E4, and once starred in a short comedy horror film titled 'Attack of the Mutant Sock Freaks', in which a bunch of deranged killer socks attempt to destroy Bognor Regis.

Visit the author's website at the cunningly titled **www.davidhailwood.com** and register for a newsletter to be kept up-to-date with new releases, and get a free copy of his Dead Short anthology which contains the 'Head Case' short story that inspired Life Subtracted.

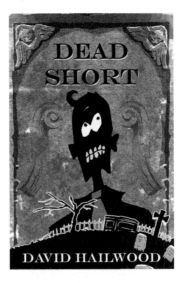